David Elginbrod
Book II

By

George Macdonald

David Elginbrod
Book II
by George Macdonald

ISBN: 978-93-61154-44-7
Published by

DOUBLE 9 BOOKS
2/13-B, Ansari Road
Daryaganj, New Delhi – 110002
info@double9books.com
www.double9books.com
Tel. 011-40042856

ABOUT THE AUTHOR

George MacDonald was a Scottish author, poet, and Christian Congregational clergyman. He established himself as a pioneering figure in modern fantasy writing and mentored fellow writer Lewis Carroll. In addition to his fairy stories, MacDonald wrote various works on Christian theology, including sermon collections. George MacDonald was born on December 10, 1824 in Huntly, Aberdeenshire, Scotland. His father, a farmer, descended from the Clan MacDonald of Glen Coe and was a direct descendant of one of the families killed in the 1692 massacre. MacDonald was raised in an exceptionally literary household: one of his maternal uncles was a renowned Celtic scholar, editor of the Gaelic Highland Dictionary, and collector of fairy stories and Celtic oral poetry. His paternal grandfather had helped to publish an edition of James Macpherson's Ossian, a contentious epic poem based on the Fenian Cycle of Celtic Mythology that contributed to the birth of European Romanticism. MacDonald's step-uncle was a Shakespeare scholar, while his paternal cousin was also a Celtic intellectual.

CONTENTS

BOOK II
ARNSTEAD

The earth hath bubbles as the water has.

MACBETH.—I.3

CHAPTER I
A NEW HOME

A wise man's home is whereso'er he's wise

JOHN MARSTON.—Antonio's Revenge.

Hugh left the North dead in the arms of grey winter, and found his new abode already alive in the breath of the west wind. As he walked up the avenue to the house, he felt that the buds were breaking all about, though, the night being dark and cloudy, the green shadows of the coming spring were invisible.

He was received at the hall-door, and shown to his room, by an old, apparently confidential, and certainly important butler; whose importance, however, was inoffensive, as founded, to all appearance, on a sense of family and not of personal dignity. Refreshment was then brought him, with the message that, as it was late, Mr. Arnold would defer the pleasure of meeting him till the morning at breakfast.

Left to himself, Hugh began to look around him. Everything suggested a contrast between his present position and that which he had first occupied about the same time of the year at Turriepuffit. He was in an old handsome room of dark wainscot, furnished like a library, with book-cases about the walls. One of them, with glass doors, had an ancient escritoire underneath, which was open, and evidently left empty for his use. A fire was burning cheerfully in an old high grate; but its light, though assisted by that of two wax candles on the table, failed to show the outlines of the room, it was so large and dark. The ceiling was rather low in proportion, and a huge beam crossed it. At one end, an open door revealed a room beyond, likewise lighted with fire and candles. Entering, he found this to be an equally old-fashioned bedroom, to which his luggage had been already conveyed.

"As far as creature comforts go," thought Hugh, "I have fallen on my feet." He rang the bell, had the tray removed, and then proceeded to examine the book-cases. He found them to contain much of the literature with which he was most desirous of making an acquaintance. A few books of the day were interspersed. The sense of having good companions in the authors around him, added greatly to his feeling of comfort; and he retired for the night filled with pleasant anticipations of his sojourn at Arnstead. All the night, however, his dreams were of wind and snow, and Margaret out in them alone. Janet was waiting in the cottage for him to bring her home. He had found her, but could not move her; for the spirit of the storm had frozen her to ice, and she was heavy as a marble statue.

When he awoke, the shadows of boughs and budding twigs were waving in changeful network-tracery, across the bright sunshine on his window-curtains. Before he was called he was ready to go down; and to amuse himself till breakfast-time, he proceeded to make another survey of the books. He concluded that these must be a colony from the mother-library; and also that the room must, notwithstanding, be intended for his especial occupation, seeing his bedroom opened out of it. Next, he looked from all the windows, to discover into what kind of a furrow on the face of the old earth he had fallen. All he could see was trees and trees. But oh! how different from the sombre, dark, changeless fir-wood at Turriepuffit! whose trees looked small and shrunken in his memory, beside this glory of boughs, breaking out into their prophecy of an infinite greenery at hand. His rooms seemed to occupy the end of a small wing at the back of the house, as well as he could judge. His sitting-room windows looked across a small space to another wing; and the windows of his bedroom, which were at right-angles to those of the former, looked full into what seemed an ordered ancient forest of gracious trees of all kinds, coming almost close to the very windows. They were the trees which had been throwing their shadows on these windows for two or three hours of the silent spring sunlight, at once so liquid and so dazzling. Then he resolved to test his faculty for discovery, by seeing whether he could find his way to the breakfast-room without a guide. In this he would have succeeded without much difficulty, for it opened from the main-entrance hall, to which the huge square-turned oak staircase, by which he had ascended, led; had it not been for the somewhat intricate nature of the passages leading from the wing in which his rooms were (evidently an older and more retired portion of the house) to the main staircase itself. After opening many doors and finding no thoroughfare, he became convinced that, in place of finding a way on, he had lost the way back. At length he came to a small stair, which led him down to a single door. This he opened, and straightway found himself in the library, a long, low, silent-looking room, every foot of the walls of which was occupied with books in varied and rich bindings. The lozenge-paned windows, with thick stone mullions, were much overgrown with ivy, throwing a cool green shadowiness into the room. One of them, however, had been altered to a more modern taste, and opened with folding-doors upon a few steps, descending into an old-fashioned, terraced garden. To approach this window he had to pass a table, lying on which he saw a paper with verses on it, evidently in a woman's hand, and apparently just written, for the ink of the corrective scores still glittered. Just as he reached the window, which stood open, a lady had almost gained it from the other side, coming up the steps from the garden. She gave a slight start when she saw him, looked away, and as instantly glanced towards him again. Then approaching him through the window, for he had retreated to allow her to enter, she bowed with a kind of studied ease, and a slight shade of something French in her manner. Her voice was very pleasing, almost bewitching; yet had, at the same time, something assumed, if not affected, in the tone. All this was discoverable, or rather spiritually palpable, in the two words she said— merely, "Mr. Sutherland?" interrogatively. Hugh bowed, and said:

"I am very glad you have found me, for I had quite lost myself. I doubt whether I should ever have reached the breakfast-room."

"Come this way," she rejoined.

As they passed the table on which the verses lay, she stopped and slipped them into a writing-case. Leading him through a succession of handsome, evidently modern passages, she brought him across the main hall to the breakfast-room, which looked in the opposite direction to the library, namely, to the front of the house. She rang the bell; the urn was brought in; and she proceeded at once to make the tea; which she did well, rising in Hugh's estimation thereby. Before he had time, however, to make his private remarks on her exterior, or his conjectures on her position in the family, Mr. Arnold entered the room, with a slow, somewhat dignified step, and a dull outlook of grey eyes from a grey head well-balanced on a tall, rather slender frame. The lady rose, and, addressing him as uncle, bade him good morning; a greeting which he returned cordially, with a kiss on her forehead. Then accosting Hugh, with a manner which seemed the more polite and cold after the tone in which he had spoken to his niece, he bade him welcome to Arnstead.

"I trust you were properly attended to last night, Mr. Sutherland? Your pupil wanted very much to sit up till you arrived, but he is altogether too delicate, I am sorry to say, for late hours, though he has an unfortunate preference for them himself. Jacob," (to the man in waiting), "is not Master Harry up yet?"

Master Harry's entrance at that moment rendered reply unnecessary.

"Good morning, Euphra," he said to the lady, and kissed her on the cheek.

"Good morning, dear," was the reply, accompanied by a pretence of returning the kiss. But she smiled with a kind of confectionary sweetness on him; and, dropping an additional lump of sugar into his tea at the same moment, placed it for him beside herself; while he went and shook hands with his father, and then glancing shyly up at Hugh from a pair of large dark eyes, put his hand in his, and smiled, revealing teeth of a pearly whiteness. The lips, however, did not contrast them sufficiently, being pale and thin, with indication of suffering in their tremulous lines. Taking his place at table, he trifled with his breakfast; and after making pretence of eating for a while, asked Euphra if he might go. She giving him leave, he hastened away.

Mr. Arnold took advantage of his retreat to explain to Hugh what he expected of him with regard to the boy.

"How old would you take Harry to be, Mr. Sutherland?"

"I should say about twelve from his size," replied Hugh; "but from his evident bad health, and intelligent expression—"

"Ah! you perceive the state he is in," interrupted Mr. Arnold, with some sadness in his voice. "You are right; he is nearly fifteen. He has not grown half-an-inch in the last twelve months."

"Perhaps that is better than growing too fast," said Hugh.

"Perhaps—perhaps; we will hope so. But I cannot help being uneasy about him. He reads too much, and I have not yet been able to help it; for he seems miserable, and without any object in life, if I compel him to leave his books."

"Perhaps we can manage to get over that in a little while."

"Besides," Mr. Arnold went on, paying no attention to what Hugh said, "I can get him to take no exercise. He does not even care for riding. I bought him a second pony a month ago, and he has not been twice on its back yet."

Hugh could not help thinking that to increase the supply was not always the best mode of increasing the demand; and that one who would not ride the first pony, would hardly be likely to ride the second. Mr. Arnold concluded with the words:

"I don't want to stop the boy's reading, but I can't have him a milksop."

"Will you let me manage him as I please, Mr. Arnold?" Hugh ventured to say.

Mr. Arnold looked full at him, with a very slight but quite manifest expression of surprise; and Hugh was aware that the eyes of the lady, called by the boy Euphra, were likewise fixed upon him penetratingly. As if he were then for the first time struck by the manly development of Hugh's frame, Mr. Arnold answered:

"I don't want you to overdo it, either. You cannot make a muscular Christian of him." (The speaker smiled at his own imagined wit.) "The boy has talents, and I want him to use them."

"I will do my best for him both ways," answered Hugh, "if you will trust me. For my part, I think the only way is to make the operation of the intellectual tendency on the one side, reveal to the boy himself his deficiency on the other. This once done, all will be well."

As he said this, Hugh caught sight of a cloudy, inscrutable dissatisfaction slightly contracting the eyebrows of the lady. Mr. Arnold, however, seemed not to be altogether displeased.

"Well," he answered, "I have my plans; but let us see first what you can do with yours. If they fail, perhaps you will oblige me by trying mine."

This was said with the decisive politeness of one who is accustomed to have his own way, and fully intends to have it—every word as articulate and deliberate as organs of speech could make it. But he seemed at the same time somewhat impressed by Hugh, and not unwilling to yield.

Throughout the conversation, the lady had said nothing, but had sat watching, or rather scrutinizing, Hugh's countenance, with a far keener and more frequent glance than, I presume, he was at all aware of. Whether or not she was satisfied with her conclusions, she allowed no sign to disclose; but, breakfast being over, rose and withdrew, turning, however, at the door, and saying:

"When you please, Mr. Sutherland, I shall be glad to show you what Harry has been doing with me; for till now I have been his only tutor."

"Thank you," replied Hugh; "but for some time we shall be quite independent of school-books. Perhaps we may require none at all. He can read, I presume, fairly well?"

"Reading is not only his forte but his fault," replied Mr. Arnold; while Euphra, fixing one more piercing look upon him, withdrew.

"Yes," responded Hugh; "but a boy may shuffle through a book very quickly, and have no such accurate perceptions of even the mere words, as to be able to read aloud intelligibly."

How little this applied to Harry, Hugh was soon to learn.

"Well, you know best about these things, I daresay. I leave it to you. With such testimonials as you have, Mr. Sutherland, I can hardly be wrong in letting you try your own plans with him. Now, I must bid you good morning. You will, in all probability, find Harry in the library."

CHAPTER II
HARRY'S NEW HORSE

Spielender Unterricht heisst nicht, dem Kinde Anstrengungen ersparen und abnehmen, sondern eine Leidenschaft in ihm erwecken, welche ihm die stärksten aufnöthigt und erleichtert.

JEAN PAUL.—Die Unsichtbare Loge.

It is not the intention of sportive instruction that the child should be spared effort, or delivered from it; but that thereby a passion should be wakened in him, which shall both necessitate and facilitate the strongest exertion.

Hugh made no haste to find his pupil in the library; thinking it better, with such a boy, not to pounce upon him as if he were going to educate him directly. He went to his own rooms instead; got his books out and arranged them,—supplying thus, in a very small degree, the scarcity of modern ones in the book-cases; then arranged his small wardrobe, looked about him a little, and finally went to seek his pupil.

He found him in the library, as he had been given to expect, coiled up on the floor in a corner, with his back against the book-shelves, and an old folio on his knees, which he was reading in silence.

"Well, Harry," said Hugh, in a half-indifferent tone, as he threw himself on a couch, "what are you reading?"

Harry had not heard him come in. He started, and almost shuddered; then looked up, hesitated, rose, and, as if ashamed to utter the name of the book, brought it to Hugh, opening it at the title-page as he held it out to him. It was the old romance of Polexander. Hugh knew nothing about it; but, glancing over some of the pages, could not help wondering that the boy should find it interesting.

"Do you like this very much?" said he.

"Well—no. Yes, rather."

"I think I could find you something more interesting in the book-shelves."

"Oh! please, sir, mayn't I read this?" pleaded Harry, with signs of distress in his pale face.

"Oh, yes, certainly, if you wish. But tell me why you want to read it so very much."

"Because I have set myself to read it through."

Hugh saw that the child was in a diseased state of mind, as well as of body.

"You should not set yourself to read anything, before you know whether it is worth reading."

"I could not help it. I was forced to say I would."

"To whom?"

"To myself. Mayn't I read it?"

"Certainly," was all Hugh's answer; for he saw that he must not pursue the subject at present: the boy was quite hypochondriacal. His face was keen, with that clear definition of feature which suggests superior intellect. He was, though very small for his age, well proportioned, except that his head and face were too large. His forehead indicated thought; and Hugh could not doubt that, however uninteresting the books which he read might be, they must have afforded him subjects of mental activity. But he could not help seeing as well, that this activity, if not altered in its direction and modified in its degree, would soon destroy itself, either by ruining his feeble constitution altogether, or, which was more to be feared, by irremediably injuring the action of the brain. He resolved, however, to let him satisfy his conscience by reading the book; hoping, by the introduction of other objects of thought and feeling, to render it so distasteful, that he would be in little danger of yielding a similar pledge again, even should the temptation return, which Hugh hoped to prevent.

"But you have read enough for the present, have you not?" said he, rising, and approaching the book-shelves.

"Yes; I have been reading since breakfast."

"Ah! there's a capital book. Have you ever read it—Gulliver's Travels?"

"No. The outside looked always so uninteresting."

"So does Polexander's outside."

"Yes. But I couldn't help that one."

"Well, come along. I will read to you."

"Oh! thank you. That will be delightful. But must we not go to our lessons?"

"I'm going to make a lesson of this. I have been talking to your papa; and we're going to begin with a holiday, instead of ending with one. I must get better acquainted with you first, Harry, before I can teach you right. We must be friends, you know."

The boy crept close up to him, laid one thin hand on his knee, looked in his face for a moment, and then, without a word, sat down on the couch close beside him. Before an hour had passed, Harry was laughing heartily at Gulliver's adventures amongst the Lilliputians. Having arrived at this point of success, Hugh ceased reading, and began to talk to him.

"Is that lady your cousin?"

"Yes. Isn't she beautiful?"

"I hardly know yet. I have not got used to her enough yet. What is her name?"

"Oh! such a pretty name—Euphrasia."

"Is she the only lady in the house?"

"Yes; my mamma is dead, you know. She was ill for a long time, they say; and she died when I was born."

The tears came in the poor boy's eyes. Hugh thought of his own father, and put his hand on Harry's shoulder. Harry laid his head on Hugh's shoulder.

"But," he went on, "Euphra is so kind to me! And she is so clever too! She knows everything."

"Have you no brothers or sisters?"

"No, none. I wish I had."

"Well, I'll be your big brother. Only you must mind what I say to you; else I shall stop being him. Is it a bargain?"

"Yes, to be sure!" cried Harry in delight; and, springing from the couch, he began hopping feebly about the room on one foot, to express his pleasure.

"Well, then, that's settled. Now, you must come and show me the horses—your ponies, you know—and the pigs—"

"I don't like the pigs—I don't know where they are."

"Well, we must find out. Perhaps I shall make some discoveries for you. Have you any rabbits?"

"No."

"A dog though, surely?"

"No. I had a canary, but the cat killed it, and I have never had a pet since."

"Well, get your cap, and come out with me. I will wait for you here."

Harry walked away—he seldom ran. He soon returned with his cap, and they sallied out together.

Happening to look back at the house, when a few paces from it, Hugh thought he saw Euphra standing at the window of a back staircase. They made the round of the stables, and the cow-house, and the poultry-yard; and even the pigs, as proposed, came in for a share of their attention. As they approached the stye, Harry turned away his head with a look of disgust. They were eating out of the trough.

"They make such a nasty noise!" he said.

"Yes, but just look: don't they enjoy it?" said Hugh.

Harry looked at them. The notion of their enjoyment seemed to dawn upon him as something quite new. He went nearer and nearer to the stye. At last a smile broke out over his countenance.

"How tight that one curls his tail!" said he, and burst out laughing.

"How dreadfully this boy must have been mismanaged!" thought Hugh to himself. "But there is no fear of him now, I hope."

By this time they had been wandering about for more than an hour; and Hugh saw, by Harry's increased paleness, that he was getting tired.

"Here, Harry, get on my back, my boy, and have a ride. You're tired."

And Hugh knelt down.

Harry shrunk back.

"I shall spoil your coat with my shoes."

"Nonsense! Rub them well on the grass there. And then get on my back directly."

Harry did as he was bid, and found his tutor's broad back and strong arms a very comfortable saddle. So away they went, wandering about for a long time, in their new relation of horse and his rider. At length they got into the middle of a long narrow avenue, quite neglected, overgrown with weeds, and obstructed with rubbish. But the trees were fine beeches, of great growth and considerable age. One end led far into a wood, and the other towards the house, a small portion of which could be seen at the end, the avenue appearing to reach close up to it.

"Don't go down this," said Harry.

"Well, it's not a very good road for a horse certainly, but I think I can go it. What a beautiful avenue! Why is it so neglected?"

"Don't go down there, please, dear horse."

Harry was getting wonderfully at home with Hugh already.

"Why?" asked Hugh.

"They call it the Ghost's Walk, and I don't much like it. It has a strange distracted look!"

"That's a long word, and a descriptive one too," thought Hugh; but, considering that there would come many a better opportunity of combating the boy's fears than now, he simply said: "Very well, Harry," —and proceeded to leave the avenue by the other side. But Harry was not yet satisfied.

"Please, Mr. Sutherland, don't go on that side, just now. Ride me back, please. It is not safe, they say, to cross her path. She always follows any one who crosses her path."

Hugh laughed; but again said, "Very well, my boy;" and, returning, left the avenue by the side by which he had entered it.

"Shall we go home to luncheon now?" said Harry.

"Yes," replied Hugh. "Could we not go by the front of the house? I should like very much to see it."

"Oh, certainly," said Harry, and proceeded to direct Hugh how to go; but evidently did not know quite to his own satisfaction. There being, however, but little foliage yet, Hugh could discover his way pretty well. He promised himself many a delightful wander in the woody regions in the evenings.

They managed to get round to the front of the house, not without some difficulty; and then Hugh saw to his surprise that, although not imposing in appearance, it was in extent more like a baronial residence than that of a simple gentleman. The front was very long, apparently of all ages, and of all possible styles of architecture, the result being somewhat mysterious and eminently picturesque. All kinds of windows; all kinds of projections and recesses; a house here, joined to a hall there; here a pointed gable, the very bell on the top overgrown and apparently choked with ivy; there a wide front with large bay windows; and next a turret of old stone, with not a shred of ivy upon it, but crowded over with grey-green lichens, which looked as if the stone itself had taken to growing; multitudes of roofs, of all shapes and materials, so that one might very easily be lost amongst the chimneys and gutters and dormer windows and pinnacles—made up the appearance of the house on the outside to Hugh's first inquiring glance, as he paused at a little distance with Harry on his back, and scanned the wonderful pile before him. But as he looked at the house of Arnstead, Euphra was looking at him with the boy on his back, from one of the smaller windows. Was she making up her mind?

"You are as kind to me as Euphra," said Harry, as Hugh set him down in the hall. "I've enjoyed my ride very much, thank you, Mr. Sutherland. I am sure Euphra will like you very much—she likes everybody."

CHAPTER III
EUPHRASIA

then purged with Euphrasy and Rue
The visual nerve, for he had much to see.
Paradise Lost, b. xi.

Soft music came to mine ear. It was like the rising breeze, that whirls, at first, the thistle's beard; then flies, dark-shadowy, over the grass. It was the maid of Fuärfed wild: she raised the nightly song; for she knew that my soul was a stream, that flowed at pleasant sounds.

Ossian.—Oina-Morul.

Harry led Hugh by the hand to the dining-room, a large oak hall with Gothic windows, and an open roof supported by richly carved woodwork, in the squares amidst which were painted many escutcheons parted by fanciful devices. Over the high stone carving above the chimney hung an old piece of tapestry, occupying the whole space between that and the roof. It represented a hunting-party of ladies and gentlemen, just setting out. The table looked very small in the centre of the room, though it would have seated twelve or fourteen. It was already covered for luncheon; and in a minute Euphra entered and took her place without a word. Hugh sat on one side and Harry on the other. Euphra, having helped both to soup, turned to Harry and said, "Well, Harry, I hope you have enjoyed your first lesson."

"Very much," answered Harry with a smile. "I have learned pigs and horseback."

"The boy is positively clever," thought Hugh.

"Mr. Sutherland"—he continued, "has begun to teach me to like creatures."

"But I thought you were very fond of your wild-beast book, Harry."

"Oh! yes; but that was only in the book, you know. I like the stories about them, of course. But to like pigs, you know, is quite different. They are so ugly and ill-bred. I like them though."

"You seem to have quite gained Harry already," said Euphra, glancing at Hugh, and looking away as quickly.

"We are very good friends, and shall be, I think," replied he.

Harry looked at him affectionately, and said to him, not to Euphra, "Oh! yes, that we shall, I am sure." Then turning to the lady—"Do you know, Euphra, he is my big brother?"

"You must mind how you make new relations, though, Harry; for you know that would make him my cousin."

"Well, you will be a kind cousin to him, won't you?"

"I will try," replied Euphra, looking up at Hugh with a naïve expression of shyness, and the slightest possible blush.

Hugh began to think her pretty, almost handsome. His next thought was to wonder how old she was. But about this he could not at once make up his mind. She might be four-and-twenty; she might be two-and-thirty. She had black, lustreless hair, and eyes to match, as far as colour was concerned—but they could sparkle, and probably flash upon occasion; a low forehead, but very finely developed in the faculties that dwell above the eyes; slender but very dark eyebrows—just black arched lines in her rather sallow complexion; nose straight, and nothing remarkable—"an excellent thing in woman," a mouth indifferent when at rest, but capable of a beautiful laugh. She was rather tall, and of a pretty enough figure; hands good; feet invisible. Hugh came to these conclusions rapidly enough, now that his attention was directed to her; for, though naturally unobservant, his perception was very acute as soon as his attention was roused.

"Thank you," he replied to her pretty speech. "I shall do my best to deserve it."

"I hope you will, Mr. Sutherland," rejoined she, with another arch look. "Take some wine, Harry."

She poured out a glass of sherry, and gave it to the boy, who drank it with some eagerness. Hugh could not approve of this, but thought it too early to interfere. Turning to Harry, he said:

"Now, Harry, you have had rather a tiring morning. I should like you to go and lie down a while."

"Very well, Mr. Sutherland," replied Harry, who seemed rather deficient in combativeness, as well as other boyish virtues. "Shall I lie down in the library?"

"No—have a change."

"In my bed-room?"

"No, I think not. Go to my room, and lie on the couch till I come to you."

Harry went; and Hugh, partly for the sake of saying something, and partly to justify his treatment of Harry, told Euphra, whose surname he did not yet know, what they had been about all the morning, ending with some remark on the view of the house in front. She heard the account of their proceedings with apparent indifference, replying only to the remark with which he closed it:

"It is rather a large house, is it not, for three—I beg your pardon, for four persons to live in, Mr. Sutherland?"

"It is, indeed; it quite bewilders me."

"To tell the truth, I don't quite know above the half of it myself."

Hugh thought this rather a strange assertion, large as the house was; but she went on:

"I lost myself between the housekeeper's room and my own, no later than last week."

I suppose there was a particle of truth in this; and that she had taken a wrong turning in an abstracted fit. Perhaps she did not mean it to be taken as absolutely true.

"You have not lived here long, then?"

"Not long for such a great place. A few years. I am only a poor relation."

She accompanied this statement with another swift uplifting of the eyelids. But this time her eyes rested for a moment on Hugh's, with something of a pleading expression; and when they fell, a slight sigh followed. Hugh felt that he could not quite understand her. A vague suspicion crossed his mind that she was bewitching him, but vanished instantly. He replied to her communication by a smile, and the remark:

"You have the more freedom, then.—Did you know Harry's mother?" he added, after a pause.

"No. She died when Harry was born. She was very beautiful, and, they say, very clever, but always in extremely delicate health. Between ourselves, I doubt if there was much sympathy—that is, if my uncle and she quite understood each other. But that is an old story."

A pause followed. Euphra resumed:

"As to the freedom you speak of, Mr. Sutherland, I do not quite know what to do with it. I live here as if the place were my own, and give what orders I please. But Mr. Arnold shows me little attention—he is so occupied with one thing and another, I hardly know what; and if he did, perhaps I should get tired of him. So, except when we have visitors, which is not very often, the time hangs rather heavy on my hands."

"But you are fond of reading—and writing, too, I suspect;" Hugh ventured to say.

She gave him another of her glances, in which the apparent shyness was mingled with something for which Hugh could not find a name. Nor did he suspect, till long after, that it was in reality slyness, so tempered with archness, that, if discovered, it might easily pass for an expression playfully assumed.

"Oh! yes," she said; "one must read a book now and then; and if a verse"—again a glance and a slight blush—"should come up from nobody knows where, one may as well write it down. But, please, do not take me for a literary lady. Indeed, I make not the slightest pretensions. I don't know what I should do without Harry; and indeed, indeed, you must not steal him from me, Mr. Sutherland."

"I should be very sorry," replied Hugh. "Let me beg you, as far as I have a right to do so, to join us as often and as long as you please. I will go and see how he is. I am sure the boy only wants thorough rousing, alternated with perfect repose."

He went to his own room, where he found Harry, to his satisfaction, fast asleep on the sofa. He took care not to wake him, but sat down beside him to read till his sleep should be over. But, a moment after, the boy opened his eyes with a start and a shiver, and gave a slight cry. When he saw Hugh he jumped up, and with a smile which was pitiful to see upon a scared face, said:

"Oh! I am so glad you are there."

"What is the matter, dear Harry?"

"I had a dreadful dream."

"What was it?"

"I don't know. It always comes. It is always the same. I know that. And yet I can never remember what it is."

Hugh soothed him as well as he could; and he needed it, for the cold drops were standing on his forehead. When he had grown calmer, he went and fetched Gulliver, and, to the boy's great delight, read to him till dinner-time. Before the first bell rang, he had quite recovered, and indeed seemed rather interested in the approach of dinner.

Dinner was an affair of some state at Arnstead. Almost immediately after the second bell had rung, Mr. Arnold made his appearance in the drawing-room, where the others were already waiting for him. This room had nothing of the distinctive character of the parts of the house which Hugh had already seen. It was merely a handsome modern room, of no great size. Mr. Arnold led Euphra to dinner, and Hugh followed with Harry.

Mr. Arnold's manner to Hugh was the same as in the morning—studiously polite, without the smallest approach to cordiality. He addressed him as an equal, it is true; but an equal who could never be in the smallest danger of thinking he meant it. Hugh, who, without having seen a great deal of the world, yet felt much the same wherever he was, took care to give him all that he seemed to look for, as far at least as was consistent with his own self-respect. He soon discovered that he was one of those men, who, if you will only grant their position, and acknowledge their authority, will allow you to have much your own way in everything. His servants had found this out long ago, and almost everything about the house was managed as they pleased; but as the oldest of them were respectable family servants, nothing went very far wrong. They all, however, waited on Euphra with an assiduity that showed she was, or could be, quite mistress when and where she pleased. Perhaps they had found out that she had great influence with Mr. Arnold; and certainly he seemed very fond of her indeed, after a stately fashion. She spoke to the servants with peculiar gentleness; never said, if you please; but always, thank you. Harry never asked for anything, but always looked to Euphra, who gave the necessary order. Hugh saw that the boy was quite dependent upon her, seeming of himself scarcely capable of originating the simplest action. Mr. Arnold, however, dull as he was, could not help seeing that Harry's manner was livelier than usual, and seemed pleased at the slight change already visible for the better. Turning to Hugh he said:

"Do you find Harry very much behind with his studies, Mr. Sutherland?"

"I have not yet attempted to find out," replied Hugh.

"Not?" said Mr. Arnold, with surprise.

"No. If he be behind, I feel confident it will not be for long."

"But," began Mr. Arnold, pompously; and then he paused.

"You were kind enough to say, Mr. Arnold, that I might try my own plans with him first. I have been doing so."

"Yes—certainly. But—"

Here Harry broke in with some animation:

"Mr. Sutherland has been my horse, carrying me about on his back all the morning—no, not all the morning—but an hour, or an hour and a half—or was it two hours, Mr. Sutherland?"

"I really don't know, Harry," answered Hugh; "I don't think it matters much."

Harry seemed relieved, and went on:

"He has been reading Gulliver's Travels to me—oh, such fall! And we have been to see the cows and the pigs; and Mr. Sutherland has been teaching me to jump. Do you know, papa, he jumped right over the pony's back without touching it."

Mr. Arnold stared at the boy with lustreless eyes and hanging checks. These grew red, as if he were going to choke. Such behaviour was quite inconsistent with the dignity of Arnstead and its tutor, who had been recommended to him as a thorough gentleman. But for the present he said nothing; probably because he could think of nothing to say.

"Certainly Harry seems better already," interposed Euphra.

"I cannot help thinking Mr. Sutherland has made a good beginning."

Mr. Arnold did not reply, but the cloud wore away from his face by degrees; and at length he asked Hugh to take a glass of wine with him.

When Euphra rose from the table, and Harry followed her example, Hugh thought it better to rise as well. Mr. Arnold seemed to hesitate whether or not to ask him to resume his seat and have a glass of claret. Had he been a little wizened pedagogue, no doubt he would have insisted on his company, sure of acquiescence from him in every sentiment he might happen to utter. But Hugh really looked so very much like a gentleman, and stated his own views, or adopted his own plans, with so much independence, that Mr. Arnold judged it safer to keep him at arm's length for a season at least, till he should thoroughly understand his position—not that of a guest, but that of his son's tutor, belonging to the household of Arnstead only on approval.

On leaving the dining-room, Hugh hesitated, in his turn, whether to betake himself to his own room, or to accompany Euphra to the drawing-room, the door of which stood open on the opposite side of the hall, revealing a brightness and warmth, which the chill of the evening, and the lowness of the fire in the dining-room, rendered quite enticing. But Euphra, who was half-across the hall, seeming to divine his thoughts, turned, and said, "Are you not going to favour us with your company, Mr. Sutherland?"

"With pleasure," replied Hugh; but, to cover his hesitation, added, "I will be with you presently;" and ran up stairs to his own room. "The old gentleman sits on his dignity—can hardly be said to stand on it," thought he, as he went. "The poor relation, as she calls herself, treats me like a guest. She is mistress here, however; that is clear enough."

As he descended the stairs to the drawing-room, a voice rose through the house, like the voice of an angel. At least so thought Hugh, hearing it for the first time. It seemed to take his breath away, as he stood for a moment on the stairs, listening. It was only Euphra singing The Flowers of the Forest. The drawing-room door was still open, and her voice rang through the wide lofty hall. He entered almost on tip-toe, that he might lose no thread of the fine tones. —Had she chosen the song of Scotland out of compliment to him? —She saw him enter, but went on without hesitating even. In the high notes, her voice had that peculiar vibratory richness which belongs to the nightingale's; but he could not help thinking that the low tones were deficient both in quality and volume. The expression and execution, however, would have made up for a thousand defects. Her very soul seemed brooding over the dead upon Flodden field, as she sang this most wailful of melodies —this embodiment of a nation's grief. The song died away as if the last breath had gone with it; failing as it failed, and ceasing with its inspiration, as if the voice that sang lived only for and in the song. A moment of intense silence followed. Then, before Hugh had half recovered from the former, with an almost grand dramatic recoil, as if the second sprang out of the first, like an eagle of might out of an ocean of weeping, she burst into Scots wha hae. She might have been a new Deborah, heralding her nation to battle. Hugh was transfixed, turned icy cold, with the excitement of his favourite song so sung. —Was that a glance of satisfied triumph with which Euphra looked at him for a single moment? —She sang the rest of the song as if the battle were already gained; but looked no more at Hugh.

The excellence of her tones, and the lambent fluidity of her transitions, if I may be allowed the phrase, were made by her art quite subservient to the expression, and owed their chief value to the share they bore in producing it. Possibly there was a little too much of the dramatic in her singing, but it was all in good taste; and, in a word, Hugh had never heard such singing before. As soon as she had finished, she rose, and shut the piano.

"Do not, do not," faltered Hugh, seeking to arrest her hand, as she closed the instrument.

"I can sing nothing after that," she said with emotion, or perhaps excitement; for the trembling of her voice might be attributed to either cause. "Do not ask me."

Hugh respectfully desisted; but after a few minutes' pause ventured to remark:

"I cannot understand how you should be able to sing Scotch songs so well. I never heard any but Scotch women sing them, even endurably, before: your singing of them is perfect."

"It seems to me," said Euphra, speaking as if she would rather have remained silent, "that a true musical penetration is independent of styles and nationalities. It can perceive, or rather feel, and reproduce, at the same moment. If the music speaks Scotch, the musical nature hears Scotch. It can take any shape, indeed cannot help taking any shape, presented to it."

Hugh was yet further astonished by this criticism from one whom he had been criticising with so much carelessness that very day.

"You think, then," said he, modestly, not as if he would bring her to book, but as really seeking to learn from her, "that a true musical nature can pour itself into the mould of any song, in entire independence of association and education?"

"Yes; in independence of any but what it may provide for itself."

Euphrasia, however, had left one important element unrepresented in the construction of her theory—namely, the degree of capability which a mind may possess of sympathy with any given class of feelings. The blossom of the mind, whether it flower in poetry, music, or any other art, must be the exponent of the nature and condition of that whose blossom it is. No mind, therefore, incapable of sympathising with the feelings whence it springs, can interpret the music of another. And Euphra herself was rather a remarkable instance of this forgotten fact.

Further conversation on the subject was interrupted by the entrance of Mr. Arnold, who looked rather annoyed at finding Hugh in the drawing-room, and ordered Harry off to bed, with some little asperity of tone. The boy rose at once, rang the bell, bade them all good night, and went. A servant met him at the door with a candle, and accompanied him.

Thought Hugh: "Here are several things to be righted at once. The boy must not have wine; and he must have only one dinner a-day—especially if he is ordered to bed so early. I must make a man of him if I can."

He made inquiries, and, with some difficulty, found out where the boy slept. During the night he was several times in Harry's room, and once in happy time to wake him from a nightmare dream. The boy was so overcome with terror, that Hugh got into bed beside him and comforted him to sleep in his arms. Nor did he leave him till it was time to get up, when he stole back to his own quarters, which, happily, were at no very great distance.

I may mention here, that it was not long before Hugh succeeded in stopping the wine, and reducing the dinner to a mouthful of supper. Harry, as far as he was concerned, yielded at once; and his father only held out long enough to satisfy his own sense of dignity.

CHAPTER IV
THE CAVE IN THE STRAW

All knowledge and wonder (which is the seed of knowledge) is an impression of pleasure in itself.

LORD BACON.—Advancement of Learning.

The following morning dawned in a cloud; which, swathed about the trees, wetted them down to the roots, without having time to become rain. They drank it in like sorrow, the only material out of which true joy can be fashioned. This cloud of mist would yet glimmer in a new heaven, namely, in the cloud of blooms which would clothe the limes and the chestnuts and the beeches along the ghost's walk. But there was gloomy weather within doors as well; for poor Harry was especially sensitive to variations of the barometer, without being in the least aware of the fact himself. Again Hugh found him in the library, seated in his usual corner, with Polexander on his knees. He half dropped the book when Hugh entered, and murmured with a sigh:

"It's no use; I can't read it."

"What's the matter, Harry?" said his tutor.

"I should like to tell you, but you will laugh at me."

"I shall never laugh at you, Harry."

"Never?"

"No, never."

"Then tell me how I can be sure that I have read this book."

"I do not quite understand you."

"All! I was sure nobody could be so stupid as I am. Do you know, Mr. Sutherland, I seem to have read a page from top to bottom sometimes, and when I come to the bottom I know nothing about it, and doubt whether I have read it at all; and then I stare at it all over again, till I grow so queer, and sometimes nearly scream. You see I must be able to say I have read the book."

"Why? Nobody will ever ask you."

"Perhaps not; but you know that is nothing. I want to know that I have read the book—really and truly read it."

Hugh thought for a moment, and seemed to see that the boy, not being strong enough to be a law to himself, just needed a benign law from without, to lift him from the chaos of feeble and conflicting notions and impulses within, which generated a false law of slavery. So he said:

"Harry, am I your big brother?"

"Yes, Mr. Sutherland."

"Then, ought you to do what I wish, or what you wish yourself?"

"What you wish, sir."

"Then I want you to put away that book for a month at least."

"Oh, Mr. Sutherland! I promised."

"To whom?"

"To myself." "But I am above you; and I want you to do as I tell you. Will you, Harry?"

"Yes."

"Put away the book, then."

Harry sprang to his feet, put the book on its shelf, and, going up to Hugh, said,

"You have done it, not me."

"Certainly, Harry."

The notions of a hypochondriacal child will hardly be interesting to the greater part of my readers; but Hugh learned from this a little lesson about divine law which he never forgot.

"Now, Harry," added he, "you must not open a book till I allow you."

"No poetry, either?" said poor Harry; and his face fell.

"I don't mind poetry so much; but of prose I will read as much to you as will be good for you. Come, let us have a bit of Gulliver again."

"Oh, how delightful!" cried Harry. "I am so glad you made me put away that tiresome book. I wonder why it insisted so on being read."

Hugh read for an hour, and then made Harry put on his cloak, notwithstanding the rain, which fell in a slow thoughtful spring shower. Taking the boy again on his back, he carried him into the woods. There he told him how the drops of wet sank into the ground, and then went running about through it in every direction, looking for seeds: which were all thirsty little things, that wanted to grow, and could not, till a drop came and gave them drink. And he told him how the rain-drops were made up in the skies, and then came down, like millions of angels, to do what they were told in the dark earth. The good drops went into all the cellars and dungeons of the earth, to let out the imprisoned flowers. And he told him how the seeds, when they had drunk the rain-drops, wanted another kind of drink next, which was much thinner and much stronger, but could not do them any good till they had drunk the rain first.

"What is that?" said Harry. "I feel as if you were reading out of the Bible, Mr. Sutherland."

"It is the sunlight," answered his tutor. "When a seed has drunk of the water, and is not thirsty any more, it wants to breathe next; and then the sun sends a long, small finger of fire down into the grave where the seed is lying; and it touches the seed, and something inside the seed begins to move instantly and to grow bigger and bigger, till it sends two green blades out of it into the earth, and through the earth into the air; and then it can breathe. And then it sends roots down into the earth; and the roots keep drinking water, and the leaves keep breathing the air, and the sun keeps them alive and busy; and so a great tree grows up, and God looks at it, and says it is good."

"Then they really are living things?" said Harry.

"Certainly."

"Thank you, Mr. Sutherland. I don't think I shall dislike rain so much any more."

Hugh took him next into the barn, where they found a great heap of straw. Recalling his own boyish amusements, he made him put off his cloak, and help to make a tunnel into this heap. Harry was delighted—the straw was so nice, and bright, and dry, and clean. They drew it out by handfuls, and thus excavated a round tunnel to the distance of six feet or so; when Hugh proceeded to more extended operations. Before it was time to go to lunch, they had cleared half of a hollow sphere, six feet in diameter, out of the heart of the heap.

After lunch, for which Harry had been very unwilling to relinquish the straw hut, Hugh sent him to lie down for a while; when he fell fast asleep as before. After he had left the room, Euphra said:

"How do you get on with Harry, Mr. Sutherland?"

"Perfectly to my satisfaction," answered Hugh.

"Do you not find him very slow?"

"Quite the contrary."

"You surprise me. But you have not given him any lessons yet."

"I have given him a great many, and he is learning them very fast."

"I fear he will have forgotten all my poor labours before you take up the work where we left it. When will you give him any book-lessons?"

"Not for a while yet."

Euphra did not reply. Her silence seemed intended to express dissatisfaction; at least so Hugh interpreted it.

"I hope you do not think it is to indulge myself that I manage Master Harry in this peculiar fashion," he said. "The fact is, he is a very peculiar child, and may turn out a genius or a weakling, just as he is managed. At least so it appears to me at present. May I ask where you left the work you were doing with him?"

"He was going through the Eton grammar for the third time," answered Euphra, with a defiant glance, almost of dislike, at Hugh. "But I need not enumerate his studies, for I daresay you will not take them up at all after my fashion. I only assure you I have been a very exact disciplinarian. What he knows, I think you will find he knows thoroughly."

So saying, Euphra rose, and with a flush on her cheek, walked out of the room in a more stately manner than usual.

Hugh felt that he had, somehow or other, offended her. But, to tell the truth, he did not much care, for her manner had rather irritated him. He retired to his own room, wrote to his mother, and, when Harry awoke, carried him again to the barn for an hour's work in the straw. Before it grew dusk, they had finished a little, silent, dark chamber, as round as they could make it, in the heart of the straw. All the excavated material they had thrown on the top, reserving only a little to close up the entrance when they pleased.

The next morning was still rainy; and when Hugh found Harry in the library as usual, he saw that the clouds had again gathered over the boy's spirit. He was pacing about the room in a very odd manner. The carpet was divided diamond-wise in a regular pattern. Harry's steps were, for the most part, planted upon every third diamond, as he slowly crossed the floor in a variety of directions; for, as on previous occasions, he had not perceived the entrance of his tutor. But, every now and then, the boy would make the most sudden and irregular change in his mode of progression, setting his foot on the most unexpected diamond, at one time the nearest to him, at another the farthest within his reach. When he looked up, and saw his tutor watching him, he neither started nor blushed: but, still retaining on his countenance the perplexed, anxious expression which Hugh had remarked, said to him:

"How can God know on which of those diamonds I am going to set my foot next?"

"If you could understand how God knows, Harry, then you would know yourself; but before you have made up your mind, you don't know which you will choose; and even then you only know on which you intend to set your foot; for you have often changed your mind after making it up."

Harry looked as puzzled as before.

"Why, Harry, to understand how God understands, you would need to be as wise as he is; so it is no use trying. You see you can't quite understand me, though I have a real meaning in what I say."

"Ah! I see it is no use; but I can't bear to be puzzled."

"But you need not be puzzled; you have no business to be puzzled. You are trying to get into your little brain what is far too grand and beautiful to get into it. Would you not think it very stupid to puzzle yourself how to put a hundred horses into a stable with twelve stalls?"

Harry laughed, and looked relieved.

"It is more unreasonable a thousand times to try to understand such things. For my part, it would make me miserable to think that there was nothing but what I could understand. I should feel as if I had no room anywhere. Shall we go to our cave again?"

"Oh! yes, please," cried Harry; and in a moment he was on Hugh's back once more, cantering joyously to the barn.

After various improvements, including some enlargement of the interior, Hugh and Harry sat down together in the low yellow twilight of their cave, to enjoy the result of their labours. They could just see, by the light from the tunnel, the glimmer of the golden hollow all about them. The rain was falling heavily out-of-doors; and they could hear the sound of the multitudinous drops of the broken cataract of the heavens like the murmur of the insects in a summer wood. They knew that everything outside was rained upon, and was again raining on everything beneath it, while they were dry and warm.

"This is nice!" exclaimed Harry, after a few moments of silent enjoyment.

"This is your first lesson in architecture," said Hugh.

"Am I to learn architecture?" asked Harry, in a rueful tone.

"It is well to know how things came to be done, if you should know nothing more about them, Harry. Men lived in the cellars first of all, and next on the ground floor; but they could get no further till they joined the two, and then they could build higher."

"I don't quite understand you, sir."

"I did not mean you should, Harry."

"Then I don't mind, sir. But I thought architecture was building."

"So it is; and this is one way of building. It is only making an outside by pulling out an inside, instead of making an inside by setting up an outside."

Harry thought for a while, and then said joyfully:

"I see it, sir! I see it. The inside is the chief thing—not the outside."

"Yes, Harry; and not in architecture only. Never forget that."

They lay for some time in silence, listening to the rain. At length Harry spoke:

"I have been thinking of what you told me yesterday, Mr. Sutherland, about the rain going to look for the seeds that were thirsty for it. And now I feel just as if I were a seed, lying in its little hole in the earth, and hearing the rain-drops pattering down all about it, waiting—oh, so thirsty!—for some kind drop to find me out, and give me itself to drink. I wonder what kind of flower I should grow up," added he, laughing.

"There is more truth than you think, in your pretty fancy, Harry," rejoined Hugh, and was silent—self-rebuked; for the memory of David came back upon him, recalled by the words of the boy; of David, whom he loved and honoured with the best powers of his nature, and whom yet he had neglected and seemed to forget; nay, whom he had partially forgotten— he could not deny. The old man, whose thoughts were just those of a wise child, had said to him once:

"We ken no more, Maister Sutherlan', what we're growin' till, than that neep-seed there kens what a neep is, though a neep it will be. The only odds is, that we ken that we dinna ken, and the neep-seed kens nothing at all aboot it. But ae thing, Maister Sutherlan', we may be sure o': that, whatever it be, it will be worth God's makin' an' our growin'."

A solemn stillness fell upon Hugh's spirit, as he recalled these words; out of which stillness, I presume, grew the little parable which follows; though Hugh, after he had learned far more about the things therein hinted at, could never understand how it was, that he could have put so much more into it, than he seemed to have understood at that period of his history.

For Harry said:

"Wouldn't this be a nice place for a story, Mr. Sutherland? Do you ever tell stories, sir?"

"I was just thinking of one, Harry; but it is as much yours as mine, for you sowed the seed of the story in my mind."

"Do you mean a story that never was in a book—a story out of your own head? Oh! that will be grand!"

"Wait till we see what it will be, Harry; for I can't tell you how it will turn out."

After a little further pause, Hugh began:

"Long, long ago, two seeds lay beside each other in the earth, waiting. It was cold, and rather wearisome; and, to beguile the time, the one found means to speak to the other.

"'What are you going to be?' said the one.

"'I don't know,' answered the other.

"'For me,' rejoined the first, 'I mean to be a rose. There is nothing like a splendid rose. Everybody will love me then!'

"'It's all right,' whispered the second; and that was all he could say; for somehow when he had said that, he felt as if all the words in the world were used up. So they were silent again for a day or two.

"'Oh, dear!' cried the first, 'I have had some water. I never knew till it was inside me. I'm growing! I'm growing! Good-bye!'

"'Good-bye!' repeated the other, and lay still; and waited more than ever.

"The first grew and grew, pushing itself straight up, till at last it felt that it was in the open air, for it could breathe. And what a delicious breath that was! It was rather cold, but so refreshing. The flower could see nothing, for it was not quite a flower yet, only a plant; and they never see till their eyes come, that is, till they open their blossoms—then they are flowers quite. So it grew and grew, and kept its head up very steadily, meaning to see the sky the first thing, and leave the earth quite behind as well as beneath it. But somehow or other, though why it could not tell, it felt very much inclined to cry. At length it opened its eye. It was morning, and the sky was over its head; but, alas! itself was no rose—only a tiny white flower. It felt yet more inclined to hang down its head and to cry; but it still resisted, and tried hard to open its eye wide, and to hold its head upright, and to look full at the sky.

"'I will be a star of Bethlehem at least!' said the flower to itself.

"But its head felt very heavy; and a cold wind rushed over it, and bowed it down towards the earth. And the flower saw that the time of the singing of birds was not come, that the snow covered the whole land, and that there was not a single flower in sight but itself. And it half-closed its leaves in terror and the dismay of loneliness. But that instant it remembered what the other flower used to say; and it said to itself: 'It's all right; I will be what I can.' And thereon it yielded to the wind, drooped its head to the earth, and looked no more on the sky, but on the snow. And straightway the wind stopped, and the cold died away, and the snow sparkled like pearls and diamonds; and the flower knew that it was the holding of its head up that had hurt it so; for that its body came of the snow, and that its name was Snow-drop. And so it said once more, 'It's all right!' and waited in perfect peace. All the rest it needed was to hang its head after its nature."

"And what became of the other?" asked Harry.

"I haven't done with this one yet," answered Hugh. "I only told you it was waiting. One day a pale, sad-looking girl, with thin face, large eyes, and long white hands, came, hanging her head like the snowdrop, along the snow where the flower grew. She spied it, smiled joyously, and saying, 'Ah! my little sister, are you come?' stooped and plucked the snowdrop. It trembled and died in her hand; which was a heavenly death for a snowdrop; for had it not cast a gleam of summer, pale as it had been itself, upon the heart of a sick girl?"

"And the other?" repeated Harry.

"The other had a long time to wait; but it did grow one of the loveliest roses ever seen. And at last it had the highest honour ever granted to a flower: two lovers smelled it together, and were content with it."

Harry was silent, and so was Hugh; for he could not understand himself quite. He felt, all the time he was speaking, is if he were listening to David, instead of talking himself. The fact was, he was only expanding, in an imaginative soil, the living seed which David had cast into it. There seemed to himself to be more in his parable than he had any right to invent. But is it not so with all stories that are rightly rooted in the human?

"What a delightful story, Mr. Sutherland!" said Harry, at last. "Euphra tells me stories sometimes; but I don't think I ever heard one I liked so much. I wish we were meant to grow into something, like the flower-seeds."

"So we are, Harry."

"Are we indeed? How delightful it would be to think that I am only a seed, Mr. Sutherland! Do you think I might think so?"

"Yes, I do."

"Then, please, let me begin to learn something directly. I haven't had anything disagreeable to do since you came; and I don't feel as if that was right."

Poor Harry, like so many thousands of good people, had not yet learned that God is not a hard task-master.

"I don't intend that you should have anything disagreeable to do, if I can help it. We must do such things when they come to us; but we must not make them for ourselves, or for each other."

"Then I'm not to learn any more Latin, am I?" said Harry, in a doubtful kind of tone, as if there were after all a little pleasure in doing what he did not like.

"Is Latin so disagreeable, Harry?"

"Yes; it is rule after rule, that has nothing in it I care for. How can anybody care for Latin? But I am quite ready to begin, if I am only a seed— really, you know."

"Not yet, Harry. Indeed, we shall not begin again—I won't let you—till you ask me with your whole heart, to let you learn Latin."

"I am afraid that will be a long time, and Euphra will not like it."

"I will talk to her about it. But perhaps it will not be so long as you think. Now, don't mention Latin to me again, till you are ready to ask me, heartily, to teach you. And don't give yourself any trouble about it either. You never can make yourself like anything."

Harry was silent. They returned to the house, through the pouring rain; Harry, as usual, mounted on his big brother.

As they crossed the hall, Mr. Arnold came in. He looked surprised and annoyed. Hugh set Harry down, who ran upstairs to get dressed for dinner; while he himself half-stopped, and turned towards Mr. Arnold. But Mr. Arnold did not speak, and so Hugh followed Harry.

Hugh spent all that evening, after Harry had gone to bed, in correcting his impressions of some of the chief stories of early Roman history; of which stories he intended commencing a little course to Harry the next day.

Meantime there was very little intercourse between Hugh and Euphra, whose surname, somehow or other, Hugh had never inquired after. He disliked asking questions about people to an uncommon degree, and so preferred waiting for a natural revelation. Her later behaviour had repelled him, impressing him with the notion that she was proud, and that she had made up her mind, notwithstanding her apparent frankness at first, to keep him at a distance. That she was fitful, too, and incapable of showing much tenderness even to poor Harry, he had already concluded in his private judgment-hall. Nor could he doubt that, whether from wrong theories, incapacity, or culpable indifference, she must have taken very bad measures indeed with her young pupil.

The next day resembled the two former; with this difference, that the rain fell in torrents. Seated in their strawy bower, they cared for no rain. They were safe from the whole world, and all the tempers of nature.

Then Hugh told Harry about the slow beginnings and the mighty birth of the great Roman people. He told him tales of their battles and conquests; their strifes at home, and their wars abroad. He told him stories of their grand men, great with the individuality of their nation and their own. He told him their characters, their peculiar opinions and grounds of action, and the results of their various schemes for their various ends. He told him about their love to their country, about their poetry and their religion; their courage, and their hardihood; their architecture, their clothes, and their armour; their customs and their laws; but all in such language, or mostly in such language, as one boy might use in telling another of the same age; for Hugh possessed the gift of a general simplicity of thought, one of the most valuable a man can have. It cost him a good deal of labour (well-repaid in itself, not to speak of the evident delight of Harry), to make himself perfectly competent for this; but he had a good foundation of knowledge to work upon.

This went on for a long time after the period to which I am now more immediately confined. Every time they stopped to rest from their rambles or games — as often, in fact, as they sat down alone, Harry's constant request was:

"Now, Mr. Sutherland, mightn't we have something more about the Romans?"

And Mr. Sutherland gave him something more. But all this time he never uttered the word — Latin.

CHAPTER V
LARCH AND OTHER HUNTING

For there is neither buske nor hay In May, that it n'ill shrouded bene, And it with newé leavés wrene; These woodés eke recoveren grene, That drie in winter ben to sene, And the erth waxeth proud withall, For swoté dewes that on it fall, And the poore estate forget, In which that winter had it set: And than becomes the ground so proude, That it wol have a newé shroude, And maketh so queint his robe and faire, That it hath hewes an hundred paire, Of grasse and floures, of Ind and Pers, And many hewés full divers: That is the robe I mean, ywis, Through which the ground to praisen is.

CHAUCER'S translation of the Romaunt of the Rose.

So passed the three days of rain. After breakfast the following morning, Hugh went to find Harry, according to custom, in the library. He was reading.

"What are you reading, Harry?" asked he.

"A poem," said Harry; and, rising as before, he brought the book to Hugh. It was Mrs. Hemans's Poems.

"You are fond of poetry, Harry."

"Yes, very."

"Whose poems do you like best?"

"Mrs. Hemans's, of course. Don't you think she is the best, sir?"

"She writes very beautiful verses, Harry. Which poem are you reading now?"

"Oh! one of my favourites—The Voice of Spring."

"Who taught you to like Mrs. Hemans?"

"Euphra, of course."

"Will you read the poem to me?"

Harry began, and read the poem through, with much taste and evident enjoyment; an enjoyment which seemed, however, to spring more from the music of the thought and its embodiment in sound, than from sympathy with the forms of nature called up thereby. This was shown by his mode of reading, in which the music was everything, and the sense little or nothing. When he came to the line,

"And the larch has hung all his tassels forth,"
he smiled so delightedly, that Hugh said:

"Are you fond of the larch, Harry?"

"Yes, very."

"Are there any about here?"

"I don't know. What is it like?"

"You said you were fond of it."

"Oh, yes; it is a tree with beautiful tassels, you know. I think I should like to see one. Isn't it a beautiful line?"

"When you have finished the poem, we will go and see if we can find one anywhere in the woods. We must know where we are in the world, Harry—what is all round about us, you know."

"Oh, yes," said Harry; "let us go and hunt the larch."

"Perhaps we shall meet Spring, if we look for her—perhaps hear her voice, too."

"That would be delightful," answered Harry, smiling. And away they went.

I may just mention here that Mrs. Hemans was allowed to retire gradually, till at last she was to be found only in the more inaccessible recesses of the library-shelves; while by that time Harry might be heard, not all over the house, certainly, but as far off as outside the closed door of the library, reading aloud to himself one or other of Macaulay's ballads, with an evident enjoyment of the go in it. A story with drum and trumpet accompaniment was quite enough, for the present, to satisfy Harry; and Macaulay could give him that, if little more.

As they went across the lawn towards the shrubbery, on their way to look for larches and Spring, Euphra joined them in walking dress. It was a lovely morning.

"I have taken you at your word, you see, Mr. Sutherland," said she. "I don't want to lose my Harry quite."

"You dear kind Euphra!" said Harry, going round to her side and taking her hand. He did not stay long with her, however, nor did Euphra seem particularly to want him.

"There was one thing I ought to have mentioned to you the other night, Mr. Sutherland; and I daresay I should have mentioned it, had not Mr. Arnold interrupted our tête-à-tête. I feel now as if I had been guilty of claiming far more than I have a right to, on the score of musical insight. I have Scotch blood in me, and was indeed born in Scotland, though I left it before I was a year old. My mother, Mr. Arnold's sister, married a gentleman who was half Sootch; and I was born while they were on a visit to his relatives, the Camerons of Lochnie. His mother, my grandmother, was a Bohemian lady, a countess with sixteen quarterings—not a gipsy, I beg to say."

Hugh thought she might have been, to judge from present appearances.

But how was he to account for this torrent of genealogical information, into which the ice of her late constraint had suddenly thawed? It was odd that she should all at once volunteer so much about herself. Perhaps she had made up one of those minds which need making up, every now and then, like a monthly magazine; and now was prepared to publish it. Hugh responded with a question:

"Do I know your name, then, at last? You are Miss Cameron?"

"Euphrasia Cameron; at your service, sir." And she dropped a gay little courtesy to Hugh, looking up at him with a flash of her black diamonds.

"Then you must sing to me to-night."

"With all the pleasure in gipsy-land," replied she, with a second courtesy, lower than the first; taking for granted, no doubt, his silent judgment on her person and complexion.

By this time they had reached the woods in a different quarter from that which Hugh had gone through the other day with Harry. And here, in very deed, the Spring met them, with a profusion of richness to which Hugh was quite a stranger. The ground was carpeted with primroses, and anemones, and other spring flowers, which are the loveliest of all flowers. They were drinking the sunlight, which fell upon them through the budded boughs. By the time the light should be hidden from them by the leaves, which are the clouds of the lower firmament of the woods, their need of it would be gone: exquisites in living, they cared only for the delicate morning of the year.

"Do look at this darling, Mr. Sutherland!" exclaimed Euphrasia suddenly, as she bent at the root of a great beech, where grew a large bush of rough leaves, with one tiny but perfectly-formed primrose peeping out between. "Is it not a little pet?—all eyes—all one eye staring out of its curtained bed to see what ever is going on in the world.—You had better lie down again: it is not a nice place."

She spoke to it as if it had been a kitten or a baby. And as she spoke, she pulled the leaves yet closer over the little starer so as to hide it quite.

As they went on, she almost obtrusively avoided stepping on the flowers, saying she almost felt cruel, or at least rude, when she did so. Yet she trailed her dress over them in quite a careless way, not lifting it at all. This was a peculiarity of hers, which Hugh never understood till he understood herself.

All about in shady places, the ferns were busy untucking themselves from their grave-clothes, unrolling their mysterious coils of life, adding continually to the hidden growth as they unfolded the visible. In this, they were like the other revelations of God the Infinite. All the wild lovely things were coming up for their month's life of joy. Orchis-harlequins, cuckoo-plants, wild arums, more properly lords-and-ladies, were coming, and coming—slowly; for had they not a long way to come, from the valley of the shadow of death into the land of life? At last the wanderers came upon a whole company of bluebells—not what Hugh would have called bluebells, for the bluebells of Scotland are the single-poised harebells—but wild hyacinths, growing in a damp and shady spot, in wonderful luxuriance. They were quite three feet in height, with long, graceful, drooping heads; hanging down from them, all along one side, the largest and loveliest of bells—one lying close above the other, on the lower part; while they parted thinner and thinner as they rose towards the lonely one at the top. Miss Cameron went into ecstasies over these; not saying much, but breaking up what she did say with many prettily passionate pauses.

She had a very happy turn for seeing external resemblances, either humorous or pathetic; for she had much of one element that goes to the making of a poet—namely, surface impressibility.

"Look, Harry; they are all sad at having to go down there again so soon. They are looking at their graves so ruefully."

Harry looked sad and rather sentimental immediately. When Hugh glanced at Miss Cameron, he saw tears in her eyes.

"You have nothing like this in your country, have you, Mr. Sutherland?" said she, with an apparent effort.

"No, indeed," answered Hugh.

And he said no more. For a vision rose before him of the rugged pine-wood and the single primrose; and of the thoughtful maiden, with unpolished speech and rough hands, and—but this he did not see—a soul slowly refining itself to a crystalline clearness. And he thought of the grand old grey-haired David, and of Janet with her quaint motherhood, and of all the blessed bareness of the ancient time—in sunlight and in snow; and he felt again that he had forgotten and forsaken his friends.

"How the fairies will be ringing the bells in these airy steeples in the moonlight!" said Miss Cameron to Harry, who was surprised and delighted with it all. He could not help wondering, however, after he went to bed that night, that Euphra had never before taken him to see these beautiful things, and had never before said anything half so pretty to him, as the least pretty thing she had said about the flowers that morning when they were out with Mr. Sutherland. Had Mr. Sutherland anything to do with it? Was he giving Euphra a lesson in flowers such as he had given him in pigs?

Miss Cameron presently drew Hugh into conversation again, and the old times were once more forgotten for a season. They were worthy of distinguishing note—that trio in those spring woods: the boy waking up to feel that flowers and buds were lovelier in the woods than in verses; Euphra finding everything about her sentimentally useful, and really delighting in the prettinesses they suggested to her; and Hugh regarding the whole chiefly as a material and means for reproducing in verse such impressions of delight as he had received and still received from all (but the highest) poetry about nature. The presence of Harry and his necessities was certainly a saving influence upon Hugh; but, however much he sought to realize Harry's life, he himself, at this period of his history, enjoyed everything artistically far more than humanly.

Margaret would have walked through all this infant summer without speaking at all, but with a deep light far back in her quiet eyes. Perhaps she would not have had many thoughts about the flowers. Rather she would have thought the very flowers themselves; would have been at home with them, in a delighted oneness with their life and expression. Certainly she would have walked through them with reverence, and would not have petted or patronised nature by saying pretty things about her children. Their life would have entered into her, and she would have hardly known it from her own. I daresay Miss Cameron would have called a mountain a darling or a beauty. But there are other ways of showing affection than by patting and petting—though Margaret, for her part, would have needed no art-expression, because she had the things themselves. It is not always those who utter best who feel most; and the dumb poets are sometimes dumb because it would need the "large utterance of the early gods" to carry their thoughts through the gates of speech.

But the fancy and skin-sympathy of Miss Cameron began already to tell upon Hugh. He knew very little of women, and had never heard a woman talk as she talked. He did not know how cheap this accomplishment is, and took it for sensibility, imaginativeness, and even originality. He thought she was far more en rapport with nature than he was. It was much easier to make this mistake after hearing the really delightful way in which she sang. Certainly she could not have sung so, perhaps not even have talked so, except she had been capable of more; but to be capable of more, and to be able for more, are two very distinct conditions.

Many walks followed this, extending themselves farther and farther from home, as Harry's strength gradually improved. It was quite remarkable how his interest in everything external increased, in exact proportion as he learned to see into the inside or life of it. With most children, the interest in the external comes first, and with many ceases there. But it is in reality only a shallower form of the deeper sympathy; and in those cases where it does lead to a desire after the hidden nature of things, it is perhaps the better beginning of the two. In such exceptional cases as Harry's, it is of unspeakable importance that both the difference and the identity should be recognized; and in doing so, Hugh became to Harry his big brother indeed, for he led him where he could not go alone.

As often as Mr. Arnold was from home, which happened not unfrequently, Miss Cameron accompanied them in their rambles. She gave as her reason for doing so only on such occasions, that she never liked to be out of the way when her uncle might want her. Traces of an inclination to quarrel with Hugh, or even to stand upon her dignity, had all but vanished; and as her vivacity never failed her, as her intellect was always active, and as by the exercise of her will she could enter sympathetically, or appear to enter, into everything, her presence was not in the least a restraint upon them.

On one occasion, when Harry had actually run a little way after a butterfly, Hugh said to her:

"What did you mean, Miss Cameron, by saying you were only a poor relation? You are certainly mistress of the house."

"On sufferance, yes. But I am only a poor relation. I have no fortune of my own."

"But Mr. Arnold does not treat you as such."

"Oh! no. He likes me. He is very kind to me.—He gave me this ring on my last birthday. Is it not a beauty?"

She pulled off her glove and showed a very fine diamond on a finger worthy of the ornament.

"It is more like a gentleman's, is it not?" she added, drawing it off. "Let me see how it would look on your hand."

She gave the ring to Hugh; who, laughing, got it with some difficulty just over the first joint of his little finger, and held it up for Euphra to see.

"Ah! I see I cannot ask you to wear it for me," said she. "I don't like it myself. I am afraid, however," she added, with an arch look, "my uncle would not like it either—on your finger. Put it on mine again."

Holding her hand towards Hugh, she continued:

"It must not be promoted just yet. Besides, I see you have a still better one of your own."

As Hugh did according to her request, the words sprang to his lips, "There are other ways of wearing a ring than on the finger." But they did not cross the threshold of speech. Was it the repression of them that caused that strange flutter and slight pain at the heart, which he could not quite understand?

CHAPTER VI
FATIMA

Those lips that Love's own hand did make Breathed forth the sound that said, "I hate," To me that languished for her sake: But when she saw my woeful state, Straight in her heart did mercy come, Chiding that tongue that, ever sweet, Was used in giving gentle doom, And taught it thus anew to greet: "I hate" she altered with an end, That followed it as gentle day Doth follow night, who, like a fiend, From heaven to hell is flown away. "I hate" from hate away she threw, And saved my life, saying—"Not you."

SHAKSPERE

Mr. Arnold was busy at home for a few days after this, and Hugh and Harry had to go out alone. One day, when the wind was rather cold, they took refuge in the barn; for it was part of Hugh's especial care that Harry should be rendered hardy, by never being exposed to more than he could bear without a sense of suffering. As soon as the boy began to feel fatigue, or cold, or any other discomfort, his tutor took measures accordingly.

Harry would have crept into the straw-house; but Hugh said, pulling a book out of his pocket,

"I have a poem here for you, Harry. I want to read it to you now; and we can't see in there."

They threw themselves down on the straw, and Hugh, opening a volume of Robert Browning's Poems, read the famous ride from Ghent to Aix. He knew the poem well, and read it well. Harry was in raptures.

"I wish I could read that as you do," said he.

"Try," said Hugh.

Harry tried the first verse, and threw the book down in disgust with himself.

"Why cannot I read it?" said he.

"Because you can't ride."

"I could ride, if I had such a horse as that to ride upon."

"But you could never have such a horse as that except you could ride, and ride well, first. After that, there is no saying but you might get one. You might, in fact, train one for yourself—till from being a little foal it became your own wonderful horse."

"Oh! that would be delightful! Will you teach me horses as well, Mr. Sutherland?"

"Perhaps I will."

That evening, at dinner, Hugh said to Mr. Arnold:

"Could you let me have a horse to-morrow morning, Mr. Arnold?"

Mr. Arnold stared a little, as he always did at anything new. But Hugh went on:

"Harry and I want to have a ride to-morrow; and I expect we shall like it so much, that we shall want to ride very often."

"Yes, that we shall!" cried Harry.

"Could not Mr. Sutherland have your white mare, Euphra?" said Mr. Arnold, reconciled at once to the proposal.

"I would rather not, if you don't mind, uncle. My Fatty is not used to such a burden as I fear Mr. Sutherland would prove. She drops a little now, on the hard road."

The fact was, Euphra would want Fatima.

"Well, Harry," said Mr. Arnold, graciously pleased to be facetious, "don't you think your Welsh dray-horse could carry Mr. Sutherland?"

"Ha! ha! ha! Papa, do you know, Mr. Sutherland set him up on his hind legs yesterday, and made him walk on them like a dancing-dog. He was going to lift him, but he kicked about so when he felt himself leaving the ground, that he tumbled Mr. Sutherland into the horse-trough."

Even the solemn face of the butler relaxed into a smile, but Mr. Arnold's clouded instead. His boy's tutor ought to be a gentleman.

"Wasn't it fun, Mr. Sutherland?"

"It was to you, you little rogue!" said Sutherland, laughing.

"And how you did run home, dripping like a water-cart!—and all the dogs after you!"

Mr. Arnold's monotonous solemnity soon checked Harry's prattle.

"I will see, Mr. Sutherland, what I can do to mount you."

"I don't care what it is," said Hugh; who though by no means a thorough horseman, had been from boyhood in the habit of mounting everything in the shape of a horse that he could lay hands upon, from a cart-horse upwards and downwards.

"There's an old bay that would carry me very well."

"That is my own horse, Mr. Sutherland."

This stopped the conversation in that direction. But next morning after breakfast, an excellent chestnut horse was waiting at the door, along with Harry's new pony. Mr. Arnold would see them go off. This did not exactly suit Miss Cameron, but if she frowned, it was when nobody saw her. Hugh put Harry up himself, told him to stick fast with his knees, and then mounted his chestnut. As they trotted slowly down the avenue, Euphrasia heard Mr. Arnold say to himself, "The fellow sits well, at all events." She took care to make herself agreeable to Hugh by reporting this, with the omission of the initiatory epithet, however.

Harry returned from his ride rather tired, but in high spirits.

"Oh, Euphra!" he cried, "Mr. Sutherland is such a rider! He jumps hedges and ditches and everything. And he has promised to teach me and my pony to jump too. And if I am not too tired, we are to begin to-morrow, out on the common. Oh! jolly!"

The little fellow's heart was full of the sense of growing life and strength, and Hugh was delighted with his own success. He caught sight of a serpentine motion in Euphra's eyebrows, as she bent her face again over the work from which she had lifted it on their entrance. He addressed her.

"You will be glad to hear that Harry has ridden like a man."

"I am glad to hear it, Harry."

Why did she reply to the subject of the remark, and not to the speaker? Hugh perplexed himself in vain to answer this question; but a very small amount of experience would have made him able to understand at once as much of her behaviour as was genuine. At luncheon she spoke only in reply; and then so briefly, as not to afford the smallest peg on which to hang a response.

"What can be the matter?" thought Hugh. "What a peculiar creature she is! But after what has passed between us, I can't stand this."

When dinner was over that evening, she rose as usual and left the room, followed by Hugh and Harry; but as soon as they were in the drawing-room, she left it; and, returning to the dining-room, resumed her seat at the table.

"Take a glass of claret, Euphra, dear?" said Mr. Arnold.

"I will, if you please, uncle. I should like it. I have seldom a minute with you alone now."

Evidently flattered, Mr. Arnold poured out a glass of claret, rose and carried it to his niece himself, and then took a chair beside her.

"Thank you, dear uncle," she said, with one of her bewitching flashes of smile.

"Harry has been getting on bravely with his riding, has he not?" she continued.

"So it would appear."

Harry had been full of the story of the day at the dinner-table, where he still continued to present himself; for his father would not be satisfied without hint. It was certainly good moral training for the boy, to sit there almost without eating; and none the worse that he found it rather hard sometimes. He talked much more freely now, and asked the servants for anything he wanted without referring to Euphra. Now and then he would glance at her, as if afraid of offending her; but the cords which bound him to her were evidently relaxing; and she saw it plainly enough, though she made no reference to the unpleasing fact.

"I am only a little fearful, uncle, lest Mr. Sutherland should urge the boy to do more than his strength will admit of. He is exceedingly kind to him, but he has evidently never known what weakness is himself."

"True, there is danger of that. But you see he has taken him so entirely into his own hands. I don't seem to be allowed a word in the matter of his education any more." Mr. Arnold spoke with the peevishness of weak importance. "I wish you would take care that he does not carry things too far, Euphra."

This was just what Euphra wanted.

"I think, if you do not disapprove, uncle, I will have Fatima saddled to-morrow morning, and go with them myself."

"Thank you, my love; I shall be much obliged to you." The glass of claret was soon finished after this. A little more conversation about nothing followed, and Euphra rose the second time, and returned to the drawing-room. She found it unoccupied. She sat down to the piano, and sang song after song—Scotch, Italian, and Bohemian. But Hugh did not make his appearance. The fact was, he was busy writing to his mother, whom he had rather neglected since he came. Writing to her made him think of David, and he began a letter to him too; but it was never finished, and never sent.

He did not return to the drawing-room that evening. Indeed, except for a short time, while Mr. Arnold was drinking his claret, he seldom showed himself there. Had Euphra repelled him too much—hurt him? She would make up for it to-morrow.

Breakfast was scarcely over, when the chestnut and the pony passed the window, accompanied by a lovely little Arab mare, broad-chested and light-limbed, with a wonderfully small head. She was white as snow, with keen, dark eyes. Her curb-rein was red instead of white. Hearing their approach, and begging her uncle to excuse her, Euphra rose from the table, and left the room; but re-appeared in a wonderfully little while, in a well-fitted riding-habit of black velvet, with a belt of dark red leather clasping a waist of the roundest and smallest. Her little hat, likewise black, had a single long, white feather, laid horizontally within the upturned brim, and drooping over it at the back. Her white mare would be just the right pedestal for the dusky figure—black eyes, tawny skin, and all. As she stood ready to mount, and Hugh was approaching to put her up, she called the groom, seemed just to touch his hand, and was in the saddle in a moment, foot in stirrup, and skirt falling over it. Hugh thought she was carrying out the behaviour of yesterday, and was determined to ask her what it meant. The little Arab began to rear and plunge with pride, as soon as she felt her mistress on her back; but she seemed as much at home as if she had been on the music-stool, and patted her arching neck, talking to her in the same tone almost in which she had addressed the flowers.

"Be quiet, Fatty dear; you're frightening Mr. Sutherland."

But Hugh, seeing the next moment that she was in no danger, sprang into his saddle. Away they went, Fatima infusing life and frolic into the equine as Euphra into the human portion of the cavalcade. Having reached the common, out of sight of the house, Miss Cameron, instead of looking after Harry, lest he should have too much exercise, scampered about like a wild girl, jumping everything that came in her way, and so exciting Harry's pony, that it was almost more than he could do to manage it, till at last Hugh had to beg her to go more quietly, for Harry's sake. She drew up alongside of them at once, and made her mare stand as still as she could, while Harry made his first essay upon a little ditch. After crossing it two or three times, he gathered courage; and setting his pony at a larger one beyond, bounded across it beautifully.

"Bravo! Harry!" cried both Euphra and Hugh. Harry galloped back, and over it again; then came up to them with a glow of proud confidence on his pale face.

"You'll be a horseman yet, Harry," said Hugh.

"I hope so," said Harry, in an aspiring tone, which greatly satisfied his tutor. The boy's spirit was evidently reviving. Euphra must have managed him ill. Yet she was not in the least effeminate herself. It puzzled Hugh a good deal. But he did not think about it long; for Harry cantering away in front, he had an opportunity of saying to Euphra:

"Are you offended with me, Miss Cameron?"

"Offended with you! What do you mean? A girl like me offended with a man like you?"

She looked two and twenty as she spoke; but even at that she was older than Hugh. He, however, certainly looked considerably older than he really was.

"What makes you think so?" she added, turning her face towards him.

"You would not speak to me when we came home yesterday."

"Not speak to you?—I had a little headache—and perhaps I was a little sullen, from having been in such bad company all the morning."

"What company had you?" asked Hugh, gazing at her in some surprise.

"My own," answered she, with a lovely laugh, thrown full in his face. Then after a pause: "Let me advise you, if you want to live in peace, not to embark on that ocean of discovery."

"What ocean? what discovery?" asked Hugh, bewildered, and still gazing.

"The troubled ocean of ladies' looks," she replied. "You will never be able to live in the same house with one of our kind, if it be necessary to your peace to find out what every expression that puzzles you may mean."

"I did not intend to be inquisitive—it really troubled me."

"There it is. You must never mind us. We show so much sooner than men—but, take warning, there is no making out what it is we do show. Your faces are legible; ours are so scratched and interlined, that you had best give up at once the idea of deciphering them."

Hugh could not help looking once more at the smooth, simple, naïve countenance shining upon him.

"There you are at it again," she said, blushing a little, and turning her head away. "Well, to comfort you, I will confess I was rather cross yesterday—because—because you seemed to have been quite happy with only one of your pupils."

As she spoke the words, she gave Fatima the rein, and bounded off, overtaking Harry's pony in a moment. Nor did she leave her cousin during all the rest of their ride.

Most women in whom the soul has anything like a chance of reaching the windows, are more or less beautiful in their best moments. Euphra's best was when she was trying to fascinate. Then she was—fascinating. During the first morning that Hugh spent at Arnstead, she had probably been making up her mind whether, between her and Hugh, it was to be war to the knife, or fascination. The latter had carried the day, and was now carrying him. But had she calculated that fascination may re-act as well?

Hugh's heart bounded, like her Arab steed, as she uttered the words last recorded. He gave his chestnut the rein in his turn, to overtake her; but Fatima's canter quickened into a gallop, and, inspirited by her companionship, and the fact that their heads were turned stablewards, Harry's pony, one of the quickest of its race, laid itself to the ground, and kept up, taking three strides for Fatty's two, so that Hugh never got within three lengths of them till they drew rein at the hall-door, where the grooms were waiting them. Euphra was off her mare in a moment, and had almost reached her own room before Hugh and Harry had crossed the hall. She came down to luncheon in a white muslin dress, with the smallest possible red spot in it; and, taking her place at the table, seemed to Hugh to have put off not only her riding habit, but the self that was in it as well; for she chatted away in the most unconcerned and easy manner possible, as if she had not been out of her room all the morning. She had ridden so hard, that she had left her last speech in the middle of the common, and its mood with it; and there seemed now no likelihood of either finding its way home.

CHAPTER VII
THE PICTURE GALLERY

the house is crencled to and fro,
And hath so queint waies for to go,
For it is shapen as the mase is wrought.

CHAUCER—Legend of Ariadne.

Luncheon over, and Harry dismissed as usual to lie down, Miss Cameron said to Hugh:

"You have never been over the old house yet, I believe, Mr. Sutherland. Would you not like to see it?"

"I should indeed," said Hugh. "It is what I have long hoped for, and have often been on the point of begging."

"Come, then; I will be your guide—if you will trust yourself with a madcap like me, in the solitudes of the old hive."

"Lead on to the family vaults, if you will," said Hugh.

"That might be possible, too, from below. We are not so very far from them. Even within the house there is an old chapel, and some monuments worth looking at. Shall we take it last?"

"As you think best," answered Hugh.

She rose and rang the bell. When it was answered,

"Jacob," she said, "get me the keys of the house from Mrs. Horton."

Jacob vanished, and reappeared with a huge bunch of keys. She took them.

"Thank you. They should not be allowed to get quite rusty, Jacob."

"Please, Miss, Mrs. Horton desired me to say, she would have seen to them, if she had known you wanted them."

"Oh! never mind. Just tell my maid to bring me an old pair of gloves."

Jacob went; and the maid came with the required armour.

"Now, Mr. Sutherland. Jane, you will come with us. No, you need not take the keys. I will find those I want as we go."

She unlocked a door in the corner of the hall, which Hugh had never seen open. Passing through a long low passage, they came to a spiral staircase of stone, up which they went, arriving at another wide hall, very dusty, but in perfect repair. Hugh asked if there was not some communication between this hall and the great oak staircase.

"Yes," answered Euphra; "but this is the more direct way."

As she said this, he felt somehow as if she cast on him one of her keenest glances; but the place was very dusky, and he stood in a spot where the light fell upon him from an opening in a shutter, while she stood in deep shadow.

"Jane, open that shutter."

The girl obeyed; and the entering light revealed the walls covered with paintings, many of them apparently of no value, yet adding much to the effect of the place. Seeing that Hugh was at once attracted by the pictures, Euphra said:

"Perhaps you would like to see the picture gallery first?"

Hugh assented. Euphra chose key after key, and opened door after door, till they came into a long gallery, well lighted from each end. The windows were soon opened.

"Mr. Arnold is very proud of his pictures, especially of his family portraits; but he is content with knowing he has them, and never visits them except to show them; or perhaps once or twice a year, when something or other keeps him at home for a day, without anything particular to do."

In glancing over the portraits, some of them by famous masters, Hugh's eyes were arrested by a blonde beauty in the dress of the time of Charles II. There was such a reality of self-willed boldness as well as something worse in her face, that, though arrested by the picture, Hugh felt ashamed of looking at it in the presence of Euphra and her maid. The pictured woman almost put him out of countenance, and yet at the same time fascinated him. Dragging his eyes from it, he saw that Jane had turned her back upon it, while Euphra regarded it steadily.

"Open that opposite window, Jane," said she; "there is not light enough on this portrait."

Jane obeyed. While she did so, Hugh caught a glimpse of her face, and saw that the formerly rosy girl was deadly pale. He said to Euphra:

"Your maid seems ill, Miss Cameron."

"Jane, what is the matter with you?"

She did not reply, but, leaning against the wall, seemed ready to faint.

"The place is close," said her mistress. "Go into the next room there," — she pointed to a door — "and open the window. You will soon be well."

"If you please, Miss, I would rather stay with you. This place makes me feel that strange."

She had come but lately, and had never been over the house before.

"Nonsense!" said Miss Cameron, looking at her sharply. "What do you mean?"

"Please, don't be angry, Miss; but the first night e'er I slept here, I saw that very lady — "

"Saw that lady!"

"Well, Miss, I mean, I dreamed that I saw her; and I remembered her the minute I see her up there; and she give me a turn like. I'm all right now, Miss."

Euphra fixed her eyes on her, and kept them fixed, till she was very nearly all wrong again. She turned as pale as before, and began to draw her breath hard.

"You silly goose!" said Euphra, and withdrew her eyes; upon which the girl began to breathe more freely.

Hugh was making some wise remarks in his own mind on the unsteady condition of a nature in which the imagination predominates over the powers of reflection, when Euphra turned to him, and began to tell him that that was the picture of her three or four times great-grandmother, painted by Sir Peter Lely, just after she was married.

"Isn't she fair?" said she. — "She turned nun at last, they say."

"She is more fair than honest," thought Hugh. "It would take a great deal of nun to make her into a saint." But he only said, "She is more beautiful than lovely. What was her name?"

"If you mean her maiden name, it was Halkar — Lady Euphrasia Halkar — named after me, you see. She had foreign blood in her, of course; and, to tell the truth, there were strange stories told of her, of more sorts than one. I know nothing of her family. It was never heard of in England, I believe, till after the Restoration."

All the time Euphra was speaking, Hugh was being perplexed with that most annoying of perplexities — the flitting phantom of a resemblance, which he could not catch. He was forced to dismiss it for the present, utterly baffled.

"Were you really named after her, Miss Cameron?"

"No, no. It is a family name with us. But, indeed, I may be said to be named after her, for she was the first of us who bore it. You don't seem to like the portrait."

"I do not; but I cannot help looking at it, for all that."

"I am so used to the lady's face," said Euphra, "that it makes no impression on me of any sort. But it is said," she added, glancing at the maid, who stood at some distance, looking uneasily about her—and as she spoke she lowered her voice to a whisper—"it is said, she cannot lie still."

"Cannot lie still! What do you mean?"

"I mean down there in the chapel," she answered, pointing.

The Celtic nerves of Hugh shuddered. Euphra laughed; and her voice echoed in silvery billows, that broke on the faces of the men and women of old time, that had owned the whole; whose lives had flowed and ebbed in varied tides through the ancient house; who had married and been given in marriage; and gone down to the chapel below—below the prayers and below the psalms—and made a Sunday of all the week.

Ashamed of his feeling of passing dismay, Hugh said, just to say something:

"What a strange ornament that is! Is it a brooch or a pin? No, I declare it is a ring—large enough for three cardinals, and worn on her thumb. It seems almost to sparkle. Is it ruby, or carbuncle, or what?"

"I don't know: some clumsy old thing," answered Euphra, carelessly.

"Oh! I see," said Hugh; "it is not a red stone. The glow is only a reflection from part of her dress. It is as clear as a diamond. But that is impossible—such a size. There seems to me something curious about it; and the longer I look at it, the more strange it appears."

Euphra stole another of her piercing glances at him, but said nothing.

"Surely," Hugh went on, "a ring like that would hardly be likely to be lost out of the family? Your uncle must have it somewhere."

Euphra laughed; but this laugh was very different from the last. It rattled rather than rang.

"You are wonderfully taken with a bauble—for a man of letters, that is, Mr. Sutherland. The stone may have been carried down any one of the hundred streams into which a family river is always dividing."

"It is a very remarkable ornament for a lady's finger, notwithstanding," said Hugh, smiling in his turn.

"But we shall never get through the pictures at this rate," remarked Euphra; and going on, she directed Hugh's attention now to this, now to that portrait, saying who each was, and mentioning anything remarkable in the history of their originals. She manifested a thorough acquaintance with the family story, and made, in fact, an excellent show-woman. Having gone nearly to the other end of the gallery,

"This door," said she, stopping at one, and turning over the keys, "leads to one of the oldest portions of the house, the principal room in which is said to have belonged especially to the lady over there."

As she said this, she fixed her eyes once more on the maid.

"Oh! don't ye now, Miss," interrupted Jane. "Hannah du say as how a whitey-blue light shines in the window of a dark night, sometimes—that lady's window, you know, Miss. Don't ye open the door—pray, Miss."

Jane seemed on the point of falling into the same terror as before.

"Really, Jane," said her mistress, "I am ashamed of you; and of myself, for having such silly servants about me."

"I beg your pardon, Miss, but—"

"So Mr. Sutherland and I must give up our plan of going over the house, because my maid's nerves are too delicate to permit her to accompany us. For shame!"

"Oh, du ye now go without me!" cried the girl, clasping her hands.

"And you will wait here till we come back?"

"Oh! don't ye leave me here. Just show me the way out."

And once more she turned pale as death.

"Mr. Sutherland, I am very sorry, but we must put off the rest of our ramble till another time. I am, like Hamlet, very vilely attended, as you see. Come, then, you foolish girl," she added, more mildly.

The poor maid, what with terror of Lady Euphrasia, and respect for her mistress, was in a pitiable condition of moral helplessness. She seemed almost too frightened to walk behind them. But if she had been in front it would have been no better; for, like other ghost-fearers, she seemed to feel very painfully that she had no eyes in her back.

They returned as they came; and Jane receiving the keys to take to the housekeeper, darted away. When she reached Mrs. Horton's room, she sank on a chair in hysterics.

"I must get rid of that girl, I fear," said Miss Cameron, leading the way to the library; "she will infect the whole household with her foolish terrors.

We shall not hear the last of this for some time to come. We had a fit of it the same year I came; and I suppose the time has come round for another attack of the same epidemic."

"What is there about the room to terrify the poor thing?"

"Oh! they say it is haunted; that is all. Was there ever an old house anywhere over Europe, especially an old family house, but was said to be haunted? Here the story centres in that room—or at least in that room and the avenue in front of its windows."

"Is that the avenue called the Ghost's Walk?"

"Yes. Who told you?"

"Harry would not let me cross it."

"Poor boy! This is really too bad. He cannot stand anything of that kind, I am sure. Those servants!"

"Oh! I hope we shall soon get him too well to be frightened at anything. Are these places said to be haunted by any particular ghost?"

"Yes. By Lady Euphrasia—Rubbish!"

Had Hugh possessed a yet keener perception of resemblance, he would have seen that the phantom-likeness which haunted him in the portrait of Euphrasia Halkar, was that of Euphrasia Cameron—by his side all the time. But the mere difference of complexion was sufficient to throw him out— insignificant difference as that is, beside the correspondence of features and their relations. Euphra herself was perfectly aware of the likeness, but had no wish that Hugh should discover it.

As if the likeness, however, had been dimly identified by the unconscious part of his being, he sat in one corner of the library sofa, with his eyes fixed on the face of Euphra, as she sat in the other. Presently he was made aware of his unintentional rudeness, by seeing her turn pale as death, and sink back in the sofa. In a moment she started up, and began pacing about the room, rubbing her eyes and temples. He was bewildered and alarmed.

"Miss Cameron, are you ill?" he exclaimed.

She gave a kind of half-hysterical laugh, and said:

"No—nothing worth speaking of. I felt a little faint, that was all. I am better now."

She turned full towards him, and seemed to try to look all right; but there was a kind of film over the clearness of her black eyes.

"I fear you have headache."

"A little, but it is nothing. I will go and lie down."

"Do, pray; else you will not be well enough to appear at dinner."

She retired, and Hugh joined Hairy.

Euphra had another glass of claret with her uncle that evening, in order to give her report of the morning's ride.

"Really, there is not much to be afraid of, uncle. He takes very good care of Harry. To be sure, I had occasion several times to check him a little; but he has this good quality in addition to a considerable aptitude for teaching, that he perceives a hint, and takes it at once."

Knowing her uncle's formality, and preference for precise and judicial modes of expression, Euphra modelled her phrase to his mind.

"I am glad he has your good opinion so far, Euphra; for I confess there is something about the youth that pleases me. I was afraid at first that I might be annoyed by his overstepping the true boundaries of his position in my family: he seems to have been in good society, too. But your assurance that he can take a hint, lessens my apprehension considerably. To-morrow, I will ask him to resume his seat after dessert."

This was not exactly the object of Euphra's qualified commendation of Hugh. But she could not help it now.

"I think, however, if you approve, uncle, that it will be more prudent to keep a little watch over the riding for a while. I confess, too, I should be glad of a little more of that exercise than I have had for some time: I found my seat not very secure to-day."

"Very desirable on both considerations, my love."

And so the conference ended.

CHAPTER VIII
NEST-BUILDING

If you will have a tree bear more fruit than it hath used to do, it is not anything you can do to the boughs, but it is the stirring of the earth, and putting new mould about the roots, that must work it.

LORD BACON'S Advancement of Learning, b. ii.

In a short time Harry's health was so much improved, and consequently the strength and activity of his mind so much increased, that Hugh began to give him more exact mental operations to perform. But as if he had been a reader of Lord Bacon, which as yet he was not, and had learned from him that "wonder is the seed of knowledge," he came, by a kind of sympathetic instinct, to the same conclusion practically, in the case of Harry. He tried to wake a question in him, by showing him something that would rouse his interest. The reply to this question might be the whole rudiments of a science.

Things themselves should lead to the science of them. If things are not interesting in themselves, how can any amount of knowledge about them be? To be sure, there is such a thing as a purely or abstractly intellectual interest—the pleasure of the mere operation of the intellect upon the signs of things; but this must spring from a highly exercised intellectual condition, and is not to be expected before the pleasures of intellectual motion have been experienced through the employment of its means for other ends. Whether this is a higher condition or not, is open to much disquisition.

One day Hugh was purposely engaged in taking the altitude of the highest turret of the house, with an old quadrant he had found in the library, when Harry came up.

"What are you doing, big brother?" said he; for now that he was quite at home with Hugh, there was a wonderful mixture of familiarity and respect in him, that was quite bewitching.

"Finding out how high your house is, little brother," answered Hugh.

"How can you do it with that thing? Will it measure the height of other things besides the house?"

"Yes, the height of a mountain, or anything you like."

"Do show me how."

Hugh showed him as much of it as he could.

"But I don't understand it."

"Oh! that is quite another thing. To do that, you must learn a great many things—Euclid to begin with."

That very afternoon Harry began Euclid, and soon found quite enough of interest on the road to the quadrant, to prevent him from feeling any tediousness in its length.

Of an afternoon Hugh had taken to reading Shakspere to Harry. Euphra was always a listener. On one occasion Harry said:

"I am so sorry, Mr. Sutherland, but I don't understand the half of it. Sometimes when Euphra and you are laughing,—and sometimes when Euphra is crying," added he, looking at her slyly, "I can't understand what it is all about. Am I so very stupid, Mr. Sutherland?" And he almost cried himself.

"Not a bit of it, Harry, my boy; only you must learn a great many other things first."

"How can I learn them? I am willing to learn anything. I don't find it tire me now as it used."

"There are many things necessary to understand Shakspere that I cannot teach you, and that some people never learn. Most of them will come of themselves. But of one thing you may be sure, Harry, that if you learn anything, whatever it be, you are so far nearer to understanding Shakspere."

The same afternoon, when Harry had waked from his siesta, upon which Hugh still insisted, they went out for a walk in the fields. The sun was half way down the sky, but very hot and sultry.

"I wish we had our cave of straw to creep into now," said Harry. "I felt exactly like the little field-mouse you read to me about in Burns's poems, when we went in that morning, and found it all torn up, and half of it carried away. We have no place to go to now for a peculiar own place; and the consequence is, you have not told me any stories about the Romans for a whole week."

"Well, Harry, is there any way of making another?"

"There's no more straw lying about that I know of," answered Harry; "and it won't do to pull the inside out of a rick, I am afraid."

"But don't you think it would be pleasant to have a change now; and as we have lived underground, or say in the snow like the North people, try living in the air, like some of the South people?"

"Delightful!" cried Harry.—"A balloon?"

"No, not quite that. Don't you think a nest would do?"

"Up in a tree?"

"Yes."

Harry darted off for a run, as the only means of expressing his delight. When he came back, he said:

"When shall we begin, Mr. Sutherland?"

"We will go and look for a place at once; but I am not quite sure when we shall begin yet. I shall find out to-night, though."

They left the fields, and went into the woods in the neighbourhood of the house, at the back. Here the trees had grown to a great size, some of them being very old indeed. They soon fixed upon a grotesque old oak as a proper tree in which to build their nest; and Harry, who, as well as Hugh, had a good deal of constructiveness in his nature, was so delighted, that the heat seemed to have no more influence upon him; and Hugh, fearful of the reaction, was compelled to restrain his gambols.

Pursuing their way through the dark warp of the wood, with its golden weft of crossing sunbeams, Hugh began to tell Harry the story of the killing of Cæsar by Brutus and the rest, filling up the account with portions from Shakspere. Fortunately, he was able to give the orations of Brutus and Antony in full. Harry was in ecstasy over the eloquence of the two men.

"Well, what language do you think they spoke, Harry?" said Hugh.

"Why," said Harry, hesitating, "I suppose—" then, as if a sudden light broke upon him—"Latin of course. How strange!"

"Why strange?"

"That such men should talk such a dry, unpleasant language."

"I allow it is a difficult language, Harry; and very ponderous and mechanical; but not necessarily dry or unpleasant. The Romans, you know, were particularly fond of law in everything; and so they made a great many laws for their language; or rather, it grew so, because they were of that sort. It was like their swords and armour generally, not very graceful, but very strong;—like their architecture too, Harry. Nobody can ever understand what a people is, without knowing its language. It is not only that we find all these stories about them in their language, but the language itself is more like them than anything else can be. Besides, Harry, I don't believe you know anything about Latin yet."

"I know all the declensions and conjugations."

"But don't you think it must have been a very different thing to hear it spoken?"

"Yes, to be sure—and by such men. But how ever could they speak it?"

"They spoke it just as you do English. It was as natural to them. But you cannot say you know anything about it, till you read what they wrote in it; till your ears delight in the sound of their poetry;—"

"Poetry?"

"Yes; and beautiful letters; and wise lessons; and histories and plays."

"Oh! I should like you to teach me. Will it be as hard to learn always as it is now?"

"Certainly not. I am sure you will like it."

"When will you begin me?"

"To-morrow. And if you get on pretty well, we will begin our nest, too, in the afternoon."

"Oh, how kind you are! I will try very hard."

"I am sure you will, Harry."

Next morning, accordingly, Hugh did begin him, after a fashion of his own; namely, by giving him a short simple story to read, finding out all the words with him in the dictionary, and telling him what the terminations of the words signified; for he found that he had already forgotten a very great deal of what, according to Euphra, he had been thoroughly taught. No one can remember what is entirely uninteresting to him.

Hugh was as precise about the grammar of a language as any Scotch Professor of Humanity, old Prosody not excepted; but he thought it time enough to begin to that, when some interest in the words themselves should have been awakened in the mind of his pupil. He hated slovenliness as much as any one; but the question was, how best to arrive at thoroughness in the end, without losing the higher objects of study; and not how, at all risks, to commence teaching the lesson of thoroughness at once, and so waste on the shape of a pin-head the intellect which, properly directed, might arrive at the far more minute accuracies of a steam-engine. The fault of Euphra in teaching Harry, had been that, with a certain kind of tyrannical accuracy, she had determined to have the thing done—not merely decently and in order, but prudishly and pedantically; so that she deprived progress of the pleasure which ought naturally to attend it. She spoiled the walk to the distant outlook, by stopping at every step, not merely to pick flowers, but to botanise on the weeds, and to calculate the distance advanced. It is quite true that we ought to learn to do things irrespective of the reward; but plenty of opportunities will be given in the progress of life, and in much higher kinds of action, to exercise our sense of duty in severe loneliness. We have no right to turn intellectual exercises into pure operations of conscience: these ought to involve essential duty; although no doubt there is plenty of room for mingling duty with those; while, on the other hand, the highest act of suffering self-denial is not without its accompanying reward. Neither is there any exercise of the higher intellectual powers in learning the mere grammar of a language, necessary as it is for a means. And language having been made before grammar, a language must be in some measure understood, before its grammar can become intelligible.

Harry's weak (though true and keen) life could not force its way into any channel. His was a nature essentially dependent on sympathy. It could flow into truth through another loving mind: left to itself, it could not find the way, and sank in the dry sand of ennui and self-imposed obligations. Euphra was utterly incapable of understanding him; and the boy had been dying for lack of sympathy, though neither he nor any one about him had suspected the fact.

There was a strange disproportion between his knowledge and his capacity. He was able, when his attention was directed, his gaze fixed, and his whole nature supported by Hugh, to see deep into many things, and his remarks were often strikingly original; but he was one of the most ignorant boys, for his years, that Hugh had ever come across. A long and severe illness, when he was just passing into boyhood, had thrown him back far into his childhood; and he was only now beginning to show that he had anything of the boy-life in him. Hence arose that unequal development which has been sufficiently evident in the story.

In the afternoon, they went to the wood, and found the tree they had chosen for their nest. To Harry's intense admiration, Hugh, as he said, went up the tree like a squirrel, only he was too big for a bear even. Just one layer of foliage above the lowest branches, he came to a place where he thought there was a suitable foundation for the nest. From the ground Harry could scarcely see him, as, with an axe which he had borrowed for the purpose (for there was a carpenter's work-shop on the premises), he cut away several small branches from three of the principal ones; and so had these three as rafters, ready dressed and placed, for the foundation of the nest. Having made some measurements, he descended; and repairing with Harry to the work-shop, procured some boarding and some tools, which

Harry assisted in carrying to the tree. Ascending again, and drawing up his materials, by the help of Harry, with a piece of string, Hugh in a very little while had a level floor, four feet square, in the heart of the oak tree, quite invisible from below—buried in a cloud of green leaves. For greater safety, he fastened ropes as handrails all around it from one branch to another. And now nothing remained but to construct a bench to sit on, and such a stair as Harry could easily climb. The boy was quite restless with anxiety to get up and see the nest; and kept calling out constantly to know if he might not come up yet. At length Hugh allowed him to try; but the poor boy was not half strong enough to climb the tree without help. So Hugh descended, and with his aid Harry was soon standing on the new-built platform.

"I feel just like an eagle," he cried; but here his voice faltered, and he was silent.

"What is the matter, Harry?" said his tutor.

"Oh, nothing," replied he; "only I didn't exactly know whereabouts we were till I got up here."

"Whereabouts are we, then?"

"Close to the end of the Ghost's Walk."

"But you don't mind that now, surely, Harry?"

"No, sir; that is, not so much as I used."

"Shall I take all this down again, and build our nest somewhere else?"

"Oh, no, if you don't think it matters. It would be a great pity, after you have taken so much trouble with it. Besides, I shall never be here without you; and I do not think I should be afraid of the ghost herself, if you were with me."

Yet Harry shuddered involuntarily at the thought of his own daring speech.

"Very well, Harry, my boy; we will finish it here. Now, if you stand there, I will fasten a plank across here between these two stumps—no, that won't do exactly. I must put a piece on to this one, to raise it to a level with the other—then we shall have a seat in a few minutes."

Hammer and nails were busy again; and in a few minutes they sat down to enjoy the "soft pipling cold" which swung all the leaves about like little trap-doors that opened into the Infinite. Harry was highly contented. He drew a deep breath of satisfaction as, looking above and beneath and all about him, he saw that they were folded in an almost impenetrable net of foliage, through which nothing could steal into their sanctuary, save "the chartered libertine, the air," and a few stray beams of the setting sun, filtering through the multitudinous leaves, from which they caught a green tint as they passed.

"Fancy yourself a fish," said Hugh, "in the depth of a cavern of sea weed, which floats about in the slow swinging motion of the heavy waters."

"What a funny notion!"

"Not so absurd as you may think, Harry; for just as some fishes crawl about on the bottom of the sea, so do we men at the bottom of an ocean of air; which, if it be a thinner one, is certainly a deeper one."

"Then the birds are the swimming fishes, are they not?"

"Yes, to be sure."

"And you and I are two mermen—doing what? Waiting for mother mermaid to give us our dinner. I am getting hungry. But it will be a long time before a mermaid gets up here, I am afraid."

"That reminds me," said Hugh, "that I must build a stair for you, Master Harry; for you are not merman enough to get up with a stroke of your scaly tail. So here goes. You can sit there till I fetch you."

Nailing a little rude bracket here and there on the stem of the tree, just where Harry could avail himself of hand-hold as well, Hugh had soon finished a strangely irregular staircase, which it took Harry two or three times trying, to learn quite off.

CHAPTER IX
GEOGRAPHY POINT

I will fetch you a tooth-picker now from the farthest inch of Asia; bring you the length of Prester John's foot; fetch you a hair off the great Cham's beard; do you any embassage to the Pigmies.

Much Ado about Nothing.

The next day, after dinner, Mr. Arnold said to the tutor:

"Well, Mr. Sutherland, how does Harry get on with his geography?"

Mr. Arnold, be it understood, had a weakness for geography.

"We have not done anything at that yet, Mr. Arnold."

"Not done anything at geography! And the boy getting quite robust now! I am astonished, Mr. Sutherland. Why, when he was a mere child, he could repeat all the counties of England."

"Perhaps that may be the reason for the decided distaste he shows for it now, Mr. Arnold. But I will begin to teach him at once, if you desire it."

"I do desire it, Mr. Sutherland. A thorough geographical knowledge is essential to the education of a gentleman. Ask me any question you please, Mr. Sutherland, on the map of the world, or any of its divisions."

Hugh asked a few questions, which Mr. Arnold answered at once.

"Pooh! pooh!" said he, "this is mere child's play. Let me ask you some, Mr. Sutherland."

His very first question posed Hugh, whose knowledge in this science was not by any means minute.

"I fear I am no gentleman," said he, laughing; "but I can at least learn as well as teach. We shall begin to-morrow."

"What books have you?"

"Oh! no books, if you please, just yet. If you are satisfied with Harry's progress so far, let me have my own way in this too."

"But geography does not seem your strong point."

"No; but I may be able to teach it all the better from feeling the difficulties of a learner myself."

"Well, you shall have a fair trial."

Next morning Hugh and Harry went out for a walk to the top of a hill in the neighbourhood. When they reached it, Hugh took a small compass from his pocket, and set it on the ground, contemplating it and the horizon alternately.

"What are you doing, Mr. Sutherland?"

"I am trying to find the exact line that would go through my home," said he.

"Is that funny little thing able to tell you?"

"Yes; this along with other things. Isn't it curious, Harry, to have in my pocket a little thing with a kind of spirit in it, that understands the spirit that is in the big world, and always points to its North Pole?"

"Explain it to me."

"It is nearly as much a mystery to me as to you."

"Where is the North Pole?"

"Look, the little thing points to it."

"But I will turn it away. Oh! it won't go. It goes back and back, do what I will."

"Yes, it will, if you turn it away all day long. Look, Harry, if you were to go straight on in this direction, you would come to a Laplander, harnessing his broad-horned reindeer to his sledge. He's at it now, I daresay. If you were to go in this line exactly, you would go through the smoke and fire of a burning mountain in a land of ice. If you were to go this way, straight on, you would find yourself in the middle of a forest with a lion glaring at your feet, for it is dark night there now, and so hot! And over there, straight on, there is such a lovely sunset. The top of a snowy mountain is all pink with light, though the sun is down—oh! such colours all about, like fairyland! And there, there is a desert of sand, and a camel dying, and all his companions just disappearing on the horizon. And there, there is an awful sea, without a boat to be seen on it, dark and dismal, with huge rocks all about it, and waste borders of sand—so dreadful!"

"How do you know all this, Mr. Sutherland? You have never walked along those lines, I know, for you couldn't."

"Geography has taught me."

"No, Mr. Sutherland!" said Harry, incredulously. "Well, shall we travel along this line, just across that crown of trees on the hill?"

"Yes, do let us."

"Then," said Hugh, drawing a telescope from his pocket, "this hill is henceforth Geography Point, and all the world lies round about it. Do you know we are in the very middle of the earth?"

"Are we, indeed?"

"Yes. Don't you know any point you like to choose on a ball is the middle of it?"

"Oh! yes—of course."

"Very well. What lies at the bottom of the hill down there?"

"Arnstead, to be sure."

"And what beyond there?"

"I don't know."

"Look through here."

"Oh! that must be the village we rode to yesterday—I forget the name of it."

Hugh told him the name; and then made him look with the telescope all along the receding line to the trees on the opposite hill. Just as he caught them, a voice beside them said:

"What are you about, Harry?"

Hugh felt a glow of pleasure as the voice fell on his ear.

It was Euphra's.

"Oh!" replied Harry, "Mr. Sutherland is teaching me geography with a telescope. It's such fun!"

"He's a wonderful tutor, that of yours, Harry!"

"Yes, isn't he just? But," Harry went on, turning to Hugh, "what are we to do now? We can't get farther for that hill."

"Ah! we must apply to your papa now, to lend us some of his beautiful maps. They will teach us what lies beyond that hill. And then we can read in some of his books about the places; and so go on and on, till we reach the beautiful, wide, restless sea; over which we must sail in spite of wind and tide—straight on and on, till we come to land again. But we must make a great many such journeys before we really know what sort of a place we are living in; and we shall have ever so many things to learn that will surprise us."

"Oh! it will be nice!" cried Harry.

After a little more geographical talk, they put up their instruments, and began to descend the hill. Harry was in no need of Hugh's back now, but Euphra was in need of his hand. In fact, she spelled for its support.

"How awkward of me! I am stumbling over the heather shamefully!"

She was, in fact, stumbling over her own dress, which she would not hold up. Hugh offered his hand; and her small one seemed quite content to be swallowed up in his large one.

"Why do you never let me put you on your horse?" said Hugh. "You always manage to prevent me somehow or other. The last time, I just turned my head, and, behold! when I looked, you were gathering your reins."

"It is only a trick of independence, Hugh—Mr. Sutherland—I beg your pardon."

I can make no excuse for Euphra, for she had positively never heard him called Hugh: there was no one to do so. But, the slip had not, therefore, the less effect; for it sounded as if she had been saying his name over and over again to herself.

"I beg your pardon," repeated Euphra, hastily; for, as Hugh did not reply, she feared her arrow had swerved from its mark.

"For a sweet fault, Euphra—I beg your pardon—Miss Cameron."

"You punish me with forgiveness," returned she, with one of her sweetest looks.

Hugh could not help pressing the little hand.

Was the pressure returned? So slight, so airy was the touch, that it might have been only the throb of his own pulses, all consciously vital about the wonderful woman-hand that rested in his. If he had claimed it, she might easily have denied it, so ethereal and uncertain was it. Yet he believed in it. He never dreamed that she was exercising her skill upon him. What could be her object in bewitching a poor tutor? Ah! what indeed?

Meantime this much is certain, that she was drawing Hugh closer and closer to her side; that a soothing dream of delight had begun to steal over his spirit, soon to make it toss in feverous unrest—as the first effects of some poisons are like a dawn of tenfold strength. The mountain wind blew from her to him, sometimes sweeping her garments about him, and bathing him in their faint sweet odours—odours which somehow seemed to belong to her whom they had only last visited; sometimes, so kindly strong did it blow, compelling her, or at least giving her excuse enough, to leave his hand and cling closely to his arm. A fresh spring began to burst from the very bosom of what had seemed before a perfect summer. A spring to summer! What would the following summer be? Ah! and what the autumn? And what the winter? For if the summer be tenfold summer, then must the winter be tenfold winter.

But though knowledge is good for man, foreknowledge is not so good.

And, though Love be good, a tempest of it in the brain will not ripen the fruits like a soft steady wind, or waft the ships home to their desired haven.

Perhaps, what enslaved Hugh most, was the feeling that the damsel stooped to him, without knowing that she stooped. She seemed to him in every way above him. She knew so many things of which he was ignorant; could say such lovely things; could, he did not doubt, write lovely verses; could sing like an angel; (though Scotch songs are not of essentially angelic strain, nor Italian songs either, in general; and they were all that she could do); was mistress of a great rich wonderful house, with a history; and, more than all, was, or appeared to him to be—a beautiful woman. It was true that his family was as good as hers; but he had disowned his family—so his pride declared; and the same pride made him despise his present position, and look upon a tutor's employment as—as—well, as other people look upon it; as a rather contemptible one in fact, especially for a young, powerful, six-foot fellow.

The influence of Euphrasia was not of the best upon him from the first; for it had greatly increased this feeling about his occupation. It could not affect his feelings towards Harry; so the boy did not suffer as yet. But it set him upon a very unprofitable kind of castle-building: he would be a soldier like his father; he would leave Arnstead, to revisit it with a sword by his side, and a Sir before his name. Sir Hugh Sutherland would be somebody even in the eyes of the master of Arnstead. Yes, a six-foot fellow, though he may be sensible in the main, is not, therefore, free from small vanities, especially if he be in love. But how leave Euphra?

Again I outrun my story.

CHAPTER X
ITALIAN

Per me si va nella città dolente

DANTE

Through me thou goest into the city of grief.

Of necessity, with so many shafts opened into the mountain of knowledge, a far greater amount of time must be devoted by Harry and his tutor to the working of the mine, than they had given hitherto. This made a considerable alteration in the intercourse of the youth and the lady; for, although Euphra was often present during school-hours, it must be said for Hugh that, during those hours, he paid almost all his attention to Harry; so much of it, indeed, that perhaps there was not enough left to please the lady. But she did not say so. She sat beside them in silence, occupied with her work, and saving up her glances for use. Now and then she would read; taking an opportunity sometimes, but not often, when a fitting pause occurred, to ask him to explain some passage about which she was in doubt. It must be conceded that such passages were well chosen for the purpose; for she was too wise to do her own intellect discredit by feigning a difficulty where she saw none; intellect being the only gift in others for which she was conscious of any reverence.

By-and-by she began to discontinue these visits to the schoolroom. Perhaps she found them dull. Perhaps—but we shall see.

One morning, in the course of their study—Euphra not present—Hugh had occasion to go from his own room, where, for the most part, they carried on the severer portion of their labours, down to the library for a book, to enlighten them upon some point on which they were in doubt. As he was passing an open door, Euphra's voice called him. He entered, and found himself in her private sitting-room. He had not known before where it was.

"I beg your pardon, Mr. Sutherland, for calling you, but I am at this moment in a difficulty. I cannot manage this line in the Inferno. Do help me."

She moved the book towards him, as he now stood by her side, she remaining seated at her table. To his mortification, he was compelled to confess his utter ignorance of the language.

"Oh! I am disappointed," said Euphra.

"Not so much as I am," replied Hugh. "But could you spare me one or two of your Italian books?"

"With pleasure," she answered, rising and going to her bookshelves.

"I want only a grammar, a dictionary, and a New Testament."

"There they are," she said, taking them down one after the other, and bringing them to him. "I daresay you will soon get up with poor stupid me."

"I shall do my best to get within hearing of your voice, at least, in which Italian must be lovely."

No reply, but a sudden droop of the head.

"But," continued Hugh, "upon second thoughts, lest I should be compelled to remain dumb, or else annoy your delicate ear with discordant sounds, just give me one lesson in the pronunciation. Let me hear you read a little first."

"With all my heart."

Euphra began, and read delightfully; for she was an excellent Italian scholar. It was necessary that Hugh should look over the book. This was difficult while he remained standing, as she did not offer to lift it from the table. Gradually, therefore, and hardly knowing how, he settled into a chair by her side. Half-an-hour went by like a minute, as he listened to the silvery tones of her voice, breaking into a bell-like sound upon the double consonants of that sweet lady-tongue. Then it was his turn to read and be corrected, and read again and be again corrected. Another half-hour glided away, and yet another. But it must be confessed he made good use of the time—if only it had been his own to use; for at the end of it he could pronounce Italian very tolerably—well enough, at least, to keep him from fixing errors in his pronunciation, while studying the language alone. Suddenly he came to himself, and looked up as from a dream. Had she been bewitching him? He was in Euphra's room—alone with her. And the door was shut—how or when? And—he looked at his watch—poor little Harry had been waiting his return from the library, for the last hour and a half. He was conscience-stricken. He gathered up the books hastily, thanked Euphra in the same hurried manner, and left the room with considerable disquietude, closing the door very gently, almost guiltily, behind him.

I am afraid Euphra had been perfectly aware that he knew nothing about Italian. Did she see her own eyes shine in the mirror before her, as he closed the door? Was she in love with him, then?

When Hugh returned with the Italian books, instead of the encyclopædia he had gone to seek, he found Harry sitting where he had left him, with his arms and head on the table, fast asleep.

"Poor boy!" said Hugh to himself; but he could not help feeling glad he was asleep. He stole out of the room again, passed the fatal door with a longing pain, found the volume of his quest in the library, and, returning with it, sat down beside Harry. There he sat till he awoke.

When he did awake at last, it was almost time for luncheon. The shame-faced boy was exceedingly penitent for what was no fault, while Hugh could not relieve him by confessing his. He could only say:

"It was my fault, Harry dear. I stayed away too long. You were so nicely asleep, I would not wake you. You will not need a siesta, that is all."

He was ashamed of himself, as he uttered the false words to the true-hearted child. But this, alas! was not the end of it all.

Desirous of learning the language, but far more desirous of commending himself to Euphra, Hugh began in downright earnest. That very evening, he felt that he had a little hold of the language. Harry was left to his own resources. Nor was there any harm in this in itself: Hugh had a right to part of every day for his own uses. But then, he had been with Harry almost every evening, or a great part of it, and the boy missed him much; for he was not yet self-dependent. He would have gone to Euphrasia, but somehow she happened to be engaged that evening. So he took refuge in the library, where, in the desolation of his spirit, Polexander began, almost immediately, to exercise its old dreary fascination upon him. Although he had not opened the book since Hugh had requested him to put it away, yet he had not given up the intention of finishing it some day; and now he took it down, and opened it listlessly, with the intention of doing something towards the gradual redeeming of the pledge he had given to himself. But he found it more irksome than ever. Still he read on; till at length he could discover no meaning at all in the sentences. Then he began to doubt whether he had read the words. He fixed his attention by main force on every individual word; but even then he began to doubt whether he could say he had read the words, for he might have missed seeing some of the letters composing each word. He grew so nervous and miserable over it, almost counting every letter, that at last he burst into tears, and threw the book down.

His intellect, which in itself was excellent, was quite of the parasitic order, requiring to wind itself about a stronger intellect, to keep itself in the region of fresh air and possible growth. Left to itself, its weak stem could not raise it above the ground: it would grow and mass upon the earth, till it decayed and corrupted, for lack of room, light, and air. But, of course, there was no danger in the meantime. This was but the passing sadness of an occasional loneliness.

He crept to Hugh's room, and received an invitation to enter, in answer to his gentle knock; but Hugh was so absorbed in his new study, that he hardly took any notice of him, and Harry found it almost as dreary here as in the study. He would have gone out, but a drizzling rain was falling; and he shrank into himself at the thought of the Ghost's Walk. The dinner-bell was a welcome summons.

Hugh, inspirited by the reaction from close attention, by the presence of Euphra, and by the desire to make himself generally agreeable, which sprung from the consciousness of having done wrong, talked almost brilliantly, delighting Euphra, overcoming Harry with reverent astonishment, and even interesting slow Mr. Arnold. With the latter Hugh had been gradually becoming a favourite; partly because he had discovered in him what he considered high-minded sentiments; for, however stupid and conventional Mr. Arnold might be, he had a foundation of sterling worthiness of character. Euphra, instead of showing any jealousy of this growing friendliness, favoured it in every way in her power, and now and then alluded to it in her conversations with Hugh, as affording her great satisfaction.

"I am so glad he likes you!" she would say.

"Why should she be glad?" thought Hugh.

This gentle claim of a kind of property in him, added considerably to the strength of the attraction that drew him towards her, as towards the centre of his spiritual gravitation; if indeed that could be called spiritual which had so little of the element of moral or spiritual admiration, or even approval, mingled with it. He never felt that Euphra was good. He only felt that she drew him with a vague force of feminine sovereignty—a charm which he could no more resist or explain, than the iron could the attraction of the loadstone. Neither could he have said, had he really considered the matter, that she was beautiful—only that she often, very often, looked beautiful. I suspect if she had been rather ugly, it would have been all the same for Hugh.

He pursued his Italian studies with a singleness of aim and effort that carried him on rapidly. He asked no assistance from Euphra, and said nothing to her about his progress. But he was so absorbed in it, that it drew him still further from his pupil. Of course he went out with him, walking or riding every day that the weather would permit; and he had regular school hours with him within doors. But during the latter, while Harry was doing something on his slate, or writing, or learning some lesson (which kind of work happened oftener now than he could have approved of), he would take up his Italian; and, notwithstanding Harry's quiet hints that he had finished what had been set him, remain buried in it for a long time. When he woke at last to the necessity of taking some notice of the boy, he would only appoint him something else to occupy him again, so as to leave himself free to follow his new bent. Now and then he would become aware of his blameable neglect, and make a feeble struggle to rectify what seemed to be growing into a habit—and one of the worst for a tutor; but he gradually sank back into the mire, for mire it was, comforting himself with the resolution that as soon as he was able to read Italian without absolutely spelling his way, he would let Euphra see what progress he had made, and then return with renewed energy to Harry's education, keeping up his own new accomplishment by more moderate exercise therein. It must not be supposed, however, that a long course of time passed in this way. At the end of a fortnight, he thought he might venture to request Euphra to show him the passage which had perplexed her. This time he knew where she was—in her own room; for his mind had begun to haunt her whereabouts. He knocked at her door, heard the silvery, thrilling, happy sound, "Come in;" and entered trembling.

"Would you show me the passage in Dante that perplexed you the other day?"

Euphra looked a little surprised; but got the book and pointed it out at once.

Hugh glanced at it. His superior acquaintance with the general forms of language enabled him, after finding two words in Euphra's larger dictionary, to explain it, to her immediate satisfaction.

"You astonish me," said Euphra.

"Latin gives me an advantage, you see," said Hugh modestly.

"It seems to be very wonderful, nevertheless."

These were sweet sounds to Hugh's ear. He had gained his end. And she hers.

"Well," she said, "I have just come upon another passage that perplexes me not a little. Will you try your powers upon that for me?"

So saying, she proceeded to find it.

"It is school-time," said Hugh "I fear I must not wait now."

"Pooh! pooh! Don't make a pedagogue of yourself. You know you are here more as a guardian—big brother, you know—to the dear child. By the way, I am rather afraid you are working him a little more than his constitution will stand."

"Do you think so?" returned Hugh quite willing to be convinced. "I should be very sorry."

"This is the passage," said Euphra.

Hugh sat down once more at the table beside her. He found this morsel considerably tougher than the last. But at length he succeeded in pulling it to pieces and reconstructing it in a simpler form for the lady. She was full of thanks and admiration. Naturally enough, they went on to the next line, and the next stanza, and the next and the next; till—shall I be believed?—they had read a whole canto of the poem. Euphra knew more words by a great many than Hugh; so that, what with her knowledge of the words, and his insight into the construction, they made rare progress.

"What a beautiful passage it is!" said Euphra.

"It is indeed," responded Hugh; "I never read anything more beautiful."

"I wonder if it would be possible to turn that into English. I should like to try."

"You mean verse, of course?"

"To be sure."

"Let us try, then. I will bring you mine when I have finished it. I fear it will take some time, though, to do it well. Shall it be in blank verse, or what?"

"Oh! don't you think we had better keep the Terza Rima of the original?"

"As you please. It will add much to the difficulty."

"Recreant knight! will you shrink from following where your lady leads?"

"Never! so help me, my good pen!" answered Hugh, and took his departure, with burning cheeks and a trembling at the heart. Alas! the morning was gone. Harry was not in his study: he sought and found him in the library, apparently buried in Polexander.

"I am so glad you are come," said Harry; "I am so tired."

"Why do you read that stupid book, then?"

"Oh! you know, I told you."

"Tut! tut! nonsense! Put it away," said Hugh, his dissatisfaction with himself making him cross with Harry, who felt, in consequence, ten times more desolate than before. He could not understand the change.

If it went ill before with the hours devoted to common labour, it went worse now. Hugh seized every gap of time, and widened its margins shamefully, in order to work at his translation. He found it very difficult to render the Italian in classical and poetic English. The three rhyming words, and the mode in which the stanzas are looped together, added greatly to the difficulty. Blank verse he would have found quite easy compared to this. But he would not blench. The thought of her praise, and of the yet better favour he might gain, spurred him on; and Harry was the sacrifice. But he would make it all up to him, when this was once over. Indeed, he would.

Thus he baked cakes of clay to choke the barking of Cerberian conscience. But it would growl notwithstanding.

The boy's spirit was sinking; but Hugh did not or would not see it. His step grew less elastic. He became more listless, more like his former self—sauntering about with his hands in his pockets. And Hugh, of course, found himself caring less about him; for the thought of him, rousing as it did the sense of his own neglect, had become troublesome. Sometimes he even passed poor Harry without speaking to him.

Gradually, however, he grew still further into the favour of Mr. Arnold, until he seemed to have even acquired some influence with him. Mr. Arnold would go out riding with them himself sometimes, and express great satisfaction, not only with the way Harry sat his pony, for which he accorded Hugh the credit due to him, but with the way in which Hugh managed his own horse as well. Mr. Arnold was a good horseman, and his praise was especially grateful to Hugh, because Euphra was always near, and always heard it. I fear, however, that his progress in the good graces of Mr. Arnold, was, in a considerable degree, the result of the greater anxiety to please, which sprung from the consciousness of not deserving approbation. Pleasing was an easy substitute for well-doing. Not acceptable to himself, he had the greater desire to be acceptable to others; and so reflect the side-beams of a false approbation on himself—who needed true light and would be ill-provided for with any substitute. For a man who is received as a millionaire can hardly help feeling like one at times, even if he knows he has overdrawn his banker's account. The necessity to Hugh's nature of feeling right, drove him to this false mode of producing the false impression. If one only wants to feel virtuous, there are several royal roads to that end. But, fortunately, the end itself would be unsatisfactory if gained; while not one of these roads does more than pretend to lead even to that land of delusion.

The reaction in Hugh's mind was sometimes torturing enough. But he had not strength to resist Euphra, and so reform.

Well or ill done, at length his translation was finished. So was Euphra's. They exchanged papers for a private reading first; and arranged to meet afterwards, in order to compare criticisms.

CHAPTER XI
THE FIRST MIDNIGHT

Well, if anything be damned,
It will be twelve o'clock at night; that twelve
Will never scape.

CYRIL TOURNEUR.—The Revenger's Tragedy.

Letters arrived at Arnstead generally while the family was seated at breakfast. One morning, the post-bag having been brought in, Mr. Arnold opened it himself, according to his unvarying custom; and found, amongst other letters, one in an old-fashioned female hand, which, after reading it, he passed to Euphra.

"You remember Mrs. Elton, Euphra?"

"Quite well, uncle—a dear old lady!"

But the expression which passed across her face, rather belied her words, and seemed to Hugh to mean: "I hope she is not going to bore us again."

She took care, however, to show no sign with regard to the contents of the letter; but, laying it beside her on the table, waited to hear her uncle's mind first.

"Poor, dear girl!" said he at last. "You must try to make her as comfortable as you can. There is consumption in the family, you see," he added, with a meditative sigh.

"Of course I will, uncle. Poor girl! I hope there is not much amiss though, after all."

But, as she spoke, an irrepressible flash of dislike, or displeasure of some sort, broke from her eyes, and vanished. No one but himself seemed to Hugh to have observed it; but he was learned in the lady's eyes, and their weather-signs. Mr. Arnold rose from the table and left the room, apparently to write an answer to the letter. As soon as he was gone, Euphra gave the letter to Hugh. He read as follows:—

MY DEAR MR. ARNOLD

"Will you extend the hospitality of your beautiful house to me and my young friend, who has the honour of being your relative, Lady Emily Lake? For some time her health has seemed to be failing, and she is ordered to spend the winter abroad, at Pau, or somewhere in the south of France. It is considered highly desirable that in the meantime she should have as much change as possible; and it occurred to me, remembering the charming month I passed at your seat, and recalling the fact that Lady Emily is cousin only once removed to your late most lovely wife, that there would be no impropriety in writing to ask you whether you could, without inconvenience, receive us as your guests for a short time. I say us; for the dear girl has taken such a fancy to unworthy old me, that she almost refuses to set out without me. Not to be cumbersome either to our friends or ourselves, we shall bring only our two maids, and a steady old man-servant, who has been in my family for many years.—I trust you will not hesitate to refuse my request, should I happen to have made it at an unsuitable season; assured, as you must be, that we cannot attribute the refusal to any lack of hospitality or friendliness on your part. At all events, I trust you will excuse what seems—now I have committed it to paper—a great liberty, I hope not presumption, on mine. I am, my dear Mr. Arnold,

"Yours most sincerely,

"HANNAH ELTON"

Hugh refolded the letter, and laid it down without remark. Harry had left the room.

"Isn't it a bore?" said Euphra.

Hugh answered only by a look. A pause followed.

"Who is Mrs. Elton?" he said at last.

"Oh, a good-hearted creature enough. Frightfully prosy."

"But that is a well-written letter?"

"Oh, yes. She is famed for her letter-writing; and, I believe, practises every morning on a slate. It is the only thing that redeems her from absolute stupidity."

Euphra, with her taper fore-finger, tapped the table-cloth impatiently, and shifted back in her chair, as if struggling with an inward annoyance.

"And what sort of person is Lady Emily?" asked Hugh.

"I have never seen her. Some blue-eyed milk-maid with a title, I suppose. And in a consumption, too! I presume the dear girl is as religious as the old one.—Good heavens! what shall we do?" she burst out at length; and, rising from her chair, she paced about the room hurriedly, but all the time with a gliding kind of footfall, that would have shaken none but the craziest floor.

"Dear Euphra!" Hugh ventured to say, "never mind. Let us try to make the best of it."

She stopped in her walk, turned towards him, smiled as if ashamed and delighted at the same moment, and slid out of the room. Had Euphra been the same all through, she could hardly have smiled so without being in love with Hugh.

That morning he sought her again in her room. They talked over their versions of Dante. Hugh's was certainly the best, for he was more practised in such things than Euphra. He showed her many faults, which she at once perceived to be faults, and so rose in his estimation. But at the same time there were individual lines and passages of hers, which he considered not merely better than the corresponding lines and passages, but better than any part of his version. This he was delighted to say; and she seemed as delighted that he should think so. A great part of the morning was spent thus.

"I cannot stay longer," said Hugh.

"Let us read for an hour, then, after we come up stairs to-night."

"With more pleasure than I dare to say."

"But you mean what you do say?"

"You can doubt it no more than myself."

Yet he did not like Euphra's making the proposal. No more did he like the flippant, almost cruel way in which she referred to Lady Emily's illness. But he put it down to annoyance and haste—got over it somehow—anyhow; and began to feel that if she were a devil he could not help loving her, and would not help it if he could. The hope of meeting her alone that night, gave him spirit and energy with Harry; and the poor boy was more cheery and active than he had been for some time. He thought his big brother was going to love him again as at the first. Hugh's treatment of his pupil might still have seemed kind from another, but Harry felt it a great change in him.

In the course of the day, Euphra took an opportunity of whispering to him:

"Not in my room—in the library." I presume she thought it would be more prudent, in the case of any interruption.

After dinner that evening, Hugh did not go to the drawingroom with Mr. Arnold, but out into the woods about the house. It was early in the twilight; for now the sun set late. The month was June; and the even a rich, dreamful, rosy even—the sleep of a gorgeous day. "It is like the soul of a gracious woman," thought Hugh, charmed into a lucid interval of passion by the loveliness of the nature around him. Strange to tell, at that moment, instead of the hushed gloom of the library, towards which he was hoping and leaning in his soul, there arose before him the bare, stern, leafless pine-wood—for who can call its foliage leaves?—with the chilly wind of a northern spring morning blowing through it with a wailing noise of waters; and beneath a weird fir-tree, lofty, gaunt, and huge, with bare goblin arms, contorted sweepily, in a strange mingling of the sublime and the grotesque— beneath this fir-tree, Margaret sitting on one of its twisted roots, the very image of peace, with a face that seemed stilled by the expected approach of a sacred and unknown gladness; a face that would blossom the more gloriously because its joy delayed its coming. And above it, the tree shone a "still," almost "awful red," in the level light of the morning.

The vision came and passed, for he did not invite its stay: it rebuked him to the deepest soul. He strayed in troubled pleasure, restless and dissatisfied. Woods of the richest growth were around him; heaps on heaps of leaves floating above him like clouds, a trackless wilderness of airy green, wherein one might wish to dwell for ever, looking down into the vaults and aisles of the long-ranging boles beneath. But no peace could rest on his face; only, at best, a false mask, put on to hide the trouble of the unresting heart. Had he been doing his duty to Harry, his love for Euphra, however unworthy she might be, would not have troubled him thus.

He came upon an avenue. At the further end the boughs of the old trees, bare of leaves beneath, met in a perfect pointed arch, across which were barred the lingering colours of the sunset, transforming the whole into a rich window full of stained glass and complex tracery, closing up a Gothic aisle in a temple of everlasting worship. A kind of holy calm fell upon him as he regarded the dim, dying colours; and the spirit of the night, a something that is neither silence nor sound, and yet is like both, sank into his soul, and made a moment of summer twilight there. He walked along the avenue for some distance; and then, leaving it, passed on through the woods.— Suddenly it flashed upon him that he had crossed the Ghost's Walk. A slight but cold shudder passed through the region of his heart. Then he laughed at himself, and, as it were in despite of his own tremor, turned, and crossed yet again the path of the ghost.

A spiritual epicure in his pleasures, he would not spoil the effect of the coming meeting, by seeing Euphra in the drawingroom first: he went to his own study, where he remained till the hour had nearly arrived. He tried to write some verses. But he found that, although the lovely form of its own Naiad lay on the brink of the Well of Song, its waters would not flow: during the sirocco of passion, its springs withdraw into the cool caves of the Life beneath. At length he rose, too much preoccupied to mind his want of success; and, going down the back stair, reached the library. There he seated himself, and tried to read by the light of his chamber-candle. But it was scarcely even an attempt, for every moment he was looking up to the door by which he expected her to enter.

Suddenly an increase of light warned him that she was in the room. How she had entered he could not tell. One hand carried her candle, the light of which fell on her pale face, with its halo of blackness—her hair, which looked like a well of darkness, that threatened to break from its bonds and overflood the room with a second night, dark enough to blot out that which was now looking in, treeful and deep, at the uncurtained windows. The other hand was busy trying to incarcerate a stray tress which had escaped from its net, and made her olive shoulders look white beside it.

"Let it alone," said Hugh, "let it be beautiful."

But she gently repelled the hand he raised to hers, and, though she was forced to put down her candle first, persisted in confining the refractory tress; then seated herself at the table, and taking from her pocket the manuscript which Hugh had been criticising in the morning, unfolded it, and showed him all the passages he had objected to, neatly corrected or altered. It was wonderfully done for the time she had had. He went over it all with her again, seated close to her, their faces almost meeting as they followed the lines. They had just finished it, and were about to commence reading from the original, when Hugh, who missed a sheet of Euphra's translation, stooped under the table to look for it. A few moments were spent in the search, before he discovered that Euphra's foot was upon it. He begged her to move a little, but received no reply either by word or act. Looking up in some alarm, he saw that she was either asleep or in a faint. By an impulse inexplicable to himself at the time, he went at once to the windows, and drew down the green blinds. When he turned towards her again, she was reviving or awaking, he could not tell which.

"How stupid of me to go to sleep!" she said. "Let us go on with our reading."

They had read for about half an hour, when three taps upon one of the windows, slight, but peculiar, and as if given with the point of a finger, suddenly startled them. Hugh turned at once towards the windows; but, of course, he could see nothing, having just lowered the blinds. He turned again towards Euphra. She had a strange wild look; her lips were slightly parted, and her nostrils wide; her face was rigid, and glimmering pale as death from the cloud of her black hair.

"What was it?" said Hugh, affected by her fear with the horror of the unknown. But she made no answer, and continued staring towards one of the windows. He rose and was about to advance to it, when she caught him by the hand with a grasp of which hers would have been incapable except under the influence of terror. At that moment a clock in the room began to strike. It was a slow clock, and went on deliberately, striking one...two... three...till it had struck twelve. Every stroke was a blow from the hammer of fear, and his heart was the bell. He could not breathe for dread so long as the awful clock was striking. When it had ended, they looked at each other again, and Hugh breathed once.

"Euphra!" he sighed.

But she made no answer; she turned her eyes again to one of the windows. They were both standing. He sought to draw her to him, but she yielded no more than a marble statue.

"I crossed the Ghost's Walk to-night," said he, in a hard whisper, scarcely knowing that he uttered it, till he heard his own words. They seemed to fall upon his ear as if spoken by some one outside the room. She looked at him once more, and kept looking with a fixed stare. Gradually her face became less rigid, and her eyes less wild. She could move at last.

"Come, come," she said, in a hurried whisper. "Let us go—no, no, not that way;"—as Hugh would have led her towards the private stair—"let us go the front way, by the oak staircase."

They went up together. When they reached the door of her room, she said, "Good night," without even looking at him, and passed in. Hugh went on, in a state of utter bewilderment, to his own apartment; shut the door and locked it—a thing he had never done before; lighted both the candles on his table; and then walked up and down the room, trying, like one aware that he is dreaming, to come to his real self.

"Pshaw!" he said at last. "It was only a little bird, or a large moth. How odd it is that darkness can make a fool of one! I am ashamed of myself. I wish I had gone out at the window, if only to show Euphra I was not afraid, though of course there was nothing to be seen."

As he said this in his mind,—he could not have spoken it aloud, for fear of hearing his own voice in the solitude,—he went to one of the windows of his sitting-room, which was nearly over the library, and looked into the wood.—Could it be?—Yes.—He did see something white, gliding through the wood, away in the direction of the Ghost's Walk. It vanished; and he saw it no more.

The morning was far advanced before he could go to bed. When the first light of the aurora broke the sky, he looked out again;—and the first glimmerings of the morning in the wood were more dreadful than the deepest darkness of the past night. Possessed by a new horror, he thought how awful it would be to see a belated ghost, hurrying away in helpless haste. The spectre would be yet more terrible in the grey light of the coming day, and the azure breezes of the morning, which to it would be like a new and more fearful death, than amidst its own homely sepulchral darkness; while the silence all around—silence in light—could befit only that dread season of loneliness when men are lost in sleep, and ghosts, if they walk at all, walk in dismay.

But at length fear yielded to sleep, though still he troubled her short reign.

When he awoke, he found it so late, that it was all he could do to get down in time for breakfast. But so anxious was he not to be later than usual, that he was in the room before Mr. Arnold made his appearance. Euphra, however, was there before him. She greeted him in the usual way, quite circumspectly. But she looked troubled. Her face was very pale, and her eyes were red, as if from sleeplessness or weeping. When her uncle entered, she addressed him with more gaiety than usual, and he did not perceive that anything was amiss with her. But the whole of that day she walked as in a reverie, avoiding Hugh two or three times that they chanced to meet without a third person in the neighbourhood. Once in the forenoon—when she was generally to be found in her room—he could not refrain from trying to see her. The change and the mystery were insupportable to him. But when he tapped at her door, no answer came; and he walked back to Harry, feeling, as if, by an unknown door in his own soul, he had been shut out of the half of his being. Or rather—a wall seemed to have been built right before his eyes, which still was there wherever he went.

As to the gliding phantom of the previous night, the day denied it all, telling him it was but the coinage of his own over-wrought brain, weakened by prolonged tension of the intellect, and excited by the presence of Euphra at an hour claimed by phantoms when not yielded to sleep. This was the easiest and most natural way of disposing of the difficulty. The cloud around Euphra hid the ghost in its skirts.

Although fear in some measure returned with the returning shadows, he yet resolved to try to get Euphra to meet him again in the library that night. But she never gave him a chance of even dropping a hint to that purpose. She had not gone out with them in the morning; and when he followed her into the drawing-room, she was already at the piano. He thought he might convey his wish without interrupting the music; but as often as he approached her, she broke, or rather glided, out into song, as if she had been singing in an undertone all the while. He could not help seeing she did not intend to let him speak to her. But, all the time, whatever she sang was something she knew he liked; and as often as she spoke to him in the hearing of her uncle or cousin, it was in a manner peculiarly graceful and simple.

He could not understand her; and was more bewitched, more fascinated than ever, by seeing her through the folds of the incomprehensible, in which element she had wrapped herself from his nearer vision. She had always seemed above him—now she seemed miles away as well; a region of Paradise, into which he was forbidden to enter. Everything about her, to her handkerchief and her gloves, was haunted by a vague mystery of worshipfulness, and drew him towards it with wonder and trembling. When they parted for the night, she shook hands with him with a cool frankness, that put him nearly beside himself with despair; and when he found himself in his own room, it was some time before he could collect his thoughts. Having succeeded, however, he resolved, in spite of growing fears, to go to the library, and see whether it were not possible she might be there. He took up a candle, and went down the back stair. But when he opened the library door, a gust of wind blew his candle out; all was darkness within; a sudden horror seized him; and, afraid of yielding to the inclination to bound up the stair, lest he should go wild with the terror of pursuit, he crept slowly back, feeling his way to his own room with a determined deliberateness.—Could the library window have been left open? Else whence the gust of wind?

Next day, and the next, and the next, he fared no better: her behaviour continued the same; and she allowed him no opportunity of requesting an explanation.

CHAPTER XII
A SUNDAY

A man may be a heretic in the truth; and if he believe things only because his pastor says so, or the assembly so determines, without knowing other reason, though his belief be true, yet the very truth he holds becomes his heresy.—MILTON.—Areopagitica.

At length the expected visitors arrived. Hugh saw nothing of them till they assembled for dinner. Mrs. Elton was a benevolent old lady—not old enough to give in to being old—rather tall, and rather stout, in rich widow-costume, whose depth had been moderated by time. Her kindly grey eyes looked out from a calm face, which seemed to have taken comfort from loving everybody in a mild and moderate fashion. Lady Emily was a slender girl, rather shy, with fair hair, and a pale innocent face. She wore a violet dress, which put out her blue eyes. She showed to no advantage beside the suppressed glow of life which made Euphra look like a tropical twilight—I am aware there is no such thing, but if there were, it would be just like her.

Mrs. Elton seemed to have concentrated the motherhood of her nature, which was her most prominent characteristic, notwithstanding—or perhaps in virtue of—her childlessness, upon Lady Emily. To her Mrs. Elton was solicitously attentive; and she, on her part, received it all sweetly and gratefully, taking no umbrage at being treated as more of an invalid than she was.

Lady Emily ate nothing but chicken, and custard-pudding or rice, all the time she was at Arnstead.

The richer and more seasoned any dish, the more grateful it was to Euphra.

Mr. Arnold was a saddle-of-mutton man.

Hugh preferred roast-beef, but ate anything.

"What sort of a clergyman have you now, Mr. Arnold?" asked Mrs. Elton, at the dinner-table.

"Oh! a very respectable young gentleman, brother to Sir Richard, who has the gift, you know. A very moderate, excellent clergyman he makes, too!"

"All! but you know, Lady Emily and I"—here she looked at Lady Emily, who smiled and blushed faintly, "are very dependent on our Sundays, and"—

"We all go to church regularly, I assure you, Mrs. Elton; and of course my carriage shall be always at your disposal."

"I was in no doubt about either of those things, indeed, Mr. Arnold. But what sort of a preacher is he?"

"Ah, well! let me see.—What was the subject of his sermon last Sunday, Euphra, my dear?"

"The devil and all his angels," answered Euphra, with a wicked flash in her eyes.

"Yes, yes; so it was. Oh! I assure you, Mrs. Elton, he is quite a respectable preacher, as well as clergyman. He is an honour to the cloth."

Hugh could not help thinking that the tailor should have his due, and that Mr. Arnold gave it him.

"He is no Puseyite either," added Mr. Arnold, seeing but not understanding Mrs. Elton's baffled expression, "though he does preach once a month in his surplice."

"I am afraid you will not find him very original, though," said Hugh, wishing to help the old lady.

"Original!" interposed Mr. Arnold. "Really, I am bound to say I don't know how the remark applies. How is a man to be original on a subject that is all laid down in plain print—to use a vulgar expression—and has been commented upon for eighteen hundred years and more?"

"Very true, Mr. Arnold," responded Mrs. Elton. "We don't want originality, do we? It is only the gospel we want. Does he preach the gospel?"

"How can he preach anything else? His text is always out of some part of the Bible."

"I am glad to see you hold by the Inspiration of the Scriptures, Mr. Arnold," said Mrs. Elton, chaotically bewildered.

"Good heavens! Madam, what do you mean? Could you for a moment suppose me to be an atheist? Surely you have not become a student of German Neology?" And Mr. Arnold smiled a grim smile.

"Not I, indeed!" protested poor Mrs. Elton, moving uneasily in her seat;—"I quite agree with you, Mr. Arnold."

"Then you may take my word for it, that you will hear nothing but what is highly orthodox, and perfectly worthy of a gentleman and a clergyman, from the pulpit of Mr. Penfold. He dined with us only last week."

This last assertion was made in an injured tone, just sufficient to curl the tail of the sentence. After which, what was to be said?

Several vain attempts followed, before a new subject was started, sufficiently uninteresting to cause, neither from warmth nor stupidity, any danger of dissension, and quite worthy of being here omitted.

Dinner over, and the ceremony of tea—in Lady Emily's case, milk and water—having been observed, the visitors withdrew.

The next day was Sunday. Lady Emily came down stairs in black, which suited her better. She was a pretty, gentle creature, interesting from her illness, and good, because she knew no evil, except what she heard of from the pulpit. They walked to church, which was at no great distance, along a meadow-path paved with flags, some of them worn through by the heavy shoes of country generations. The church was one of those which are, in some measure, typical of the Church itself; for it was very old, and would have been very beautiful, had it not been all plastered over, and whitened to a smooth uniformity of ugliness—the attempt having been more successful in the case of the type. The open roof had had a French heaven added to it—I mean a ceiling; and the pillars, which, even if they were not carved—though it was impossible to come to a conclusion on that point—must yet have been worn into the beauty of age, had been filled up, and stained with yellow ochre. Even the remnants of stained glass in some of the windows, were half concealed by modern appliances for the partial exclusion of the light. The church had fared as Chaucer in the hands of Dryden. So had the truth, that flickered through the sermon, fared in the hands of the clergyman, or of the sermon-wright whose manuscript he had bought for eighteen pence—I am told that sermons are to be procured at that price—on his last visit to London. Having, although a Scotchman, had an episcopalian education, Hugh could not help rejoicing that not merely the Bible, but the Church-service as well, had been fixed beyond the reach of such degenerating influences as those which had operated on the more material embodiments of religion; for otherwise such would certainly have been the first to operate, and would have found the greatest scope in any alteration. We may hope that nothing but a true growth in such religion as needs and seeks new expression for new depth and breadth of feeling, will ever be permitted to lay the hand of change upon it—a hand, otherwise, of desecration and ruin.

The sermon was chiefly occupied with proving that God is no respecter of persons; a mark of indubitable condescension in the clergyman, the rank in society which he could claim for himself duly considered. But, unfortunately, the church was so constructed, that its area contained three platforms of position, actually of differing level; the loftiest, in the chancel, on the right hand of the pulpit, occupied by the gentry; the middle, opposite the pulpit, occupied by the tulip-beds of their servants; and the third, on the left of the pulpit, occupied by the common parishioners. Unfortunately, too, by the perpetuation of some old custom, whose significance was not worn out, all on the left of the pulpit were expected, as often as they stood up to sing—which was three times—to turn their backs to the pulpit, and so face away from the chancel where the gentry stood. But there was not much inconsistency, after all; the sermon founding its argument chiefly on the antithetical facts, that death, lowering the rich to the level of the poor, was a dead leveller; and that, on the other hand, the life to come would raise the poor to the level of the rich. It was a pity that there was no phrase in the language to justify him in carrying out the antithesis, and so balancing his sentence like a rope-walker, by saying that life was a live leveller. The sermon ended with a solemn warning: "Those who neglect the gospel-scheme, and never think of death and judgment—be they rich or poor, be they wise or ignorant—whether they dwell in the palace or the hut—shall be damned. Glory be to the Father, and to the Son, and to the Holy Ghost," &c.

Lady Emily was forced to confess that she had not been much interested in the sermon. Mrs. Elton thought he spoke plainly, but there was not much of the gospel in it. Mr. Arnold opined that people should not go to church to hear sermons, but to make the responses; whoever read prayers, it made no difference, for the prayers were the Church's, not the parson's; and for the sermon, as long as it showed the uneducated how to be saved, and taught them to do their duty in the station of life to which God had called them, and so long as the parson preached neither Puseyism nor Radicalism— (he frowned solemnly and disgustedly as he repeated the word)—nor Radicalism, it was of comparatively little moment whether he was a man of intellect or not, for he could not go wrong.

Little was said in reply to this, except something not very audible or definite, by Mrs. Elton, about the necessity of faith. The conversation, which took place at luncheon, flagged, and the visitors withdrew to their respective rooms, to comfort themselves with their Daily Portions.

At dinner, Mr. Arnold, evidently believing he had made an impression by his harangue of the morning, resumed the subject. Hugh was a little surprised to find that he had, even of a negative sort, strong opinions on the subject of religion.

"What do you think, then, Mrs. Elton, my dear madam, that a clergyman ought to preach?"

"I think, Mr. Arnold, that he ought to preach salvation by faith in the merits of the Saviour."

"Oh! of course, of course. We shall not differ about that. Everybody believes that."

"I doubt it very much.—He ought, in order that men may believe, to explain the divine plan, by which the demands of divine justice are satisfied, and the punishment due to sin averted from the guilty, and laid upon the innocent; that, by bearing our sins, he might make atonement to the wrath of a justly offended God; and so—"

"Now, my dear madam, permit me to ask what right we, the subjects of a Supreme Authority, have to inquire into the reasons of his doings? It seems to me—I should be sorry to offend any one, but it seems to me quite as presumptuous as the present arrogance of the lower classes in interfering with government, and demanding a right to give their opinion, forsooth, as to the laws by which they shall be governed; as if they were capable of understanding the principles by which kings rule, and governors decree justice.—I believe I quote Scripture."

"Are we, then, to remain in utter ignorance of the divine character?"

"What business have we with the divine character? Or how could we understand it? It seems to me we have enough to do with our own. Do I inquire into the character of my sovereign? All we have to do is, to listen to what we are told by those who are educated for such studies, whom the Church approves, and who are appointed to take care of the souls committed to their charge; to teach them to respect their superiors, and to lead honest, hard-working lives."

Much more of the same sort flowed from the oracular lips of Mr. Arnold. When he ceased, he found that the conversation had ceased also. As soon as the ladies withdrew, he said, without looking at Hugh, as he filled his glass:

"Mr. Sutherland, I hate cant."

And so he canted against it.

But the next day, and during the whole week, he seemed to lay himself out to make amends for the sharpness of his remarks on the Sunday. He was afraid he had made his guests uncomfortable, and so sinned against his own character as a host. Everything that he could devise, was brought to bear for their entertainment; daily rides in the open carriage, in which he always accompanied them, to show his estate, and the improvements he was making upon it; visits sometimes to the more deserving, as he called them, of the poor upon his property—the more deserving being the most submissive and obedient to the wishes of their lord; inspections of the schools, &c., &c.; in all of which matters he took a stupid, benevolent interest. For if people would be content to occupy the corner in which he chose to place them, he would throw them morsel after morsel, as long as ever they chose to pick it up. But woe to them if they left this corner a single pace!

Euphra made one of the party always; and it was dreary indeed for Hugh to be left in the desolate house without her, though but for a few hours. And when she was at home, she never yet permitted him to speak to her alone.

There might have been some hope for Harry in Hugh's separation from Euphra; but the result was, that, although he spent school-hours more regularly with him, Hugh was yet more dull, and uninterested in the work, than he had been before. Instead of caring that his pupil should understand this or that particular, he would be speculating on Euphra's behaviour, trying to account for this or that individual look or tone, or seeking, perhaps, a special symbolic meaning in some general remark that she had happened to let fall. Meanwhile, poor Harry would be stupifying himself with work which he could not understand for lack of some explanation or other that ought to have been given him weeks ago. Still, however, he clung to Hugh with a far-off, worshipping love, never suspecting that he could be to blame, but thinking at one time that he must be ill, at another that he himself was really too stupid, and that his big brother could not help getting tired of him. When Hugh would be wandering about the place, seeking to catch a glimpse of the skirt of Euphra's dress, as she went about with her guests, or devising how he could procure an interview with her alone, Harry would be following him at a distance, like a little terrier that had lost its master, and did not know whether this man would be friendly or not; never spying on his actions, but merely longing to be near him—for had not Hugh set him going in the way of life, even if he had now left him to walk in it alone? If Hugh could have once seen into that warm, true, pining little heart, he would not have neglected it as he did. He had no eyes, however, but for Euphra.

Still, it may be that even now Harry was able to gather, though with tears, some advantage from Hugh's neglect. He used to wander about alone; and it may be that the hints which his tutor had already given him, enabled him now to find for himself the interest belonging to many objects never before remarked. Perhaps even now he began to take a few steps alone; the waking independence of which was of more value for the future growth of his nature, than a thousand miles accomplished by the aid of the strong arm of his tutor. One certain advantage was, that the constitutional trouble of the boy's nature had now assumed a definite form, by gathering around a definite object, and blending its own shadowy being with the sorrow he experienced from the loss of his tutor's sympathy. Should that sorrow ever be cleared away, much besides might be cleared away along with it.

Meantime, nature found some channels, worn by his grief, through which her comforts, that, like waters, press on all sides, and enter at every cranny and fissure in the house of life, might gently flow into him with their sympathetic soothing. Often he would creep away to the nest which Hugh had built and then forsaken; and seated there in the solitude of the wide-bourgeoned oak, he would sometimes feel for a moment as if lifted up above the world and its sorrows, to be visited by an all-healing wind from God, that came to him, through the wilderness of leaves around him—- gently, like all powerful things.

But I am putting the boy's feelings into forms and words for him. He had none of either for them.

CHAPTER XIII
A STORM

When the mind's free,
The body's delicate: the tempest in my mind
Doth from my senses take all feeling else
Save what beats there.

King Lear.

While Harry took to wandering abroad in the afternoon sun, Hugh, on the contrary, found the bright weather so distasteful to him, that he generally trifled away his afternoons with some old romance in the dark library, or lay on the couch in his study, listless and suffering. He could neither read nor write. What he felt he must do he did; but nothing more.

One day, about noon, the weather began to change. In the afternoon it grew dark; and Hugh, going to the window, perceived with delight—the first he had experienced for many days—that a great thunder-storm was at hand. Harry was rather frightened; but under his fear, there evidently lay a deep delight. The storm came nearer and nearer; till at length a vivid flash broke from the mass of darkness over the woods, lasted for one brilliant moment, and vanished. The thunder followed, like a pursuing wild beast, close on the traces of the vanishing light; as if the darkness were hunting the light from the earth, and bellowing with rage that it could not overtake and annihilate it. Without the usual prelude of a few great drops, the rain poured at once, in continuous streams, from the dense canopy overhead; and in a few moments there were six inches of water all round the house, which the force of the falling streams made to foam, and fume, and flash like a seething torrent. Harry had crept close to Hugh, who stood looking out of the window; and as if the convulsion of the elements had begun to clear the spiritual and moral, as well as the physical atmosphere, Hugh looked down on the boy kindly, and put his arm round his shoulders. Harry nestled closer, and wished it would thunder for ever. But longing to hear his tutor's voice, he ventured to speak, looking up to his face:

"Euphra says it is only electricity, Mr. Sutherland. What is that?"

A common tutor would have seized the opportunity of explaining what he knew of the laws and operations of electricity. But Hugh had been long enough a pupil of David to feel that to talk at such a time of anything in nature but God, would be to do the boy a serious wrong. One capable of so doing would, in the presence of the Saviour himself, speculate on the nature of his own faith; or upon the death of his child, seize the opportunity of lecturing on anatomy. But before Hugh could make any reply, a flash, almost invisible from excess of light, was accompanied rather than followed by a roar that made the house shake; and in a moment more the room was filled with the terrified household, which, by an unreasoning impulse, rushed to the neighbourhood of him who was considered the strongest.— Mr. Arnold was not at home.

"Come from the window instantly, Mr. Sutherland. How can you be so imprudent!" cried Mrs. Elton, her usually calm voice elevated in command, but tremulous with fear.

"Why, Mrs. Elton," answered Hugh on whose temper, as well as conduct, recent events had had their operation, "do you think the devil makes the thunder?"

Lady Emily gave a faint shriek, whether out of reverence for the devil, or fear of God, I hesitate to decide; and flitting out of the room, dived into her bed, and drew the clothes over her head—at least so she was found at a later period of the day. Euphra walked up to the window beside Hugh, as if to show her approval of his rudeness; and stood looking out with eyes that filled their own night with home-born flashes, though her lip was pale, and quivered a little. Mrs. Elton, confounded at Hugh's reply, and perhaps fearing the house might in consequence share the fate of Sodom, notwithstanding the presence of a goodly proportion of the righteous, fled, accompanied by the housekeeper, to the wine-cellar. The rest of the household crept into corners, except the coachman, who, retaining his composure, in virtue of a greater degree of insensibility from his nearer approximation to the inanimate creation, emptied the jug of ale intended for the dinner of the company, and went out to look after his horses.

But there was one in the house who, left alone, threw the window wide open; and, with gently clasped hands and calm countenance, looked up into the heavens; and the clearness of whose eye seemed the prophetic symbol of the clearness that rose all untroubled above the turmoil of the earthly storm. Truly God was in the storm; but there was more of God in the clear heaven beyond; and yet more of Him in the eye that regarded the whole with a still joy, in which was mingled no dismay.

Euphra, Hugh, and Harry were left together, looking out upon the storm. Hugh could not speak in Harry's presence. At length the boy sat down in a dark corner on the floor, concealed from the others by a window-curtain. Hugh thought he had left the room.

"Euphra," he began.

Euphra looked round for Harry, and not seeing him, thought likewise that he had left the room: she glided away without making any answer to Hugh's invocation.

He stood for a few moments in motionless despair; then glancing round the room, and taking in all its desertedness, caught up his hat, and rushed out into the storm. It was the best relief his feelings could have had; for the sullen gloom, alternated with bursts of flame, invasions of horrid uproar, and long wailing blasts of tyrannous wind, gave him his own mood to walk in; met his spirit with its own element; widened, as it were, his microcosm to the expanse of the macrocosm around him. All the walls of separation were thrown down, and he lived, not in his own frame, but in the universal frame of nature. The world was for the time, to the reality of his feeling, what Schleiermacher, in his Monologen, describes it as being to man, an extension of the body in which he dwells. His spirit flashed in the lightning, raved in the thunder, moaned in the wind, and wept in the rain.

But this could not last long, either without or within him.

He came to himself in the woods. How far he had wandered, or whereabout he was, he did not know. The storm had died away, and all that remained was the wind and the rain. The tree-tops swayed wildly in the irregular blasts, and shook new, fitful, distracted, and momentary showers upon him. It was evening, but what hour of the evening he could not tell. He was wet to the skin; but that to a young Scotchman is a matter of little moment.

Although he had no intention of returning home for some time, and meant especially to avoid the dinner-table—for, in the mood he was in, it seemed more than he could endure—he yet felt the weakness to which we are subject as embodied beings, in a common enough form; that, namely, of the necessity of knowing the precise portion of space which at the moment we fill; a conviction of our identity not being sufficient to make us comfortable, without a knowledge of our locality. So, looking all about him, and finding where the wood seemed thinnest, he went in that direction; and soon, by forcing his way through obstacles of all salvage kinds, found himself in the high road, within a quarter of a mile of the country town next to Arnstead, removed from it about three miles. This little town he knew pretty well; and, beginning to feel exhausted, resolved to go to an inn there, dry his clothes, and then walk back in the moonlight; for he felt sure the storm would be quite over in an hour or so. The fatigue he now felt was proof enough in itself, that the inward storm had, for the time, raved itself off; and now—must it be confessed?—he wished very much for something to eat and drink.

He was soon seated by a blazing fire, with a chop and a jug of ale before him.

CHAPTER XIV
AN EVENING LECTURE

The Nightmare
Shall call thee when it walks.
MIDDLETON.—The Witch.

The inn to which Hugh had betaken himself, though not the first in the town, was yet what is called a respectable house, and was possessed of a room of considerable size, in which the farmers of the neighbourhood were accustomed to hold their gatherings. While eating his dinner, Hugh learned from the conversation around him—for he sat in the kitchen for the sake of the fire—that this room was being got ready for a lecture on Bilology, as the landlady called it. Bills in red and blue had been posted all over the town; and before he had finished his dinner, the audience had begun to arrive. Partly from curiosity about a subject of which he knew nothing, and partly because it still rained, and, having got nearly dry, he did not care about a second wetting if he could help it, Hugh resolved to make one of them. So he stood by the fire till he was informed that the lecturer had made his appearance, when he went up-stairs, paid his shilling, and was admitted to one of the front seats. The room was tolerably lighted with gas; and a platform had been constructed for the lecturer and his subjects. When the place was about half-filled, he came from another room alone—a little, thick-set, bull-necked man, with vulgar face and rusty black clothes; and, mounting the platform, commenced his lecture; if lecture it could be called, in which there seemed to be no order, and scarcely any sequence. No attempt even at a theory, showed itself in the mass of what he called facts and scientific truths; and he perpeturated the most awful blunders in his English. It will not be desired that I should give any further account of such a lecture. The lecturer himself seemed to depend chiefly for his success, upon the manifestations of his art which he proceeded to bring forward. He called his familiar by the name of Willi-am, and a stunted, pale-faced, dull-looking youth started up from somewhere, and scrambled upon the platform beside his master. Upon this tutored slave a number of experiments was performed. He was first cast into whatever abnormal condition is necessary for the operations of biology, and then compelled to make a fool of himself by exhibiting actions the most inconsistent with his real circumstances and necessities. But, aware that all this was open to the most palpable objection of collusion, the operator next invited any of the company that pleased, to submit themselves to his influences. After a pause of a few moments, a stout country fellow, florid and healthy, got up and slouched to the platform. Certainly, whatever might be the nature of the influence that was brought to bear, its operative power could not, with the least probability, be attributed to an over-activity of imagination in either of the subjects submitted to its exercise. In the latter, as well as in the former case, the operator was eminently successful; and the clown returned to his seat, looking remarkably foolish and conscious of disgrace—a sufficient voucher to most present, that in this case at least there had been no collusion. Several others volunteered their negative services; but with no one of them did he succeed so well; and in one case the failure was evident. The lecturer pretended to account for this, in making some confused and unintelligible remarks about the state of the weather, the thunder-storm, electricity, &c., of which things he evidently did not understand the best known laws.

"The blundering idiot!" growled, close to Hugh's ear, a voice with a foreign accent.

He looked round sharply.

A tall, powerful, eminently handsome man, with a face as foreign as his tone and accent, sat beside him.

"I beg your pardon," he said to Hugh; "I thought aloud."

"I should like to know, if you wouldn't mind telling me, what you detect of the blunderer in him. I am quite ignorant of these matters."

"I have had many opportunities of observing them; and I see at once that this man, though he has the natural power, is excessively ignorant of the whole subject."

This was all the answer he vouchsafed to Hugh's modest inquiry. Hugh had not yet learned that one will always fare better by concealing than by acknowledging ignorance. The man, whatever his capacity, who honestly confesses even a partial ignorance, will instantly be treated as more or less incapable, by the ordinary man who has already gained a partial knowledge, or is capable of assuming a knowledge which he does not possess. But, for God's sake! let the honest and modest man stick to his honesty and modesty, cost what they may.

Hugh was silent, and fixed his attention once more on what was going on. But presently he became aware that the foreigner was scrutinizing him with the closest attention. He knew this, somehow, without having looked round; and the knowledge was accompanied with a feeling of discomfort that caused him to make a restless movement on his seat. Presently he felt that the annoyance had ceased; but not many minutes had passed, before it again commenced. In order to relieve himself from a feeling which he could only compare to that which might be produced by the presence of the dead, he turned towards his neighbour so suddenly, that it seemed for a moment to embarrass him, his eyes being caught in the very act of devouring the stolen indulgence. But the stranger recovered himself instantly with the question:

"Will you permit me to ask of what country you are?"

Hugh thought he made the request only for the sake of covering his rudeness; and so merely answered:

"Why, an Englishman, of course."

"Ah! yes; it is not necessary to be told that. But it seems to me, from your accent, that you are a Scotchman."

"So I am."

"A Highlander?"

"I was born in the Highlands. But if you are very anxious to know my pedigree, I have no reason for concealing the fact that I am, by birth, half a Scotchman and half a Welchman."

The foreigner riveted his gaze, though but for the briefest moment sufficient to justify its being called a gaze, once more upon Hugh; and then, with a slight bow, as of acquiescence, turned towards the lecturer.

When the lecture was over, and Hugh was walking away in the midst of the withdrawing audience, the stranger touched him on the shoulder.

"You said that you would like to know more of this science: will you come to my lodging?" said he.

"With pleasure," Hugh answered; though the look with which he accompanied the words, must have been one rather of surprise.

"You are astonished that a stranger should invite you so. Ah! you English always demand an introduction. There is mine."

He handed Hugh a card: Herr von Funkelstein. Hugh happened to be provided with one in exchange.

The two walked out of the inn, along the old High Street, full of gables and all the delightful irregularities of an old country-town, till they came to a court, down which Herr von Funkelstein led the way.

He let himself in with a pass-key at a low door, and then conducted Hugh, by a stair whose narrowness was equalled by its steepness, to a room, which, though not many yards above the level of the court, was yet next to the roof of the low house. Hugh could see nothing till his conductor lighted a candle. Then he found himself in a rather large room with a shaky floor and a low roof. A chintz-curtained bed in one corner had the skin of a tiger thrown over it; and a table in another had a pair of foils lying upon it. The German—for such he seemed to Hugh—offered him a chair in the politest manner; and Hugh sat down.

"I am only in lodgings here," said the host; "so you will forgive the poverty of my establishment."

"There is no occasion for forgiveness, I assure you," answered Hugh.

"You wished to know something of the subject with which that lecturer was befooling himself and the audience at the same time."

"I shall be grateful for any enlightenment."

"Ah! it is a subject for the study of a benevolent scholar, not for such a clown as that. He jumps at no conclusions; yet he shares the fate of one who does: he flounders in the mire between. No man will make anything of it who has not the benefit of the human race at heart. Humanity is the only safe guide in matters such as these. This is a dangerous study indeed in unskilful hands."

Here a frightful caterwauling interrupted Herr von Funkelstein. The room had a storm-window, of which the lattice stood open. In front of it, on the roof, seen against a white house opposite, stood a demon of a cat, arched to half its length, with a tail expanded to double its natural thickness. Its antagonist was invisible from where Hugh sat. Von Funkelstein started up without making the slightest noise, trod as softly as a cat to the table, took up one of the foils, removed the button, and, creeping close to the window, made one rapid pass at the enemy, which vanished with a shriek of hatred and fear. He then, replacing the button, laid the foil down, and resumed his seat and his discourse. This, after dealing with generalities and commonplaces for some time, gave no sign of coming either to an end or to the point. All the time he was watching Hugh—at least so Hugh thought— as if speculating on him in general. Then appearing to have come to some conclusion, he gave his mind more to his talk, and encouraged Hugh to speak as well. The conversation lasted for nearly half an hour. At its close, Hugh felt that the stranger had touched upon a variety of interesting subjects, as one possessed of a minute knowledge of them. But he did not feel that he had gained any insight from his conversation. It seemed rather as if he had been giving him a number of psychological, social, literary, and scientific receipts. During the course of the talk, his eye had appeared to rest on Hugh by a kind of compulsion; as if by its own will it would have retired from the scrutiny, but the will of its owner was too strong for it. In seemed, in relation to him, to be only a kind of tool, which he used for a particular purpose.

At length Funkelstein rose, and, marching across the room to a cupboard, brought out a bottle and glasses, saying, in the most by-the-bye way, as he went:

"Have you the second-sight, Mr. Sutherland?"

"Certainly not, as far as I am aware."

"Ah! the Welch do have it, do they not?"

"Oh! yes, of course," answered Hugh laughing. "I should like to know, though," he added, "whether they inherit the gift as Celts or as mountaineers."

"Will you take a glass of—?"

"Of nothing, thank you," answered and interrupted Hugh. "It is time for me to be going. Indeed, I fear I have stayed too long already. Good night, Herr von Funkelstein."

"You will allow me the honour of returning your visit?"

Hugh felt he could do no less, although he had not the smallest desire to keep up the acquaintance. He wrote Arnstead on his card.

As he left the house, he stumbled over something in the court. Looking down, he saw it was a cat, apparently dead.

"Can it be the cat Herr Funkelstein made the pass at?" thought he. But presently he forgot all about it, in the visions of Euphra which filled his mind during his moonlight walk home. It just occurred to him, however, before those visions had blotted everything else from his view, that he had learned simply nothing whatever about biology from his late host.

When he reached home, he was admitted by the butler, and retired to bed at once, where he slept soundly, for the first time for many nights.

But, as he drew near his own room, he might have seen, though he saw not, a little white figure gliding away in the far distance of the long passage. It was only Harry, who could not lie still in his bed, till he knew that his big brother was safe at home.

CHAPTER XV
ANOTHER EVENING LECTURE

This Eneas is come to Paradise Out of the swolowe of Hell.

CHAUCER.—Legend of Dido.

The next day, Hugh was determined to find or make an opportunity of speaking to Euphra; and fortune seemed to favour him.—Or was it Euphra herself, in one or other of her inexplicable moods? At all events, she had that morning allowed the ladies and her uncle to go without her; and Hugh met her as he went to his study.

"May I speak to you for one moment?" said he, hurriedly, and with trembling lips.

"Yes, certainly," she replied with a smile, and a glance in his face as of wonder as to what could trouble him so much. Then turning, and leading the way, she said:

"Come into my room."

He followed her. She turned and shut the door, which he had left open behind him. He almost knelt to her; but something held him back from that.

"Euphra," he said, "what have I done to offend you?"

"Offend me! Nothing."—This was uttered in a perfect tone of surprise.

"How is it that you avoid me as you do, and will not allow me one moment's speech with you? You are driving me to distraction."

"Why, you foolish man!" she answered, half playfully, pressing the palms of her little hands together, and looking up in his face, "how can I? Don't you see how those two dear old ladies swallow me up in their faddles? Oh, dear? Oh, dear! I wish they would go. Then it would be all right again—wouldn't it?"

But Hugh was not to be so easily satisfied.

"Before they came, ever since that night—"

"Hush-sh!" she interrupted, putting her finger on his lips, and looking hurriedly round her with an air of fright, of which he could hardly judge whether it was real or assumed—"hush!"

Comforted wondrously by the hushing finger, Hugh would yet understand more.

"I am no baby, dear Euphra," he said, taking hold of the hand to which the finger belonged, and laying it on his mouth; "do not make one of me. There is some mystery in all this—at least something I do not understand."

"I will tell you all about it one day. But, seriously, you must be careful how you behave to me; for if my uncle should, but for one moment, entertain a suspicion—good-bye to you—perhaps good-bye to Arnstead. All my influence with him comes from his thinking that I like him better than anybody else. So you must not make the poor old man jealous. By the bye," she went on—rapidly, as if she would turn the current of the conversation aside—"what a favourite you have grown with him! You should have heard him talk of you to the old ladies. I might well be jealous of you. There never was a tutor like his."

Hugh's heart smote him that the praise of even this common man, proud of his own vanity, should be undeserved by him. He was troubled, too, at the flippancy with which Euphra spoke; yet not the less did he feel that he loved her passionately.

"I daresay," he replied, "he praised me as he would anything else that happened to be his. Isn't that old bay horse of his the best hack in the county?"

"You naughty man! Are you going to be satirical?"

"You claim that as your privilege, do you?"

"Worse and worse! I will not talk to you. But, seriously, for I must go— bring your Italian to—to—" She hesitated.

"To the library—why not?" suggested Hugh.

"No-o," she answered, shaking her head, and looking quite solemn.

"Well, will you come to my study? Will that please you better?"

"Yes, I will," she answered, with a definitive tone. "Good-bye, now."

She opened the door, and having looked out to see that no one was passing, told him to go. As he went, he felt as if the oaken floor were elastic beneath his tread.

It was sometime after the household had retired, however, before Euphra made her appearance at the door of his study. She seemed rather shy of entering, and hesitated, as if she felt she was doing something she ought not to do. But as soon as she had entered, and the door was shut, she appeared to recover herself quite; and they sat down at the table with their books. They could not get on very well with their reading, however. Hugh often forgot what he was about, in looking at her; and she seemed nowise inclined to avert his gazes, or check the growth of his admiration.

Rather abruptly, but apparently starting from some suggestion in the book, she said to him:

"By the bye, has Mr. Arnold ever said anything to you about the family jewels?"

"No," said Hugh. "Are there many?"

"Yes, a great many. Mr. Arnold is very proud of them, as well as of the portraits; so he treats them in the same way—keeps them locked up. Indeed he seldom allows them to see daylight, except it be as a mark of especial favour to some one."

"I should like much to see them. I have always been curious about stones. They are wonderful, mysterious things to me."

Euphra gave him a very peculiar, searching glance, as he spoke.

"Shall I," he continued, "give him a hint that I should like to see them?"

"By no means," answered Euphra, emphatically, "except he should refer to them himself. He is very jealous of his possessions—his family possessions, I mean. Poor old man! he has not much else to plume himself upon; has he?"

"He is kind to you, Euphra."

She looked at him as if she did not understand him.

"Yes. What then?"

"You ought not to be unkind to him."

"You odd creature! I am not unkind to him. I like him. But we are not getting on with our reading. What could have led me to talk about family-jewels? Oh! I see. What a strange thing the association of ideas is! There is not a very obvious connexion here; is there?"

"No. One cannot account for such things. The links in the chain of ideas are sometimes slender enough. Yet the slenderest is sufficient to enable the electric flash of thought to pass along the line."

She seemed pondering for a moment.

"That strikes me as a fine simile," she said. "You ought to be a poet yourself."

Hugh made no reply.

"I daresay you have hundreds of poems in that old desk, now?"

"I think they might be counted by tens."

"Do let me see them."

"You would not care for them."

"Wouldn't I, Hugh?"

"I will, on one condition—two conditions, I mean."

"What are they?"

"One is, that you show me yours."

"Mine?"

"Yes."

"Who told you I wrote verses? That silly boy?"

"No—I saw your verses before I saw you. You remember?"

"It was very dishonourable in you to read them."

"I only saw they were verses. I did not read a word."

"I forgive you, then. You must show me yours first, till I see whether I could venture to let you see mine. If yours were very bad indeed, then I might risk showing mine."

And much more of this sort, with which I will not weary my readers. It ended in Hugh's taking from the old escritoire a bundle of papers, and handing them to Euphra. But the reader need not fear that I am going to print any of these verses. I have more respect for my honest prose page than to break it up so. Indeed, the whole of this interview might have been omitted, but for two circumstances. One of them was, that in getting these papers, Hugh had to open a concealed portion of the escritoire, which his mathematical knowledge had enabled him to discover. It had evidently not been opened for many years before he found it. He had made use of it to hold the only treasures he had—poor enough treasures, certainly! Not a loving note, not a lock of hair even had he—nothing but the few cobwebs spun from his own brain. It is true, we are rich or poor according to what we are, not what we have. But what a man has produced, is not what he is. He may even impoverish his true self by production.

When Euphra saw him open this place, she uttered a suppressed cry of astonishment.

"Ah!" said Hugh, "you did not know of this hidie-hole, did you?"

"Indeed, I did not. I had used the desk myself, for this was a favourite room of mine before you came, but I never found that. Dear me! Let me look."

She put her hand on his shoulder and leaned over him, as he pointed out the way of opening it.

"Did you find nothing in it?" she said, with a slight tremour in her voice.

"Nothing whatever."

"There may be more places."

"No. I have accounted for the whole bulk, I believe."

"How strange!"

"But now you must give me my guerdon," said Hugh timidly.

The fact was, the poor youth had bargained, in a playful manner, and yet with an earnest, covetous heart, for one, the first kiss, in return for the poems she begged to see.

She turned her face towards him.

The second circumstance which makes the interview worth recording is, that, at this moment, three distinct knocks were heard on the window. They sprang asunder, and saw each other's face pale as death. In Euphra's, the expression of fright was mingled with one of annoyance. Hugh, though his heart trembled like a bird, leaped to the window. Nothing was to be seen but the trees that "stretched their dark arms" within a few feet of the oriel. Turning again towards Euphra, he found, to his mortification, that she had vanished—and had left the packet of poems behind her.

He replaced them in their old quarters in the escritoire; and his vague dismay at the unaccountable noises, was drowned in the bitter waters of miserable humiliation. He slept at last, from the exhaustion of disappointment.

When he awoke, however, he tried to persuade himself that he had made far too much of the trifling circumstance of her leaving the verses behind. For was she not terrified?—Why, then, did she leave him and go alone to her own room?—She must have felt that she ought not to be in his, at that hour, and therefore dared not stay.—Why dared not? Did she think the house was haunted by a ghost of propriety? What rational theory could he invent to account for the strange and repeated sounds?—He puzzled himself over it to the verge of absolute intellectual prostration.

He was generally the first in the breakfast-room; that is, after Euphra, who was always the first. She went up to him as he entered, and said, almost in a whisper:

"Have you got the poems for me? Quick!"

Hugh hesitated. She looked at him.

"No," he said at last.—"You never wanted them."

"That is very unkind; when you know I was frightened out of my wits. Do give me them."

"They are not worth giving you. Besides, I have not got them. I don't carry them in my pocket. They are in the escritoire. I couldn't leave them lying about. Never mind them."

"I have a right to them," she said, looking up at him slyly and shyly.

"Well, I gave you them, and you did not think them worth keeping. I kept my part of the bargain."

She looked annoyed.

"Never mind, dear Euphra; you shall have them, or anything else I have;—the brain that made them, if you like."

"Was it only the brain that had to do with the making of them?"

"Perhaps the heart too; but you have that already."

Her face flushed like a damask rose.

At that moment Mrs. Elton entered, and looked a little surprised. Euphra instantly said:

"I think it is rather too bad of you, Mr. Sutherland, to keep the poor boy so hard to his work, when you know he is not strong. Mrs. Elton, I have been begging a holiday for poor Harry, to let him go with us to Wotton House; but he has such a hard task-master! He will not hear of it."

The flush, which she could not get rid of all at once, was thus made to do duty as one of displeasure. Mrs. Elton was thoroughly deceived, and united her entreaties to those of Miss Cameron. Hugh was compelled to join in the deception, and pretend to yield a slow consent. Thus a holiday was extemporised for Harry, subject to the approbation of his father. This was readily granted; and Mr. Arnold, turning to Hugh, said:

"You will have nothing to do, Mr. Sutherland: had you not better join us?"

"With pleasure," replied he; "but the carriage will be full."

"You can take your horse."

"Thank you very much. I will."

The day was delightful; one of those grey summer-days, that are far better for an excursion than bright ones. In the best of spirits, mounted on a good horse, riding alongside of the carriage in which was the lady who was all womankind to him, and who, without taking much notice of him, yet contrived to throw him a glance now and then, Hugh would have been overflowingly happy, but for an unquiet, distressed feeling, which all the time made him aware of the presence of a sick conscience somewhere within. Mr. Arnold was exceedingly pleasant, for he was much taken with the sweetness and modesty of Lady Emily, who, having no strong opinions upon anything, received those of Mr. Arnold with attentive submission. He saw, or fancied he saw in her, a great resemblance to his deceased wife, to whom he had been as sincerely attached as his nature would allow. In fact, Lady Emily advanced so rapidly in his good graces, that either Euphra was, or thought fit to appear, rather jealous of her. She paid her every attention, however, and seemed to gratify Mr. Arnold by her care of the invalid. She even joined in the entreaties which, on their way home, he made with evident earnestness, for an extension of their visit to a month. Lady Emily was already so much better for the change, that Mrs. Elton made no objection to the proposal. Euphra gave Hugh one look of misery, and, turning again, insisted with increased warmth on their immediate consent. It was gained without much difficulty before they reached home.

Harry, too, was captivated by the gentle kindness of Lady Emily, and hardly took his eyes off her all the way; while, on the other hand, his delicate little attentions had already gained the heart of good Mrs. Elton, who from the first had remarked and pitied the sad looks of the boy.

CHAPTER XVI
A NEW VISITOR AND AN OLD ACQUAINTANCE

He's enough
To bring a woman to confusion,
More than a wiser man, or a far greater.

MIDDLETON.—The Witch.

When they reached the lodge, Lady Emily expressed a wish to walk up the avenue to the house. To this Mr. Arnold gladly consented. The carriage was sent round the back way; and Hugh, dismounting, gave his horse to the footman in attendance. As they drew near the house, the rest of the party having stopped to look at an old tree which was a favourite with its owner, Hugh and Harry were some yards in advance; when the former spied, approaching them from the house, the distinguished figure of Herr von Funkelstein. Saluting as they met, the visitor informed Hugh that he had just been leaving his card for him, and would call some other morning soon; for, as he was rusticating, he had little to occupy him. Hugh turned with him towards the rest of the party, who were now close at hand; when Funkelstein exclaimed, in a tone of surprise,

"What! Miss Cameron here!" and advanced with a profound obeisance, holding his hat in his hand.

Hugh thought he saw her look annoyed; but she held out her hand to him, and, in a voice indicating—still as it appeared to Hugh—some reluctance, introduced him to her uncle, with the words:

"We met at Sir Edward Laston's, when I was visiting Mrs. Elkingham, two years ago, uncle."

Mr. Arnold lifted his hat and bowed politely to the stranger. Had Euphra informed him that, although a person of considerable influence in Sir Edward's household, Herr von Funkelstein had his standing there only as Sir Edward's private secretary, Mr. Arnold's aversion to foreigners generally would not have been so scrupulously banished into the background of his behaviour. Ordinary civilities passed between them, marked by an air of flattering deference on Funkelstein's part, which might have been disagreeable to a man less uninterruptedly conscious of his own importance than Mr. Arnold; and the new visitor turned once more, as if forgetful of his previous direction, and accompanied them towards the house. Before they reached it he had, even in that short space, ingratiated himself so far with Mr. Arnold, that he asked him to stay and dine with them—an invitation which was accepted with manifest pleasure.

"Mr. Sutherland," said Mr. Arnold, "will you show your friend anything worth note about the place? He has kindly consented to dine with us; and in the meantime I have some letters to write."

"With pleasure," answered Hugh.

But all this time he had been inwardly commenting on the appearance of his friend, as Mr. Arnold called him, with the jealousy of a youth in love; for was not Funkelstein an old acquaintance of Miss Cameron? What might not have passed between them in that old hidden time?—for love is jealous of the past as well as of the future. Love, as well as metaphysics, has a lasting quarrel with time and space: the lower love fears them, while the higher defies them.—And he could not help seeing that Funkelstein was one to win favour in ladies' eyes. Very regular features and a dark complexion were lighted up by eyes as black as Euphra's, and capable of a wonderful play of light; while his form was remarkable for strength and symmetry. Hugh felt that in any company he would attract immediate attention. His long dark beard, of which just the centre was removed to expose a finely-turned chin, blew over each shoulder as often as they met the wind in going round the house. From what I have heard of him from other deponents besides Hugh, I should judge that he did well to conceal the lines of his mouth in a long moustache, which flowed into his bifurcated beard. He had just enough of the foreign in his dress to add to the appearance of fashion which it bore.

As they walked, Hugh could not help observing an odd peculiarity in the carriage of his companion. It was, that, every few steps, he gave a backward and downward glance to the right, with a sweeping bend of his body, as if he were trying to get a view of the calf of his leg, or as if he fancied he felt something trailing at his foot. So probable, from his motion, did the latter supposition seem, that Hugh changed sides to satisfy himself whether or not there was some dragging briar or straw annoying him; but no follower was to be discovered.

"You are a happy man, Mr. Sutherland," said the guest, "to live under the same roof with that beautiful Miss Cameron."

"Am I?" thought Hugh; but he only said, affecting some surprise:

"Do you think her so beautiful?"

Funkelstein's eyes were fixed upon him, as if to see the effect of his remark. Hugh felt them, and could not conform his face to the indifference of his words. But his companion only answered indifferently:

"Well, I should say so; but beauty is not, that is not beauty for us."

Whether or not there was poison in the fork of this remark, Hugh could only conjecture. He made no reply.

As they walked about the precincts of the house, Funkelstein asked many questions of Hugh, which his entire ignorance of domestic architecture made it impossible for him to answer. This seemed only to excite the questioner's desire for information to a higher pitch; and as if the very stones could reply to his demands, he examined the whole range of the various buildings constituting the house of Arnstead "as he would draw it."

"Certainly," said he, "there is at least variety enough in the style of this mass of material. There is enough for one pyramid."

"That would be rather at the expense of the variety, would it not?" said Hugh, in spiteful response to the inconsequence of the second member of Funkelstein's remark. But the latter was apparently too much absorbed in his continued inspection of the house, from every attainable point of near view, to heed the comment.

"This they call the Ghost's Walk," said Hugh.

"Ah! about these old houses there are always such tales."

"What sort of tales do you mean?"

"I mean of particular spots and their ghosts. You must have heard many such?"

"No, not I."

"I think Germany is more prolific of such stories. I could tell you plenty."

"But you don't mean you believe such things?"

"To me it is equal. I look at them entirely as objects of art."

"That is a new view of a ghost to me. An object of art? I should have thought them considerably more suitable objects previous to their disembodiment."

"Ah! you do not understand. You call art painting, don't you—or sculpture at most? I give up sculpture certainly—and painting too. But don't you think a ghost a very effective object in literature now? Confess: do you not like a ghost-story very much?"

"Yes, if it is a very good one."

"Hamlet now?"

"Ah! we don't speak of Shakspere's plays as stories. His characters are so real to us, that, in thinking of their development, we go back even to their fathers and mothers—and sometimes even speculate about their future."

"You islanders are always in earliest somehow. So are we Germans. We are all one."

"I hope you can be in earnest about dinner, then, for I hear the bell."

"We must render ourselves in the drawing-room, then? Yes."

When they entered the drawing-room, they found Miss Cameron alone. Funkelstein advanced, and addressed a few words to her in German, which Hugh's limited acquaintance with the language prevented him from catching. At the same moment, Mr. Arnold entered, and Funkelstein, turning to him immediately, proceeded, as if by way of apology for speaking in an unknown tongue, to interpret for Mr. Arnold's benefit:

"I have just been telling Miss Cameron in the language of my country, how much better she looks than when I saw her at Sir Edward Lastons."

"I know I was quite a scare-crow then," said Euphra, attempting to laugh.

"And now you are quite a decoy-duck, eh, Euphra?" said Mr. Arnold, laughing in reality at his own joke, which put him in great good-humour for the whole time of dinner and dessert.

"Thank you, uncle," said Euphra, with a prettily pretended affectation of humility. Then she added gaily:

"When did you rise on our Sussex horizon, Herr von Funkelstein?"

"Oh! I have been in the neighbourhood for a few days; but I owe my meeting with you to one of those coincidences which, were they not so pleasant—to me in this case, at least—one would think could only result from the blundering of old Dame Nature over her knitting. If I had not had the good fortune to meet Mr. Sutherland the other evening, I should have remained in utter ignorance of your neighbourhood and my own felicity, Miss Cameron. Indeed, I called now to see him, not you."

Hugh saw Mr. Arnold looking rather doubtful of the foreigner's fine speeches.

Dinner was announced. Funkelstein took Miss Cameron, Hugh Mrs. Elton, and Mr. Arnold followed with Lady Emily, who would never precede her older friend. Hugh tried to talk to Mrs. Elton, but with meagre success. He was suddenly a nobody, and felt more than he had felt for a long time what, in his present deteriorated moral state, he considered the degradation of his position. A gulf seemed to have suddenly yawned between himself and Euphra, and the loudest voice of his despairing agony could not reach across that gulf. An awful conviction awoke within him, that the woman he worshipped would scarcely receive his worship at the worth of incense now; and yet in spirit he fell down grovelling before his idol. The words "euphrasy and rue" kept ringing in his brain, coming over and over with an awful mingling of chime and toll. When he thought about it afterwards, he seemed to have been a year in crossing the hall with Mrs. Elton on his arm. But as if divining his thoughts—just as they passed through the dining-room door, Euphra looked round at him, almost over Funkelstein's shoulder, and, without putting into her face the least expression discernible by either of the others following, contrived to banish for the time all Hugh's despair, and to convince him that he had nothing to fear from Funkelstein. How it was done Hugh himself could not tell. He could not even recall the look. He only knew that he had been as miserable as one waking in his coffin, and that now he was out in the sunny air.

During dinner, Funkelstein paid no very particular attention to Euphrasia, but was remarkably polite to Lady Emily. She seemed hardly to know how to receive his attentions, but to regard him as a strange animal, which she did not know how to treat, and of which she was a little afraid. Mrs. Elton, on the contrary, appeared to be delighted with his behaviour and conversation; for, without showing the least originality, he yet had seen so much, and knew so well how to bring out what he had seen, that he was a most interesting companion. Hugh took little share in the conversation beyond listening as well as he could, to prevent himself from gazing too much at Euphra.

"Had Mr. Sutherland and you been old acquaintants then, Herr von Funkelstein?" asked Mr. Arnold, reverting to the conversation which had been interrupted by the announcement of dinner.

"Not at all. We met quite accidentally, and introduced ourselves. I believe a thunderstorm and a lecture on biology were the mediating parties between us. Was it not so, Mr. Sutherland?"

"I beg your pardon," stammered Hugh. But Mr. Arnold interposed:

"A lecture on what, did you say?"

"On biology."

Mr. Arnold looked posed. He did not like to say he did not know what the word meant; for, like many more ignorant men, he thought such a confession humiliating. Von Funkelstein hastened to his relief.

"It would be rather surprising if you were acquainted with the subject, Mr. Arnold. I fear to explain it to you, lest both Mr. Sutherland and myself should sink irrecoverably in your estimation. But young men want to know all that is going on."

Herr Funkelstein was not exactly what one would call a young man; but, as he chose to do so himself, there was no one to dispute the classification.

"Oh! of course," replied Mr. Arnold; "quite right. What, then, pray, is biology?"

"A science, falsely so called," said Hugh, who, waking up a little, wanted to join in the conversation.

"What does the word mean?" said Mr. Arnold.

Von Funkelstein answered at once:

"The science of life. But I must say, the name, as now applied, is no indication of the thing signified."

"How, then, is a gentleman to know what it is?" said Mr. Arnold, half pettishly, and forgetting that his knowledge had not extended even to the interpretation of the name.

"It is one of the sciences, true or false, connected with animal magnetism."

"Bah!" exclaimed Mr. Arnold, rather rudely.

"You would have said so, if you had heard the lecture," said Funkelstein.

The conversation had not taken this turn till quite late in the dining ceremony. Euphra rose to go; and Hugh remarked that her face was dreadfully pale. But she walked steadily out of the room.

This interrupted the course of the talk, and the subject was not resumed. Immediately after tea, which was served very soon, Funkelstein took his leave of the ladies.

"We shall be glad to see you often while in this neighbourhood," said Mr. Arnold, as he bade him good night.

"I shall, without fail, do myself the honour of calling again soon," replied he, and bowed himself out.

Lady Emily, evidently relieved by his departure, rose, and, approaching Euphra, said, in a sweet coaxing tone, which even she could hardly have resisted:

"Dear Miss Cameron, you promised to sing, for me in particular, some evening. May I claim the fulfilment of your promise?"

Euphra had recovered her complexion, and she too seemed to Hugh to be relieved by the departure of Funkelstein.

"Certainly," she answered, rising at once. "What shall I sing?"

Hugh was all ear now.

"Something sacred, if you please."

Euphra hesitated, but not long.

"Shall I sing Mozart's Agnus Dei, then?"

Lady Emily hesitated in her turn.

"I should prefer something else. I don't approve of singing popish music, however beautiful it may be."

"Well, what shall it be?"

"Something of Handel or Mendelssohn, please. Do you sing, 'I know that my Redeemer liveth?'"

"I daresay I can sing it," replied Euphra, with some petulance; and went to the piano.

This was a favourite air with Hugh; and he placed himself so as to see the singer without being seen himself, and to lose no slightest modulation of her voice. But what was his disappointment to find that oratorio-music was just what Euphra was incapable of! No doubt she sang it quite correctly; but there was no religion in it. Not a single tone worshipped or rejoiced. The quality of sound necessary to express the feeling and thought of the composer was lacking: the palace of sound was all right constructed, but of wrong material. Euphra, however, was quite unconscious of failure. She did not care for the music; but she attributed her lack of interest in it to the music itself, never dreaming that, in fact, she had never really heard it, having no inner ear for its deeper harmonies. As soon as she had finished, Lady Emily thanked her, but did not praise her more than by saying:

"I wish I had a voice like yours, Miss Cameron."

"I daresay you have a better of your own," said Euphra, falsely.

Lady Emily laughed.

"It is the poorest little voice you ever heard; yet I confess I am glad, for my own sake, that I have even that. What should I do if I never heard Handel!"

Every simple mind has a little well of beauty somewhere in its precincts, which flows and warbles, even when the owner is unheeded. The religion of Lady Emily had led her into a region far beyond the reach of her intellect, in which there sprang a constant fountain of sacred song. To it she owed her highest moods.

"Then Handel is your musician?" said Euphra. "You should not have put me to such a test. It was very unfair of you, Lady Emily."

Lady Emily laughed, as if quite amused at the idea of having done Euphra any wrong. Euphra added:

"You must sing now, Lady Emily. You cannot refuse, after the admission you have just made."

"I confess it is only fair; but I warn you to expect nothing."

She took her place at the piano, and sang—He shall feed his flock. Her health had improved so much during her sojourn at Arnstead, that, when she began to sing, the quantity of her voice surprised herself; but after all, it was a poor voice; and the execution, if clear of any great faults, made no other pretence to merit. Yet she effected the end of the music, the very result which every musician would most desire, wherein Euphra had failed utterly. This was worthy of note, and Hugh was not even yet too blind to perceive it. Lady Emily, with very ordinary intellect, and paltry religious opinions, yet because she was good herself, and religious—could, in the reproduction of the highest kind of music, greatly surpass the spirited, intellectual musician, whose voice was as superior to hers as a nightingale's to a sparrow's, and whose knowledge of music and musical power generally, surpassed hers beyond all comparison.

It must be allowed for Euphra, that she seemed to have gained some perception of the fact. Perhaps she had seen signs of emotion in Hugh's face, which he had shaded with his hand as Lady Emily sang; or perhaps the singing produced in her a feeling which she had not had when singing herself. All I know is, that the same night—while Hugh was walking up and down his room, meditating on this defect of Euphra's, and yet feeling that if she could sing only devil's music, he must love her—a tap came to the door which made him start with the suggestion of the former mysterious noises of a similar kind; that he sprang to the door; and that, instead of looking out on a vacant corridor, as he all but anticipated, he saw Euphra standing there in the dark—who said in a whisper:

"Ah! you do not love me any longer, because Lady Emily can sing psalms better than I can!"

There was both pathos and spite in the speech.

"Come in, Euphra."

"No. I am afraid I have been very naughty in coming here at all."

"Do come in. I want you to tell me something about Funkelstein."

"What do you want to know about him? I suppose you are jealous of him. Ah! you men can both be jealous and make jealous at the same moment." A little broken sigh followed. Hugh answered:

"I only want to know what he is."

"Oh! some twentieth cousin of mine."

"Mr. Arnold does not know that?"

"Oh dear! no. It is so far off I can't count it, In fact I doubt it altogether. It must date centuries back."

"His intimacy, then, is not to be accounted for by his relationship?"

"Ah! ah! I thought so. Jealous of the poor count!"

"Count?"

"Oh dear! what does it matter? He doesn't like to be called Count, because all foreigners are counts or barons, or something equally distinguished. I oughtn't to have let it out."

"Never mind. Tell me something about him."

"He is a Bohemian. I met him first, some years ago, on the continent."

"Then that was not your first meeting—at Sir Edward Laston's?"

"No."

"How candid she is!" thought Hugh.

"He calls me his cousin; but if he be mine, he is yet more Mr. Arnold's. But he does not want it mentioned yet. I am sure I don't know why."

"Is he in love with you?"

"How can I tell?" she answered archly. "By his being very jealous? Is that the way to know whether a man is in love with one? But if he is in love with me, it does not follow that I am in love with him—does it? Confess. Am I not very good to answer all your impertinent downright questions? They are as point blank as the church-catechism;—mind, I don't say as rude.— How can I be in love with two at—a—?"

She seemed to cheek herself. But Hugh had heard enough—as she had intended he should. She turned instantly, and sped—surrounded by the "low melodious thunder" of her silken garments—to her own door, where she vanished noiselessly.

"What care I for oratorios?" said Hugh to himself, as he put the light out, towards morning.

Where was all this to end? What goal had Hugh set himself? Could he not go away, and achieve renown in one of many ways, and return fit, in the eyes of the world, to claim the hand of Miss Cameron? But would he marry her if he could? He would not answer the question. He closed the ears of his heart to it, and tried to go to sleep. He slept, and dreamed of Margaret in the storm.

A few days passed without anything occurring sufficiently marked for relation. Euphra and he seemed satisfied without meeting in private. Perhaps both were afraid of carrying it too far; at least, too far to keep clear of the risk of discovery, seeing that danger was at present greater than usual. Mr. Arnold continued to be thoroughly attentive to his guests, and became more and more devoted to Lady Emily. There was no saying where it might end; for he was not an old man yet, and Lady Emily appeared to have no special admirers. Arnstead was such an abode, and surrounded with such an estate, as few even of the nobility could call their own. And a reminiscence of his first wife seemed to haunt all Mr. Arnold's contemplations of Lady Emily, and all his attentions to her. These were delicate in the extreme, evidently bringing out the best life that yet remained in a heart that was almost a fossil. Hugh made some fresh efforts to do his duty by Harry, and so far succeeded, that at least the boy made some progress—evident enough to the moderate expectations of his father. But what helped Harry as much as anything, was the motherly kindness, even tenderness, of good Mrs. Elton, who often had him to sit with her in her own room. To her he generally fled for refuge, when he felt deserted and lonely.

CHAPTER XVII
MATERIALISM alias GHOST-HUNTING

Wie der Mond sich leuchtend dränget Durch den dunkeln Wolkenflor,
Also taucht aus dunkeln Zeiten Mir ein lichtes Bild hervor.

HEINRICH HEINE

As the moon her face advances Through the darkened cloudy veil; So,
from darkened times arising, Dawns on me a vision pale.

In consequence of what Euphra had caused him to believe without
saying it, Hugh felt more friendly towards his new acquaintance; and
happening—on his side at least it did happen—to meet him a few days
after, walking in the neighbourhood, he joined him in a stroll. Mr. Arnold
met them on horseback, and invited Von Funkelstein to dine with them that
evening, to which he willingly consented. It was noticeable that no sooner
was the count within the doors of Arnstead House, than he behaved with
cordiality to every one of the company except Hugh. With him he made
no approach to familiarity of any kind, treating him, on the contrary, with
studious politeness.

In the course of the dinner, Mr. Arnold said:

"It is curious, Herr von Funkelstein, how often, if you meet with
something new to you, you fall in with it again almost immediately. I found
an article on Biology in the newspaper, the very day after our conversation
on the subject. But absurd as the whole thing is, it is quite surpassed by a
letter in to-day's Times about spirit-rapping and mediums, and what not!"

This observation of the host at once opened the whole question of those
physico-psychological phenomena to which the name of spiritualism has
been so absurdly applied. Mr. Arnold was profound in his contempt of the
whole system, if not very profound in his arguments against it. Every one
had something to remark in opposition to the notions which were so rapidly
gaining ground in the country, except Funkelstein, who maintained a rigid
silence.

This silence could not continue long without attracting the attention of
the rest of the party; upon which Mr. Arnold said:

"You have not given us your opinion on the subject, Herr von Funkelstein."

"I have not, Mr. Arnold;—I should not like to encounter the opposition of so many fair adversaries, as well as of my host."

"We are in England, sir; and every man is at liberty to say what he thinks. For my part, I think it all absurd, if not improper."

"I would not willingly differ from you, Mr. Arnold. And I confess that a great deal that finds its way into the public prints, does seem very ridiculous indeed; but I am bound, for truth's sake, to say, that I have seen more than I can account for, in that kind of thing. There are strange stories connected with my own family, which, perhaps, incline me to believe in the supernatural; and, indeed, without making the smallest pretence to the dignity of what they call a medium, I have myself had some curious experiences. I fear I have some natural proclivity towards what you despise. But I beg that my statement of my own feelings on the subject, may not interfere in the least with the prosecution of the present conversation; for I am quite capable of drawing pleasure from listening to what I am unable to agree with."

"But let us hear your arguments, strengthened by your facts, in opposition to ours; for it will be impossible to talk with a silent judge amongst us," Hugh ventured to say.

"I set up for no judge, Mr. Sutherland, I assure you; and perhaps I shall do my opinions more justice by remaining silent, seeing I am conscious of utter inability to answer the a priori arguments which you in particular have brought against them. All I would venture to say is, that an a priori argument may owe its force to a mistaken hypothesis with regard to the matter in question; and that the true Baconian method, which is the glory of your English philosophy, would be to inquire first what the thing is, by recording observations and experiments made in its supposed direction."

"At least Herr von Funkelstein has the best of the argument now, I am compelled to confess," said Hugh.

Funkelstein bowed stiffly, and was silent.

"You rouse our curiosity," said Mr. Arnold; "but I fear, after the free utterance which we have already given to our own judgments, in ignorance, of course, of your greater experience, you will not be inclined to make us wiser by communicating any of the said experience, however much we may desire to hear it."

Had he been speaking to one of less evident social standing than Funkelstein, Mr. Arnold, if dying with curiosity, would not have expressed the least wish to be made acquainted with his experiences. He would have sat in apparent indifference, but in real anxiety that some one else would draw him out, and thus gratify his curiosity without endangering his dignity.

"I do not think," replied Funkelstein, "that it is of any use to bring testimony to bear on such a matter. I have seen—to use the words of some one else, I forget whom, on a similar subject—I have seen with my own eyes what I certainly should never have believed on the testimony of another. Consequently, I have no right to expect that my testimony should be received. Besides, I do not wish it to be received, although I confess I shrink from presenting it with a certainty of its being rejected. I have no wish to make converts to my opinions."

"Really, Herr von Funkelstein, at the risk of your considering me importunate, I would beg—"

"Excuse me, Mr. Arnold. The recital of some of the matters to which you refer, would not only be painful to myself, but would be agitating to the ladies present."

"In that case, I have only to beg your pardon for pressing the matter—I hope no further than to the verge of incivility."

"In no degree approaching it, I assure you, Mr. Arnold. In proof that I do not think so, I am ready, if you wish it—although I rather dread the possible effects on the nerves of the ladies, especially as this is an old house—to repeat, with the aid of those present, certain experiments which I have sometimes found perhaps only too successful."

"Oh! I don't," said Euphra, faintly.

An expression of the opposite desire followed, however, from the other ladies. Their curiosity seemed to strive with their fears, and to overcome them.

"I hope we shall have nothing to do with it in any other way than merely as spectators?" said Mrs. Elton.

"Nothing more than you please. It is doubtful if you can even be spectators. That remains to be seen."

"Good gracious!" exclaimed Mrs. Elton.

Lady Emily looked at her with surprise—almost reproof.

"I beg your pardon, my dear; but it sounds so dreadful. What can it be?"

"Let me entreat you, ladies, not to imagine that I am urging you to anything," said Funkelstein.

"Not in the least," replied Mrs. Elton. "I was very foolish." And the old lady looked ashamed, and was silent.

"Then if you will allow me, I will make one small preparation. Have you a tool-chest anywhere, Mr. Arnold?"

"There must be tools enough about the place, I know. I will ring for Atkins."

"I know where the tool chest is," said Hugh; "and, if you will allow me a suggestion, would it not be better the servants should know nothing about this? There are some foolish stories afloat amongst them already."

"A very proper suggestion, Mr. Sutherland," said Mr. Arnold, graciously. "Will you find all that is wanted, then?"

"What tools do you want?" asked Hugh.

"Only a small drill. Could you get me an earthenware plate—not china—too?"

"I will manage that," said Euphra.

Hugh soon returned with the drill, and Euphra with the plate. The Bohemian, with some difficulty, and the remark that the English ware was very hard, drilled a small hole in the rim of the plate—a dinner-plate; then begging an H B drawing-pencil from Miss Cameron, cut off a small piece, and fitted it into the hole, making it just long enough to touch the table with its point when the plate lay in its ordinary position.

"Now I am ready," said he. "But," he added, raising his head, and looking all round the room, as if a sudden thought had struck him—"I do not think this room will be quite satisfactory."

They were now in the drawing-room.

"Choose the room in the house that will suit you," said Mr. Arnold. "The dining-room?"

"Certainly not," answered Funkelstein, as he took from his watch-chain a small compass and laid it on the table. "Not the dining-room, nor the breakfast-room—I think. Let me see—how is it situated?" He went to the hall, as if to refresh his memory, and then looked again at the compass. "No, not the breakfast-room."

Hugh could not help thinking there was more or less of the charlatan about the man.

"The library?" suggested Lady Emily.

They adjourned to the library to see. The library would do. After some further difficulty, they succeeded in procuring a large sheet of paper and fastening it down to the table by drawing-pins. Only two candles were in the great room, and it was scarcely lighted at all by them; yet Funkelstein requested that one of these should be extinguished, and the other removed to a table near the door. He then said, solemnly:

"Let me request silence, absolute silence, and quiescence of thought even."

After stillness had settled down with outspread wings of intensity, he resumed:

"Will any one, or, better, two of you, touch the plate as lightly as possible with your fingers?"

All hung back for a moment. Then Mr. Arnold came forward.

"I will," said he, and laid his fingers on the plate.

"As lightly as possible, if you please. If the plate moves, follow it with your fingers, but be sure not to push it in any direction."

"I understand," said Mr. Arnold; and silence fell again.

The Bohemian, after a pause, spoke once more, but in a foreign tongue. The words sounded first like entreaty, then like command, and at last, almost like imprecation. The ladies shuddered.

"Any movement of the vehicle?" said he to Mr. Arnold.

"If by the vehicle you mean the plate, certainly not," said Mr. Arnold solemnly. But the ladies were very glad of the pretext for attempting a laugh, in order to get rid of the oppression which they had felt for some time.

"Hush!" said Funkelstein, solemnly. — "Will no one else touch the plate, as well? It will seldom move with one. It does with me. But I fear I might be suspected of treachery, if I offered to join Mr. Arnold."

"Do not hint at such a thing. You are beyond suspicion."

What ground Mr. Arnold had for making such an assertion, was no better known to himself than to any one else present. Von Funkelstein, without another word, put the fingers of one hand lightly on the plate beside Mr. Arnold's. The plate instantly began to move upon the paper. The motion was a succession of small jerks at first; but soon it tilted up a little, and moved upon a changing point of support. Now it careered rapidly in wavy lines, sweeping back towards the other side, as often as it approached the extremity of the sheet, the men keeping their fingers in contact with it, but not appearing to influence its motion. Gradually the motion ceased. Von Funkelstein withdrew his hand, and requested that the other candle should be lighted. The paper was taken up and examined. Nothing could be discovered upon it, but a labyrinth of wavy and sweepy lines. Funkelstein pored over it for some minutes, and then confessed his inability to make a single letter out of it, still less words and sentences, as he had expected.

"But," said he, "we are at least so far successful: it moves. Let us try again. Who will try next?"

"I will," said Hugh, who had refrained at first, partly from dislike to the whole affair, partly because he shrank from putting himself forward.

A new sheet of paper was fixed. The candle was extinguished. Hugh put his fingers on the plate. In a second or two, it began to move.

"A medium!" murmured Funkelstein. He then spoke aloud some words unintelligible to the rest.

Whether from the peculiarity of his position and the consequent excitement of his imagination, or from some other cause, Hugh grew quite cold, and began to tremble. The plate, which had been careering violently for a few moments, now went more slowly, making regular short motions and returns, at right angles to its chief direction, as if letters were being formed by the pencil. Hugh shuddered, thinking he recognised the letters as they grew. The writing ceased. The candles were brought. Yes; there it was!—not plain, but easily decipherable—David Elginbrod. Hugh felt sick.

Euphra, looking on beside him, whispered:

"What an odd name! Who can it mean?"

He made no reply

Neither of the other ladies saw it; for Mrs. Elton had discovered, the moment the second candle was lighted, that Lady Emily was either asleep or in a faint. She was soon all but satisfied that she was asleep.

Hugh's opinion, gathered from what followed, was, that the Bohemian had not been so intent on the operations with the plate, as he had appeared to be; and that he had been employing part of his energy in mesmerising Lady Emily. Mrs. Elton, remembering that she had had quite a long walk that morning, was not much alarmed. Unwilling to make a disturbance, she rang the bell very quietly, and, going to the door, asked the servant who answered it, to send her maid with some eau-de-cologne. Meantime, the gentlemen had been too much absorbed to take any notice of her proceedings, and, after removing the one and extinguishing the other candle, had reverted to the plate.—Hugh was still the operator.

Von Funkelstein spoke again in an unknown tongue. The plate began to move as before. After only a second or two of preparatory gyration, Hugh felt that it was writing Turriepuffit, and shook from head to foot.

Suddenly, in the middle of the word, the plate ceased its motion, and lay perfectly still. Hugh felt a kind of surprise come upon him, as if he waked from an unpleasant dream, and saw the sun shining. The morbid excitement of his nervous system had suddenly ceased, and a healthful sense of strength and every-day life took its place.

Simultaneously with the stopping of the plate, and this new feeling which I have tried to describe, Hugh involuntarily raised his eyes towards the door of the room. In the all-but-darkness between him and the door, he saw a pale beautiful face—a face only. It was the face of Margaret Elginbrod; not, however, such as he had used to see it—but glorified. That was the only word by which he could describe its new aspect. A mist of darkness fell upon his brain, and the room swam round with him. But he was saved from falling, or attracting attention to a weakness for which he could have made no excuse, by a sudden cry from Lady Emily.

"See! see!" she cried wildly, pointing towards one of the windows.

These looked across to another part of the house, one of the oldest, at some distance.—One of its windows, apparently on the first floor, shone with a faint bluish light.

All the company had hurried to the window at Lady Emily's exclamation.

"Who can be in that part of the house?" said Mr. Arnold, angrily.

"It is Lady Euphrasia's window," said Euphra, in a low voice, the tone of which suggested, somehow, that the speaker was very cold.

"What do you mean by speaking like that?" said Mr. Arnold, forgetting his dignity. "Surely you are above being superstitious. Is it possible the servants could be about any mischief? I will discharge any one at once, that dares go there without permission."

The light disappeared, fading slowly out.

"Indeed, the servants are all too much alarmed, after what took place last year, to go near that wing—much less that room," said Euphra. "Besides, Mrs. Horton has all the keys in her own charge."

"Go yourself and get me them, Euphra. I will see at once what this means. Don't say why you want them."

"Certainly not, uncle."

Hugh had recovered almost instantaneously. Though full of amazement, he had yet his perceptive faculties sufficiently unimpaired to recognise the real source of the light in the window. It seemed to him more like moonlight than anything else; and he thought the others would have seen it to be such, but for the effect of Lady Emily's sudden exclamation. Perhaps she was under the influence of the Bohemian at the moment. Certainly they were all in a tolerable condition for seeing whatever might be required of them. True, there was no moon to be seen; and if it was the moon, why did the light go out? But he found afterwards that he had been right. The house stood upon a rising ground; and, every recurring cycle, the moon would shine, through a certain vista of trees and branches, upon Lady Euphrasia's window; provided there had been no growth of twigs to stop up the channel of the light, which was so narrow that in a few moments the moon had crossed it. A gap in a hedge made by a bull that morning, had removed the last screen.—Lady Euphrasia's window was so neglected and dusty, that it could reflect nothing more than a dim bluish shimmer.

"Will you all accompany me, ladies and gentlemen, that you may see with your own eyes that there is nothing dangerous in the house?" said Mr. Arnold.

Of course Funkelstein was quite ready, and Hugh as well, although he felt at this moment ill-fitted for ghost-hunting. The ladies hesitated; but at last, more afraid of being left behind alone, than of going with the gentlemen, they consented. Euphra brought the keys, and they commenced their march of investigation. Up the grand staircase they went, Mr. Arnold first with the keys, Hugh next with Mrs. Elton and Lady Emily, and the Bohemian, considerably to Hugh's dissatisfaction, bringing up the rear with Euphra.—This misarrangement did more than anything else could have done, to deaden for the time the distraction of feeling produced in Hugh's mind by the events of the last few minutes. Yet even now he seemed to be wandering through the old house in a dream, instead of following Mr. Arnold, whose presence might well have been sufficient to destroy any illusion, except such as a Chinese screen might superinduce; for, possessed of far less imagination than a horse, he was incapable of any terrors, but such as had to do with robbers, or fire, or chartists—which latter fear included both the former. He strode on securely, carrying a candle in one hand, and the keys in the other. Each of the other gentlemen likewise bore a light. They had to go through doors, some locked, some open, following a different route from that taken by Euphra on a former occasion.

But Mr. Arnold found the keys troublesome. He could not easily distinguish those he wanted, and was compelled to apply to Euphra. She left Funkelstein in consequence, and walked in front with her uncle. Her former companion got beside Lady Emily, and as they could not well walk four abreast, she fell behind with him. So Hugh got next to Euphra, behind her, and was comforted.

At length, by tortuous ways, across old rooms, and up and down abrupt little stairs, they reached the door of Lady Euphrasia's room. The key was found, and the door opened with some perturbation—manifest on the part of the ladies, and concealed on the part of the men. The place was quite dark. They entered; and Hugh was greatly struck with its strange antiquity. Lady Euphrasia's ghost had driven the last occupant out of it nearly a hundred years ago; but most of the furniture was much older than that, having probably belonged to Lady Euphrasia herself. The room remained just as the said last occupant had left it. Even the bed-clothes remained, folded down, as if expecting their occupant for the last hundred years. The fine linen had grown yellow; and the rich counterpane lay like a churchyard after the resurrection, full of the open graves of the liberated moths. On the wall hung the portrait of a nun in convent-attire.

"Some have taken that for a second portrait of Lady Euphrasia," said Mr. Arnold, "but it cannot be.—Euphra, we will go back through the picture gallery.—I suspect it of originating the tradition that Lady Euphrasia became a nun at last. I do not believe it myself. The picture is certainly old enough to stand for her, but it does not seem to me in the least like the other."

It was a great room, with large recesses, and therefore irregular in form. Old chairs, with remnants of enamel and gilding, and seats of faded damask, stood all about. But the beauty of the chamber was its tapestry. The walls were entirely covered with it, and the rich colours had not yet receded into the dull grey of the past, though their gorgeousness had become sombre with age. The subject was the story of Samson.

"Come and see this strange piece of furniture," said Euphra to Hugh, who had kept by her side since they entered this room.

She led him into one of the recesses, almost concealed by the bed-hangings. In it stood a cabinet of ebony, reaching nearly to the ceiling, curiously carved in high relief.

"I wish I could show you the inside of it," she went on, "but I cannot now."

This was said almost in a whisper. Hugh replied with only a look of thanks. He gazed at the carving, on whose black surface his candle made little light, and threw no shadows.

"You have looked at this before, Euphra," said he. "Explain it to me."

"I have often tried to find out what it is," she answered; "but I never could quite satisfy myself about it."

She proceeded, however, to tell him what she fancied it might mean, speaking still in the low tone which seemed suitable to the awe of the place. She got interested in showing him the relations of the different figures; and he made several suggestions as to the possible intention of the artist. More than one well-known subject was proposed and rejected.

Suddenly becoming aware of the sensation of silence, they looked up, and saw that theirs was the only light in the room. They were left alone in the haunted chamber.—They looked at each other for one moment; then said, with half-stifled voices:

"Euphra!"

"Hugh!"

Euphra seemed half amused and half perplexed. Hugh looked half perplexed and wholly pleased.

"Come, come," said Euphra, recovering herself, and leading the way to the door.

When they reached it, they found it closed and locked. Euphra raised her hand to beat on it. Hugh caught it.

"You will drive Lady Emily into fits. Did you not see how awfully pale she was?"

Euphra instantly lifted her hand again, as if she would just like to try that result. But Hugh, who was in no haste for any result, held her back.

She struggled for a moment or two, but not very strenuously, and, desisting all at once, let her arms drop by her sides.

"I fear it is too late. This is a double door, and Mr. Arnold will have locked all the doors between this and the picture-gallery. They are there now. What shall we do?"

She said this with an expression of comical despair, which would have made Hugh burst into laughter, had he not been too much pleased to laugh.

"Never mind," he said, "we will go on with our study of the cabinet. They will soon find out that we are left behind, and come back to look for us."

"Yes, but only fancy being found here!"

She laughed; but the laugh did not succeed. It could not hide a real embarrassment. She pondered, and seemed irresolute. Then with the words—"They will say we stayed behind on purpose," she moved her hand to the door, but again withdrew it, and stood irresolute.

"Let us put out the light." said Hugh laughing, "and make no answer."

"Can you starve well?"

"With you."

She murmured something to herself; then said aloud and hastily, as if she had made up her mind by the compulsion of circumstances:

"But this won't do. They are still looking at the portrait, I daresay. Come."

So saying, she went into another recess, and, lifting a curtain of tapestry, opened a door.

"Come quick," she said.

Hugh followed her down a short stair into a narrow passage, nowhere lighted from the outside. The door went to behind them, as if some one had banged it in anger at their intrusion. The passage smelt very musty, and was as quiet as death.

"Not a word of this, Hugh, as you love me. It may be useful yet."

"Not a word."

They came through a sliding panel into an empty room. Euphra closed it behind them.

"Now shade your light."

He did so. She took him by the hand. A few more turns brought them in sight of the lights of the rest of the party. As Euphra had conjectured, they were looking at the picture of Lady Euphrasia, Mr. Arnold prosing away to them, in proof that the nun could not be she. They entered the gallery without being heard; and parting a little way, one pretending to look at one picture, the other at another, crept gradually round till they joined the group. It was a piece of most successful generalship. Euphra was, doubtless, quite prepared with her story in case it should fail.

"Dear Lady Emily," said she, "how tired you look! Do let us go, uncle."

"By all means. Take my arm, Lady Emily. Euphra, will you take the keys again, and lock the doors?"

Mrs. Elton had already taken Hugh's arm, and was leading him away after Mr. Arnold and Lady Emily.

"I will not leave you behind with the spectres, Miss Cameron," said Funkelstein.

"Thank you; they will not detain me long. They don't mind being locked up."

It was some little time, however, before they presented themselves in the drawing-room, to which, and not to the library, the party had gone: they had had enough of horrors for that night.

Lest my readers should think they have had too many wonders at least, I will explain one of them. It was really Margaret Elginbrod whom Hugh had seen. Mrs. Elton was the lady in whose service she had left her home. It was nothing strange that they had not met, for Margaret knew he was in the same house, and had several times seen him, but had avoided meeting him. Neither was it a wonderful coincidence that they should be in such close proximity; for the college friend from whom Hugh had first heard of Mr. Arnold, was the son of the gentleman whom Mrs. Elton was visiting, when she first saw Margaret.

Margaret had obeyed her mistress's summons to the drawing-room, and had entered while Hugh was stooping over the plate. As the room was nearly dark, and she was dressed in black, her pale face alone caught the light and his eye as he looked up, and the giddiness which followed had prevented him from seeing more. She left the room the next moment, while they were all looking out of the window. Nor was it any exercise of his excited imagination that had presented her face as glorified. She was now a woman; and, there being no divine law against saying so, I say that she had grown a lady as well; as indeed any one might have foreseen who was capable of foreseeing it. Her whole nature had blossomed into a still, stately, lily-like beauty; and the face that Hugh saw was indeed the realised idea of the former face of Margaret.

But how did the plate move? and whence came the writing of old David's name? I must, for the present, leave the whole matter to the speculative power of each of my readers.

But Margaret was in mourning: was David indeed dead?

He was dead.—Yet his name will stand as the name of my story for pages to come; because, if he had not been in it, the story would never have been worth writing; because the influence of that ploughman is the salt of the whole; because a man's life in the earth is not to be measured by the time he is visible upon it; and because, when the story is wound up, it will be in the presence of his spirit.

Do I then believe that David himself did write that name of his?

Heaven forbid that any friend of mine should be able to believe it!

Long before she saw him, Margaret had known, from what she heard among the servants, that Master Harry's tutor could be no other than her own tutor of the old time. By and by she learned a great deal about him from Harry's talk with Mrs. Elton and Lady Emily. But she did not give the least hint that she knew him, or betray the least desire to see him.

Mrs. Elton was amusingly bewildered by the occurrences of the evening. Her theories were something astounding; and followed one another with such alarming rapidity, that had they been in themselves such as to imply the smallest exercise of the thinking faculty, she might well have been considered in danger of an attack of brain-fever. As it was, none such supervened. Lady Emily said nothing, but seemed unhappy. As for Hugh, he simply could not tell what to make of the writing. But he did not for a moment doubt that the vision he had seen was only a vision—a home-made ghost, sent out from his own creative brain. Still he felt that Margaret's face, come whence it might, was a living reproof to him; for he was losing his life in passion, sinking deeper in it day by day. His powers were deserting him. Poetry, usually supposed to be the attendant of love, had deserted him. Only by fits could he see anything beautiful; and then it was but in closest association of thought with the one image which was burning itself deeper and deeper into his mental sensorium. Come what might, he could not tear it away. It had become a part of himself—of his inner life—even while it seemed to be working the death of life. Deeper and deeper it would burn, till it reached the innermost chamber of life. Let it burn.

Yet he felt that he could not trust her. Vague hopes he had, that, by trusting, she might be made trustworthy; but he feared they were vain as well as vague. And yet he would not cast them away, for he could not cast her away.

CHAPTER XVIII
MORE MATERIALISM AND SOME SPIRITUALISM

God wisheth none should wreck on a strange shelf:
To Him man's dearer than to himself.

BEN Jonson.—The Forest: To Sir Robert Wroth.

At breakfast the following morning, the influences of the past day on the family were evident. There was a good deal of excitement, alternated with listlessness. The moral atmosphere seemed unhealthy; and Harry, although he had, fortunately for him, had nothing to do with the manifestations of the previous evening, was affected by the condition of those around him. Hugh was still careful enough of him to try to divert the conversation entirely from what he knew would have a very injurious effect upon him; and Mr. Arnold, seeing the anxious way in which he glanced now and then at his pupil, and divining the reason, by the instinct of his affection, with far more than his usual acuteness, tried likewise to turn it aside, as often as it inclined that way. Still a few words were let fall by the visitors, which made Harry stare. Hugh took him away as soon as breakfast was over.

In the afternoon, Funkelstein called to inquire after the ladies; and hoped he had no injury to their health to lay on his conscience. Mr. Arnold, who had a full allowance of curiosity, its amount being frequently in an inverse ratio to that of higher intellectual gifts, begged him to spend the rest of the day with them; but not to say a word of what had passed the day before, till after Harry had retired for the night.

Renewed conversation led to renewed experiments in the library. Hugh, however, refused to have anything more to do with the plate-writing; for he dreaded its influence on his physical nature, attributing, as I have said, the vision of Margaret to a cerebral affection. And the plate did not seem to work satisfactorily with any one else, except Funkelstein, who, for his part, had no great wish to operate. Recourse was had to a more vulgar method—that of expectant solicitation of those noises whereby the prisoners in the aërial vaults are supposed capable of communicating with those in this earthly cell. Certainly, raps were heard from some quarter or another; and when the lights were extinguished, and the crescent moon only allowed to shine in the room, some commotion was discernible amongst the furniture. Several light articles flew about. A pen-wiper alighted on Euphra's lap, and a sofa-pillow gently disarranged Mrs. Elton's cap. Most of the artillery, however, was directed against Lady Emily; and she it was who saw, in a faint stream of moonlight, a female arm uplifted towards her, from under a table, with a threatening motion. It was bare to the elbow, and draped above. It showed first a clenched fist, and next an open hand, palm outwards, making a repellent gesture. Then the back of the hand was turned, and it motioned her away, as if she had been an importunate beggar. But at this moment, one of the doors opened, and a dark figure passed through the room towards the opposite door. Everything that could be called ghostly, ceased instantaneously. The arm vanished. The company breathed more freely.

Lady Emily, who had been on the point of going into hysterics, recovered herself, and overcame the still lingering impulse: she felt as if she had awaked from a momentary aberration of the intellect. Mr. Arnold proceeded to light the candles, saying, in a righteous tone:

"I think we have had enough of this nonsense."

When the candles were lighted, there was no one to be seen in the room besides themselves. Several, Hugh amongst them, had observed the figure; but all had taken it for part of the illusive phantasmagoria. Hugh would have concluded it a variety of his vision of the former night; but others had seen it as well as he.

There was no renewal of the experiments that night. But all were in a very unhealthy state of excitement. Vague fear, vague wonder, and a certain indescribable oppression, had dimmed for the time all the clearer vision, and benumbed all the nobler faculties of the soul. Lady Emily was affected the most. Her eyes looked scared; there was a bright spot on one cheek amidst deathly paleness; and she seemed very unhappy. Mrs. Elton became alarmed, and this brought her back to a more rational condition. She persuaded Lady Emily to go to bed.

But the contagion spread; and indistinct terrors were no longer confined to the upper portions of the family. The bruit revived, which had broken out a year before—that the house was haunted. It was whispered that, the very night after these occurrences, the Ghost's Walk had been in use as the name signified: a figure in death-garments had been seen gliding along the deserted avenue, by one of the maid-servants; the truth of whose story was corroborated by the fact that, to support it, she did not hesitate to confess that she had escaped from the house, nearly at midnight, to meet one of the grooms in a part of the wood contiguous to the avenue in question.

Mr. Arnold instantly dismissed her—not on the ground of the intrigue, he took care to let her know, although that was bad enough, but because she was a fool, and spread absurd and annoying reports about the house. Mr. Arnold's usual hatred of what he called superstition, was rendered yet more spiteful by the fact, that the occurrences of the week had had such an effect on his own mind, that he was mortally afraid lest he should himself sink into the same limbo of vanity. The girl, however, was, or pretended to be, quite satisfied with her discharge, protesting she would not have staid for the world; and as the groom, whose wages happened to have been paid the day before, took himself off the same evening, it may be hoped her satisfaction was not altogether counterfeit.

"If all tales be true," said Mrs. Elton, "Lady Euphrasia is where she can't get out."

"But if she repented before she died?" said Euphra, with a muffled scorn in her tone.

"My dear Miss Cameron, do you call becoming a nun—repentance? We Protestants know very well what that means. Besides, your uncle does not believe it."

"Haven't you found out yet, dear Mrs. Elton, what my uncle's favourite phrase is?"

"No. What is it?"

"I don't believe it."

"You naughty girl!"

"I'm not naughty," answered Euphra, affecting to imitate the simplicity of a chidden child. "My uncle is so fond of casting doubt upon everything! If salvation goes by quantity, his faith won't save him."

Euphra knew well enough that Mrs. Elton was no tell-tale. The good lady had hopes of her from this moment, because she all but quoted Scripture to condemn her uncle; the verdict corresponding with her own judgment of Mr. Arnold, founded on the clearest assertions of Scripture; strengthened somewhat, it must be confessed, by the fact that the spirits, on the preceding evening but one, had rapped out the sentence: "Without faith it is impossible to please him."

Lady Emily was still in bed, but apparently more sick in mind than in body. She said she had tossed about all the previous night without once falling asleep; and her maid, who had slept in the dressing-room without waking once, corroborated the assertion. In the morning, Mrs. Elton, wishing to relieve the maid, sent Margaret to Lady Emily. Margaret arranged the bedclothes and pillows, which were in a very uncomfortable condition, sat down behind the curtain; and, knowing that it would please Lady Emily, began to sing, in what the French call a veiled voice, The Land o' the Leal. Now the air of this lovely song is the same as that of Scots wha hae; but it is the pibroch of onset changed into the coronach of repose, singing of the land beyond the battle, of the entering in of those who have fought the good fight, and fallen in the field. It is the silence after the thunder. Before she had finished, Lady Emily was fast asleep. A sweet peaceful half smile lighted her troubled face graciously, like the sunshine that creeps out when it can, amidst the rain of an autumn day, saying, "I am with you still, though we are all troubled." Finding her thus at rest, Margaret left the room for a minute, to fetch some work. When she returned, she found her tossing, and moaning, and apparently on the point of waking. As soon as she sat down by her, her trouble diminished by degrees, till she lay in the same peaceful sleep as before. In this state she continued for two or three hours, and awoke much refreshed. She held out her little hand to Margaret, and said:

"Thank you. Thank you. What a sweet creature you are!"

And Lady Emily lay and gazed in loving admiration at the face of the lady's-maid.

"Shall I send Sarah to you now, my lady?" said Margaret; "or would you like me to stay with you?"

"Oh! you, you, please—if Mrs. Elton can spare you."

"She will only think of your comfort, I know, my lady."

"That recalls me to my duty, and makes me think of her."

"But your comfort will be more to her than anything else."

"In that case you must stay, Margaret."

"With pleasure, my lady."

Mrs. Elton entered, and quite confirmed what Margaret had said.

"But," she added, "it is time Lady Emily had something to eat. Go to the cook, Margaret, and see if the beef-tea Miss Cameron ordered is ready."

Margaret went.

"What a comfort it is," said Mrs. Elton, wishing to interest Lady Emily, "that now-a-days, when infidelity is so rampant, such corroborations of Sacred Writ are springing up on all sides! There are the discoveries at Nineveh; and now these Spiritual Manifestations, which bear witness so clearly to another world."

But Lady Emily made no reply. She began to toss about as before, and show signs of inexplicable discomfort. Margaret had hardly been gone two minutes, when the invalid moaned out:

"What a time Margaret is gone!—when will she be back?"

"I am here, my love," said Mrs. Elton.

"Yes, yes; thank you. But I want Margaret."

"She will be here presently. Have patience, my dear."

"Please, don't let Miss Cameron come near me. I am afraid I am very wicked, but I can't bear her to come near me."

"No, no, dear; we will keep you to ourselves."

"Is Mr.—, the foreign gentleman, I mean—below?"

"No. He is gone."

"Are you sure? I can hardly believe it."

"What do you mean, dear? I am sure he is gone."

Lady Emily did not answer. Margaret returned. She took the beef-tea, and grew quiet again.

"You must not leave her ladyship, Margaret," whispered her mistress. "She has taken it into her head to like no one but you, and you must just stay with her."

"Very well, ma'am. I shall be most happy."

Mrs. Elton left the room. Lady Emily said:

"Read something to me, Margaret."

"What shall I read?"

"Anything you like."

Margaret got a Bible, and read to her one of her father's favourite chapters, the fortieth of Isaiah.

"I have no right to trust in God, Margaret."

"Why, my lady?"

"Because I do not feel any faith in him; and you know we cannot be accepted without faith."

"That is to make God as changeable as we are, my lady."

"But the Bible says so."

"I don't think it does; but if an angel from heaven said so, I would not believe it."

"Margaret!"

"My lady, I love God with all my heart, and I cannot bear you should think so of him. You might as well say that a mother would go away from her little child, lying moaning in the dark, because it could not see her, and was afraid to put its hand out into the dark to feel for her."

"Then you think he does care for us, even when we are very wicked. But he cannot bear wicked people."

"Who dares to say that?" cried Margaret. "Has he not been making the world go on and on, with all the wickedness that is in it; yes, making new babies to be born of thieves and murderers and sad women and all, for hundreds of years? God help us, Lady Emily! If he cannot bear wicked people, then this world is hell itself, and the Bible is all a lie, and the Saviour did never die for sinners. It is only the holy Pharisees that can't bear wicked people."

"Oh! how happy I should be, if that were true! I should not be afraid now."

"You are not wicked, dear Lady Emily; but if you were, God would bend over you, trying to get you back, like a father over his sick child. Will people never believe about the lost sheep?"

"Oh! yes; I believe that. But then—"

"You can't trust it quite. Trust in God, then, the very father of you—and never mind the words. You have been taught to turn the very words of God against himself."

Lady Emily was weeping.

"Lady Emily," Margaret went on, "if I felt my heart as hard as a stone; if I did not love God, or man, or woman, or little child, I would yet say to God in my heart: 'O God, see how I trust thee, because thou art perfect, and not changeable like me. I do not love thee. I love nobody. I am not even sorry for it. Thou seest how much I need thee to come close to me, to put thy arm round me, to say to me, my child; for the worse my state, the greater my need of my father who loves me. Come to me, and my day will dawn. My beauty and my love will come back; and oh! how I shall love thee, my God! and know that my love is thy love, my blessedness thy being.'"

As Margaret spoke, she seemed to have forgotten Lady Emily's presence, and to be actually praying. Those who cannot receive such words from the lips of a lady's-maid, must be reminded what her father was, and that she had lost him. She had had advantages at least equal to those which David the Shepherd had—and he wrote the Psalms.

She ended with:

"I do not even desire thee to come, yet come thou."

She seemed to pray entirely as Lady Emily, not as Margaret. When she had ceased, Lady Emily said, sobbing:

"You will not leave me, Margaret? I will tell you why another time."

"I will not leave you, my dear lady."

Margaret stooped and kissed her forehead. Lady Emily threw her arms round her neck, and offered her mouth to be kissed by the maid. In another minute she was fast asleep, with Margaret seated by her side, every now and then glancing up at her from her work, with a calm face, over which brooded the mist of tears.

That night, as Hugh paced up and down the floor of his study about midnight, he was awfully startled by the sudden opening of the door and the apparition of Harry in his nightshirt, pale as death, and scarcely able to articulate the words:

"The ghost! the ghost!"

He took the poor boy in his arms, held him fast, and comforted him. When he was a little soothed,

"Oh, Harry!" he said, lightly, "you've been dreaming. Where's the ghost?"

"In the Ghost's Walk," cried Harry, almost shrieking anew with terror.

"How do you know it is there?"

"I saw it from my window.—I couldn't sleep. I got up and looked out—I don't know why—and I saw it! I saw it!"

The words were followed by a long cry of terror.

"Come and show it to me," said Hugh, wanting to make light of it.

"No, no, Mr. Sutherland—please not. I couldn't go back into that room."

"Very well, dear Harry; you shan't go back. You shall sleep with me, to-night."

"Oh! thank you, thank you, dear Mr. Sutherland. You will love me again, won't you?"

This touched Hugh's heart. He could hardly refrain from tears. His old love, buried before it was dead, revived. He clasped the boy to his heart, and carried him to his own bed; then, to comfort him, undressed and lay down beside him, without even going to look if he too might not see the ghost. She had brought about one good thing at least that night; though, I fear, she had no merit in it.

Lady Emily's room likewise looked out upon the Ghost's Walk. Margaret heard the cry as she sat by the sleeping Emily; and, not knowing whence it came, went, naturally enough, in her perplexity, to the window. From it she could see distinctly, for it was clear moonlight: a white figure went gliding away along the deserted avenue. She immediately guessed what the cry had meant; but as she had heard a door bang directly after (as Harry shut his behind him with a terrified instinct, to keep the awful window in), she was not very uneasy about him. She felt besides that she must remain where she was, according to her promise to Lady Emily. But she resolved to be prepared for the possible recurrence of the same event, and accordingly revolved it in her mind. She was sure that any report of it coming to Lady Emily's ears, would greatly impede her recovery; for she instinctively felt that her illness had something to do with the questionable occupations in the library. She watched by her bedside all the night, slumbering at times, but roused in a moment by any restlessness of the patient; when she found that, simply by laying her hand on hers, or kissing her forehead, she could restore her at once to quiet sleep.

CHAPTER XIX
THE GHOST'S WALK

Thierry. — 'Tis full of fearful shadows.

Ordella. — So is sleep, sir;
Or anything that's merely ours, and mortal;
We were begotten gods else. But those fears
Feeling but once the fires of nobler thoughts,
Fly, like the shapes of clouds we form, to nothing.

BEAUMONT AND FLETCHER. — Thierry and Theodoret.

Margaret sat watching the waking of Lady Emily. Knowing how much the first thought colours the feeling of the whole day, she wished that Lady Emily should at once be aware that she was by her side.

She opened her eyes, and a smile broke over her face when she perceived her nurse. But Margaret did not yet speak to her.

Every nurse should remember that waking ought always to be a gradual operation; and, except in the most triumphant health, is never complete on the opening of the eyes.

"Margaret, I am better," said Lady Emily, at last.

"I am very glad, my lady."

"I have been lying awake for some time, and I am sure I am better. I don't see strange-coloured figures floating about the room as I did yesterday. Were you not out of the room a few minutes ago?"

"Just for one moment, my lady."

"I knew it. But I did not mind it. Yesterday, when you left me, those figures grew ten times as many, the moment you were gone. But you will stay with me to-day, too, Margaret?" she added, with some anxiety.

"I will, if you find you need me. But I may be forced to leave you a little while this evening — you must try to allow me this, dear Lady Emily."

"Of course I will. I will be quite patient, I promise you, whatever comes to me."

When Harry woke, after a very troubled sleep, from which he had often started with sudden cries of terror, Hugh made him promise not to increase the confusion of the household, by speaking of what he had seen. Harry promised at once, but begged in his turn that Hugh would not leave him all day. It did not need the pale scared face of his pupil to enforce the request; for Hugh was already anxious lest the fright the boy had had, should exercise a permanently deleterious effect on his constitution. Therefore he hardly let him out of his sight.

But although Harry kept his word, the cloud of perturbation gathered thicker in the kitchen and the servants' hall. Nothing came to the ears of their master and mistress; but gloomy looks, sudden starts, and sidelong glances of fear, indicated the prevailing character of the feelings of the household.

And although Lady Emily was not so ill, she had not yet taken a decided turn for the better, but appeared to suffer from some kind of low fever. The medical man who was called in, confessed to Mrs. Elton, that as yet he could say nothing very decided about her condition, but recommended great quiet and careful nursing. Margaret scarcely left her room, and the invalid showed far more than the ordinary degree of dependence upon her nurse. In her relation to her, she was more like a child than an invalid.

About noon she was better. She called Margaret and said to her:

"Margaret, dear, I should like to tell you one thing that annoys me very much."

"What is it, dear Lady Emily?"

"That man haunts me. I cannot bear the thought of him; and yet I cannot get rid of him. I am sure he is a bad man. Are you certain he is not here?"

"Yes, indeed, my lady. He has not been here since the day before yesterday."

"And yet when you leave me for an instant, I always feel as if he were sitting in the very seat where you were the moment before, or just coming to the door and about to open it. That is why I cannot bear you to leave me."

Margaret might have confessed to some slighter sensations of the same kind; but they did not oppress her as they did Lady Emily.

"God is nearer to you than any thought or feeling of yours, Lady Emily. Do not be afraid. If all the evil things in the universe were around us, they could not come inside the ring that he makes about us. He always keeps a place for himself and his child, into which no other being can enter."

"Oh! how you must love God, Margaret!"

"Indeed I do love him, my lady. If ever anything looks beautiful or lovely to me, then I know at once that God is that."

"But, then, what right have we to take the good of that, however true it is, when we are not beautiful ourselves?"

"That only makes God the more beautiful—in that he will pour out the more of his beauty upon us to make us beautiful. If we care for his glory, we shall be glad to believe all this about him. But we are too anxious about feeling good ourselves, to rejoice in his perfect goodness. I think we should find that enough, my lady. For, if he be good, are not we his children, and sure of having it, not merely feeling it, some day?"

Here Margaret repeated a little poem of George Herbert's. She had found his poems amongst Mrs. Elton's books, who, coming upon her absorbed in it one day, had made her a present of the volume. Then indeed Margaret had found a friend.

The poem is called Dialogue:

> "Sweetest Saviour, if my soul
> Were but worth the having—"

"Oh, what a comfort you are to me, Margaret!" Lady Emily said, after a short silence. "Where did you learn such things?"

"From my father, and from Jesus Christ, and from God himself, showing them to me in my heart."

"Ah! that is why, as often as you come into my room, even if I am very troubled, I feel as if the sun shone, and the wind blew, and the birds sang, and the tree-tops went waving in the wind, as they used to do before I was taken ill—I mean before they thought I must go abroad. You seem to make everything clear, and right, and plain. I wish I were you, Margaret."

"If I were you, my lady, I would rather be what God chose to make me, than the most glorious creature that I could think of. For to have been thought about—born in God's thoughts—and then made by God, is the dearest, grandest, most precious thing in all thinking. Is it not, my lady?"

"It is," said Lady Emily, and was silent.

The shadows of evening came on. As soon as it was dark, Margaret took her place at one of the windows hidden from Lady Emily by a bed-curtain. She raised the blind, and pulled aside one curtain, to let her have a view of the trees outside. She had placed the one candle so as not to shine either on the window or on her own eyes. Lady Emily was asleep. One hour and another passed, and still she sat there—motionless, watching.

Margaret did not know, that at another window—the one, indeed, next to her own—stood a second watcher. It was Hugh, in Harry's room: Harry was asleep in Hugh's. He had no light. He stood with his face close against the windowpane, on which the moon shone brightly. All below him the woods were half dissolved away in the moonlight. The Ghost's Walk lay full before him, like a tunnel through the trees. He could see a great way down, by the light that fell into it, at various intervals, from between the boughs overhead. He stood thus for a long time, gazing somewhat listlessly. Suddenly he became all eyes, as he caught the white glimmer of something passing up the avenue. He stole out of the room, down to the library by the back-stair, and so through the library window into the wood. He reached the avenue sideways, at some distance from the house, and peeped from behind a tree, up and down. At first he saw nothing. But, a moment after, while he was looking down the avenue, that is, away from the house, a veiled figure in white passed him noiselessly from the other direction. From the way in which he was looking at the moment, it had passed him before he saw it. It made no sound. Only some early-fallen leaves rustled as they hurried away in uncertain eddies, startled by the sweep of its trailing garments, which yet were held up by hands hidden within them. On it went. Hugh's eyes were fixed on its course. He could not move, and his heart laboured so frightfully that he could hardly breathe. The figure had not advanced far, however, before he heard a repressed cry of agony, and it sank to the earth, and vanished; while from where it disappeared, down the path, came, silently too, turning neither to the right nor the left, a second figure, veiled in black from head to foot.

"It is the nun in Lady Euphrasia's room," said Hugh to himself.

This passed him too, and, walking slowly towards the house, disappeared somewhere, near the end of the avenue. Turning once more, with reviving courage—for his blood had begun to flow more equably—Hugh ventured to approach the spot where the white figure had vanished. He found nothing there but the shadow of a huge tree. He walked through the avenue to the end, and then back to the house, but saw nothing; though he often started at fancied appearances. Sorely bewildered, he returned to his own room. After speculating till thought was weary, he lay down beside Harry, whom he was thankful to find in a still repose, and fell fast asleep.

Margaret lay on a couch in Lady Emily's room, and slept likewise; but she started wide awake at every moan of the invalid, who often moaned in her sleep.

CHAPTER XX
THE BAD MAN

She kent he was nae gentle knight,
That she had letten in;
For neither when he gaed nor cam',
Kissed he her cheek or chin.

He neither kissed her when he cam'
Nor clappit her when he gaed;
And in and out at her bower window,
The moon shone like the gleed.

Glenkindie.—Old Scotch Ballad.

When Euphra recovered from the swoon into which she had fallen—for I need hardly explain to my readers, that it was she who walked the Ghost's Walk in white—on seeing Margaret, whom, under the irresistible influences of the moonlight and a bad conscience, she took for the very being whom Euphra herself was personating—when she recovered, I say, she found herself lying in the wood, with Funkelstein, whom she had gone to meet, standing beside her. Her first words were of anger, as she tried to rise, and found she could not.

"How long, Count Halkar, am I to be your slave?"

"Till you have learned to submit."

"Have I not done all I can?"

"You have not found it. You are free from the moment you place that ring, belonging to me, in right of my family, into my hands."

I do not believe that the man really was Count Halkar, although he had evidently persuaded Euphra that such was his name and title. I think it much more probable that, in the course of picking up a mass of trifling information about various families of distinction, for which his position of secretary in several of their houses had afforded him special facilities, he had learned something about the Halkar family, and this particular ring, of which, for some reason or other, he wanted to possess himself.

"What more can I do?" moaned Euphra, succeeding at length in raising herself to a sitting posture, and leaning thus against a tree. "I shall be found out some day. I have been already seen wandering through the house at midnight, with the heart of a thief. I hate you, Count Halkar!"

A low laugh was the count's only reply.

"And now Lady Euphrasia herself dogs my steps, to keep me from the ring." She gave a low cry of agony at the remembrance.

"Miss Cameron—Euphra—are you going to give way to such folly?"

"Folly! Is it not worse folly to torture a poor girl as you do me—all for a worthless ring? What can you want with the ring? I do not know that he has it even."

"You lie. You know he has. You need not think to take me in."

"You base man! You dare not give the lie to any but a woman."

"Why?"

"Because you are a coward. You are afraid of Lady Euphrasia yourself. See there!"

Von Funkelstein glanced round him uneasily. It was only the moonlight on the bark of a silver birch. Conscious of having betrayed weakness, he grew spiteful.

"If you do not behave to me better, I will compel you. Rise up!"

After a moment's hesitation, she rose.

"Put your arms round me."

She seemed to grow to the earth, and to drag herself from it, one foot after another. But she came close up to the Bohemian, and put one arm half round him, looking to the earth all the time.

"Kiss me."

"Count Halkar!" her voice sounded hollow and harsh, as if from a dead throat—"I will do what you please. Only release me."

"Go then; but mind you resist me no more. I do not care for your kisses. You were ready enough once. But that idiot of a tutor has taken my place, I see."

"Would to God I had never seen you!—never yielded to your influence over me! Swear that I shall be free if I find you the ring."

"You find the ring first. Why should I swear? I can compel you. You know you laid yourself out to entrap me first with your arts, and I only turned upon you with mine. And you are in my power. But you shall be free, notwithstanding; and I will torture you till you free yourself. Find the ring."

"Cruel! cruel! You are doing all you can to ruin me."

"On the contrary, I am doing all I can to save myself. If you had loved me as you allowed me to think once, I should never have made you my tool."

"You would all the same."

"Take care. I am irritable to-night."

For a few moments Euphra made no reply.

"To what will you drive me?" she said at last.

"I will not go too far. I should lose my power over you if I did. I prefer to keep it."

"Inexorable man!"

"Yes."

Another despairing pause.

"What am I to do?"

"Nothing. But keep yourself ready to carry out any plan that I may propose. Something will turn up, now that I have got into the house myself. Leave me to find out the means. I can expect no invention from your brains. You can go home."

Euphra turned without another word, and went; murmuring, as if in excuse to herself:

"It is for my freedom. It is for my freedom."

Of course this account must have come originally from Euphra herself, for there was no one else to tell it. She, at least, believed herself compelled to do what the man pleased. Some of my readers will put her down as insane. She may have been; but, for my part, I believe there is such a power of one being over another, though perhaps only in a rare contact of psychologically peculiar natures. I have testimony enough for that. She had yielded to his will once. Had she not done so, he could not have compelled her; but, having once yielded, she had not strength sufficient to free herself again. Whether even he could free her, further than by merely abstaining from the exercise of the power he had gained, I doubt much.

It is evident that he had come to the neighbourhood of Arnstead for the sake of finding her, and exercising his power over her for his own ends; that he had made her come to him once, if not oftener, before he met Hugh, and by means of his acquaintance, obtained admission into Arnstead. Once admitted, he had easily succeeded, by his efforts to please, in so far ingratiating himself with Mr. Arnold, that now the house-door stood open to him, and he had even his recognised seat at the dinner-table.

CHAPTER XXI
SPIRIT VERSUS MATERIALISM

Next this marble venomed seat, Smeared with gums of glutinous heat, I touch with chaste palms moist and cold— Now the spell hath lost his hold.

MILTON.—Comas.

Next morning Lady Emily felt better, and wanted to get up: but her eyes were still too bright, and her hands too hot; and Margaret would not hear of it.

Fond as Lady Emily was in general of Mrs. Elton's society, she did not care to have her with her now, and got tired of her when Margaret was absent.

They had taken care not to allow Miss Cameron to enter the room; but to-day there was not much likelihood of her making the attempt, for she did not appear at breakfast, sending a message to her uncle that she had a bad headache, but hoped to take her place at the dinner-table.

During the day, Lady Emily was better, but restless by fits.

"Were you not out of the room for a little while last night, Margaret?" she said, rather suddenly.

"Yes, my lady. I told you I should have to go, perhaps."

"I remember I thought you had gone, but I was not in the least afraid, and that dreadful man never came near me. I do not know when you returned. Perhaps I had fallen asleep; but when I thought about you next, there you were by my bedside."

"I shall not have to leave you to-night," was all Margaret's answer.

As for Hugh, when first he woke, the extraordinary experiences of the previous night appeared to him to belong only to the night, and to have no real relation to the daylight world. But a little reflection soon convinced him of the contrary; and then he went through the duties of the day like one who had nothing to do with them. The phantoms he had seen even occupied some of the thinking space formerly appropriated by the image of Euphra, though he knew to his concern that she was ill, and confined to her room.

He had heard the message sent to Mr. Arnold, however, and so kept hoping for the dinner-hour.

With it came Euphra, very pale. Her eyes had an unsettled look, and there were dark hollows under them. She would start and look sideways without any visible cause; and was thus very different from her usual self—ordinarily remarkable for self-possession, almost to coolness, of manner and speech. Hugh saw it, and became both distressed and speculative in consequence. It did not diminish his discomfort that, about the middle of dinner, Funkelstein was announced. Was it, then, that Euphra had been tremulously expectant of him?

"This is an unforeseen pleasure, Herr von Funkelstein," said Mr. Arnold.

"It is very good of you to call it a pleasure, Mr. Arnold," said he. "Miss Cameron—but, good heavens! how ill you look!"

"Don't be alarmed. I have only caught the plague."

"Only?" was all Funkelstein said in reply; yet Hugh thought he had no right to be so solicitous about Euphra's health.

As the gentlemen sat at their wine, Mr. Arnold said:

"I am anxious to have one more trial of those strange things you have brought to our knowledge. I have been thinking about them ever since."

"Of course I am at your service, Mr. Arnold; but don't you think, for the ladies' sakes, we have had enough of it?"

"You are very considerate, Herr von Funkelstein; but they need not be present if they do not like it."

"Very well, Mr. Arnold."

They adjourned once more to the library instead of the drawing-room. Hugh went and told Euphra, who was alone in the drawing-room, what they were about. She declined going, but insisted on his leaving her, and joining the other gentlemen.

Hugh left her with much reluctance.

"Margaret," said Lady Emily, "I am certain that man is in the house."

"He is, my lady," answered Margaret.

"They are about some more of those horrid experiments, as they call them."

"I do not know."

Mrs. Elton entering the room at the moment, Margaret said:

"Do you know, ma'am, whether the gentlemen are—in the library again?"

"I don't know, Margaret. I hope not. We have had enough of that. I will go and find out, though."

"Will you take my place for a few minutes first, please, ma'am?"

Margaret had felt a growing oppression for some time. She had scarcely left the sick-room that day.

"Don't leave me, dear Margaret," said Lady Emily, imploringly.

"Only for a little while, my lady. I shall be back in less than a quarter of an hour."

"Very well, Margaret," she answered dolefully.

Margaret went out into the moonlight, and walked for ten minutes. She sought the more open parts, where the winds were. She then returned to the sick-chamber, refreshed and strong.

"Now I will go and see what the gentlemen are about," said Mrs. Elton.

The good lady did not like these proceedings, but she was irresistibly attracted by them notwithstanding. Having gone to see for Lady Emily, she remained to see for herself.

After she had left, Lady Emily grew more uneasy. Not even Margaret's presence could make her comfortable. Mrs. Elton did not return. Many minutes elapsed. Lady Emily said at last:

"Margaret, I am terrified at the idea of being left alone, I confess; but not so terrified as at the idea of what is going on in that library. Mrs. Elton will not come back. Would you mind just running down to ask her to come to me?"

"I would go with pleasure," said Margaret; "but I don't want to be seen."

Margaret did not want to be seen by Hugh. Lady Emily, with her dislike to Funkelstein, thought Margaret did not want to be seen by him.

"You will find a black veil of mine," she said, "in that wardrobe—just throw it over your head, and hold a handkerchief to your face. They will be so busy that they will never see you."

Margaret yielded to the request of Lady Emily, who herself arranged her head-dress for her.

Now I must go back a little.—When Mrs. Elton reached the room, she found it darkened, and the gentlemen seated at the table. A running fire of knocks was going on all around.

She sat down in a corner. In a minute or two, she fancied she saw strange figures moving about, generally near the floor, and very imperfectly developed. Sometimes only a hand, sometimes only a foot, shadowed itself out of the dim obscurity. She tried to persuade herself that it was all done, somehow or other, by Funkelstein, yet she could not help watching with a curious dread. She was not a very excitable woman, and her nerves were safe enough.

In a minute or two more, the table at which they were seated, began to move up and down with a kind of vertical oscillation, and several things in the room began to slide about, by short, apparently purposeless jerks. Everything threatened to assume motion, and turn the library into a domestic chaos. Mrs. Elton declared afterwards that several books were thrown about the room.—But suddenly everything was as still as the moonlight. Every chair and table was at rest, looking perfectly incapable of motion. Mrs. Elton felt that she dared not say they had moved at all, so utterly ordinary was their appearance. Not a sound was to be heard from corner or ceiling. After a moment's silence, Mrs. Elton was quite restored to her sound mind, as she said, and left the room.

"Some adverse influence is at work," said Funkelstein, with some vexation. "What is in that closet?"

So saying he approached the door of the private staircase, and opened it. They saw him start aside, and a veiled dark figure pass him, cross the library, and go out by another door.

"I have my suspicions," said Funkelstein, with a rather tremulous voice.

"And your fears too, I think. Grant it now," said Mr. Arnold.

"Granted, Mr. Arnold. Let us go to the drawing-room."

Just as Margaret had reached the library door at the bottom of the private stair, either a puff of wind from an open loophole window, or some other cause, destroyed the arrangement of the veil, and made it fall quite over her face, She stopped for a moment to readjust it. She had not quite succeeded, when Funkelstein opened the door. Without an instant's hesitation, she let the veil fall, and walked forward.

Mrs. Elton had gone to her own room, on her way to Lady Emily's. When she reached the latter, she found Margaret seated as she had left her, by the bedside. Lady Emily said:

"I did not miss you, Margaret, half so much as I expected. But, indeed, you were not many moments gone. I do not care for that man now. He can't hurt me, can he?"

"Certainly not. I hope he will give you no more trouble either, dear Lady Emily. But if I might presume to advise you, I would say—Get well as soon as you can, and leave this place."

"Why should I? You frighten me. Mr. Arnold is very kind to me."

"The place quite suits Lady Emily, I am sure, Margaret."

"But Lady Emily is not so well as when she came."

"No, but that is not the fault of the place," said Lady Emily. "I am sure it is all that horrid man's doing."

"How else will you get rid of him, then? What if he wants to get rid of you?"

"What harm can I be doing him—a poor girl like me?"

"I don't know. But I fear there is something not right going on."

"We will tell Mr. Arnold at once," said Mrs. Elton.

"But what could you tell him, ma'am? Mr. Arnold is hardly one to listen to your maid's suspicions. Dear Lady Emily, you must get well and go."

"I will try," said Lady Emily, submissive as a child.

"I think you will be able to get up for a little while to-morrow."

A tap came to the door. It was Euphrasia, inquiring after Lady Emily.

"Ask Miss Cameron to come in," said the invalid.

She entered. Her manner was much changed—was subdued and suffering.

"Dear Miss Cameron, you and I ought to change places. I am sorry to see you looking so ill," said Lady Emily.

"I have had a headache all day. I shall be quite well to-morrow, thank you."

"I intend to be so too," said Lady Emily, cheerfully.

After some little talk, Euphra went, holding her hand to her forehead. Margaret did not look up, all the time she was in the room, but went on busily with her needle.

That night was a peaceful one.

CHAPTER XXII
THE RING

shining crystal, which
Out of her womb a thousand rayons threw.

BELLAY: translated by Spenser.

The next day, Lady Emily was very nearly as well as she had proposed being. She did not, however, make her appearance below. Mr. Arnold, hearing at luncheon that she was out of bed, immediately sent up his compliments, with the request that he might be permitted to see her on his return from the neighbouring village, where he had some business. To this Lady Emily gladly consented.

He sat with her a long time, talking about various things; for the presence of the girl, reminding him of his young wife, brought out the best of the man, lying yet alive under the incrustation of self-importance, and its inevitable stupidity. At length, subject of further conversation failing,

"I wonder what we can do to amuse you, Lady Emily," said he.

"Thank you, Mr. Arnold; I am not at all dull. With my kind friend, Mrs. Elton, and—"

She would have said Margaret, but became instinctively aware that the mention of her would make Mr. Arnold open his eyes, for he did not even know her name; and that he would stare yet wider when he learned that the valued companion referred to was Mrs. Elton's maid.

Mr. Arnold left the room, and presently returned with his arms filled with all the drawing-room books he could find, with grand bindings outside, and equally grand plates inside. These he heaped on the table beside Lady Emily, who tried to look interested, but scarcely succeeded to Mr. Arnold's satisfaction, for he presently said:

"You don't seem to care much about these, dear Lady Emily. I daresay you have looked at them all already, in this dull house of ours."

This was a wonderful admission from Mr. Arnold. He pondered—then exclaimed, as if he had just made a grand discovery:

"I have it! I know something that will interest you."

"Do not trouble yourself, pray, Mr. Arnold," said Lady Emily. But he was already half way to the door.

He went to his own room, and his own strong closet therein.

Returning towards the invalid's quarters with an ebony box of considerable size, he found it rather heavy, and meeting Euphra by the way, requested her to take one of the silver handles, and help him to carry it to Lady Emily's room. She started when she saw it, but merely said:

"With pleasure, uncle."

"Now, Lady Emily," said he, as, setting down the box, he took out a curious antique enamelled key, "we shall be able to amuse you for a little while."

He opened the box, and displayed such a glitter and show as would have delighted the eyes of any lady. All kinds of strange ornaments; ancient watches—one of them a death's head in gold; cameo necklaces; pearls abundant; diamonds, rubies, and all the colours of precious stones—every one of them having some history, whether known to the owner or not; gems that had flashed on many a fair finger and many a shining neck—lay before Lady Emily's delighted eyes. But Euphrasia's eyes shone, as she gazed on them, with a very different expression from that which sparkled in Lady Emily's. They seemed to search them with fingers of lightning. Mr. Arnold chose two or three, and gave Lady Emily her choice of them.

"I could not think of depriving you."

"They are of no use to me," said Mr. Arnold, making light of the handsome offer.

"You are too kind.—I should like this ring."

"Take it then, dear Lady Emily."

Euphrasia's eyes were not on the speakers, nor was any envy to be seen in her face. She still gazed at the jewels in the box.

The chosen gem was put aside; and then, one after another, the various articles were taken out and examined. At length, a large gold chain, set with emeralds, was lifted from where it lay coiled up in a corner. A low cry, like a muffled moan, escaped from Euphrasia's lips, and she turned her head away from the box.

"What is the matter, Euphra?" said Mr. Arnold.

"A sudden shoot of pain—I beg your pardon, dear uncle. I fear I am not quite so well yet as I thought I was. How stupid of me!"

"Do sit down. I fear the weight of the box was too much for you."

"Not in the least. I want to see the pretty things."

"But you have seen them before."

"No, uncle. You promised to show them to me, but you never did."

"You see what I get by being ill," said Lady Emily.

The chain was examined, admired, and laid aside.

Where it had lain, they now observed, in the corner, a huge stone like a diamond.

"What is this?" said Lady Emily, taking it up. "Oh! I see. It is a ring. But such a ring for size, I never saw. Do look, Miss Cameron."

For Miss Cameron was not looking. She was leaning her head on her hand, and her face was ashy pale. Lady Emily tried the ring on. Any two of her fingers would go into the broad gold circlet, beyond which the stone projected far in every direction. Indeed, the ring was attached to the stone, rather than the stone set in the ring.

"That is a curious thing, is it not?" said Mr. Arnold. "It is of no value in itself, I believe; it is nothing but a crystal. But it seems to have been always thought something of in the family;—I presume from its being evidently the very ring painted by Sir Peter Lely in that portrait of Lady Euphrasia which I showed you the other day. It is a clumsy affair, is it not?"

It might have occurred to Mr. Arnold, that such a thing must have been thought something of, before its owner would have chosen to wear it when sitting for her portrait.

Lady Emily was just going to lay it down, when she spied something that made her look at it more closely.

"What curious engraving is this upon the gold?" she asked.

"I do not know, indeed," answered Mr. Arnold. "I have never observed it."

"Look at it, then—all over the gold. What at first looks only like chasing, is, I do believe, words. The character looks to me like German. I wish I could read it. I am but a poor German scholar. Do look at it, please, dear Miss Cameron."

Euphra glanced slightly at it without touching it, and said:

"I am sure I could make nothing of it.—But," she added, as if struck by a sudden thought, "as Lady Emily seems interested in it—suppose we send for Mr. Sutherland. I have no doubt he will be able to decipher it."

She rose as if she would go for him herself; but, apparently on second thoughts, went to the bell and rang it.

"Oh! do not trouble yourself," interposed Lady Emily, in a tone that showed she would like it notwithstanding.

"No trouble at all," answered Euphra and her uncle in a breath.

"Jacob," said Mr. Arnold, "take my compliments to Mr. Sutherland, and ask him to step this way."

The man went, and Hugh came.

"There's a puzzle for you, Mr. Sutherland," said Mr. Arnold, as he entered. "Decipher that inscription, and gain the favour of Lady Emily for ever."

As he spoke he put the ring in Hugh's hand. Hugh recognized it at once.

"Ah! this is Lady Euphrasia's wonderful ring," said he.

Euphra cast on him one of her sudden glances.

"What do you know about it?" said Mr. Arnold, hastily.

Euphra flashed at him once more, covertly.

"I only know that this is the ring in her portrait. Any one may see that it is a very wonderful ring indeed, by only looking at it," answered Hugh, smiling.

"I hope it is not too wonderful for you to get at the mystery of it, though, Mr. Sutherland?" said Lady Emily.

"Lady Emily is dying to understand the inscription," said Euphrasia.

By this time Hugh was turning it round and round, trying to get a beginning to the legend. But in this he met with a difficulty. The fact was, that the initial letter of the inscription could only be found by looking into the crystal held close to the eye. The words seemed not altogether unknown to him, though the characters were a little strange, and the words themselves were undivided. The dinner bell rang.

"Dear me! how the time goes in your room, Lady Emily!" said Mr. Arnold, who was never known to keep dinner waiting a moment. "Will you venture to go down with us to-day?"

"I fear I must not to-day. To-morrow, I hope. But do put up these beauties before you go. I dare not touch them without you, and it is so much more pleasure seeing them, when I have you to tell me about them."

"Well, throw them in," said Mr. Arnold, pretending an indifference he did not feel. "The reality of dinner must not be postponed to the fancy of jewels."

All this time Hugh had stood poring over the ring at the window, whither he had taken it for better light, as the shadows were falling. Euphra busied herself replacing everything in the box. When all were in, she hastily shut the lid.

"Well, Mr. Sutherland?" said Mr. Arnold.

"I seem on the point of making it out, Mr. Arnold, but I certainly have not succeeded yet."

"Confess yourself vanquished, then, and come to dinner."

"I am very unwilling to give in, for I feel convinced that if I had leisure to copy the inscription as far as I can read it, I should, with the help of my dictionary, soon supply the rest. I am very unwilling, as well, to lose a chance of the favour of Lady Emily."

"Yes, do read it, if you can. I too am dying to hear it," said Euphra.

"Will you trust me with it, Mr. Arnold? I will take the greatest care of it."

"Oh, certainly!" replied Mr. Arnold—with a little hesitation in his tone, however, of which Hugh was too eager to take any notice.

He carried it to his room immediately, and laid it beside his manuscript verses, in the hiding-place of the old escritoire. He was in the drawing-room a moment after.

There he found Euphra and the Bohemian alone.—Von Funkelstein had, in an incredibly short space of time, established himself as Hausfreund, and came and went as he pleased.—They looked as if they had been interrupted in a hurried and earnest conversation—their faces were so impassive. Yet Euphra's wore a considerably heightened colour—a more articulate indication. She could school her features, but not her complexion.

CHAPTER XXIII
THE WAGER

He...stakes this ring;
And would so, had it been a carbuncle
Of Phoebus' wheel; and might so safely, had it
Been all the worth of his car.
Cymbeline.

Hugh, of course, had an immediate attack of jealousy. Wishing to show it in one quarter, and hide it in every other, he carefully abstained from looking once in the direction of Euphra; while, throughout the dinner, he spoke to every one else as often as there was the smallest pretext for doing so. To enable himself to keep this up, he drank wine freely. As he was in general very moderate, by the time the ladies rose, it had begun to affect his brain. It was not half so potent, however, in its influences, as the parting glance which Euphra succeeded at last, as she left the room, in sending through his eyes to his heart.

Hugh sat down to the table again, with a quieter tongue, but a busier brain. He drank still, without thinking of the consequences. A strong will kept him from showing any signs of intoxication, but he was certainly nearer to that state than he had ever been in his life before.

The Bohemian started the new subject which generally follows the ladies' departure.

"How long is it since Arnstead was first said to be haunted, Mr. Arnold?"

"Haunted! Herr von Funkelstein? I am at a loss to understand you," replied Mr. Arnold, who resented any such allusion, being subversive of the honour of his house, almost as much as if it had been depreciative of his own.

"I beg your pardon, Mr. Arnold. I thought it was an open subject of remark."

"So it is," said Hugh; "every one knows that."

Mr. Arnold was struck dumb with indignation. Before he had recovered himself sufficiently to know what to say, the conversation between the other two had assumed a form to which his late experiences inclined him to listen with some degree of interest. But, his pride sternly forbidding him to join in it, he sat sipping his wine in careless sublimity.

"You have seen it yourself, then?" said the Bohemian.

"I did not say that," answered Hugh. "But I heard one of the maids say once—when—"

He paused.

This hesitation of his witnessed against him afterwards, in Mr. Arnold's judgment. But he took no notice now.—Hugh ended tamely enough:

"Why, it is commonly reported amongst the servants."

"With a blue light?—Such as we saw that night from the library window, I suppose."

"I did not say that," answered Hugh. "Besides, it was nothing of the sort you saw from the library. It was only the moon. But—"

He paused again. Von Funkelstein saw the condition he was in, and pressed him.

"You know something more, Mr. Sutherland."

Hugh hesitated again, but only for a moment.

"Well, then," he said, "I have seen the spectre myself, walking in her white grave-clothes, in the Ghost's Avenue—ha! ha!"

Funkelstein looked anxious.

"Were you frightened?" said he.

"Frightened!" repeated Hugh, in a tone of the greatest contempt. "I am of Don Juan's opinion with regard to such gentry."

"What is that?"

> "'That soul and body, on the whole,
> Are odds against a disembodied soul.'"

"Bravo!" cried the count. "You despise all these tales about Lady Euphrasia, wandering about the house with a death-candle in her hand, looking everywhere about as if she had lost something, and couldn't find it?"

"Pooh! pooh! I wish I could meet her!"

"Then you don't believe a word of it?"

"I don't say that. There would be less of courage than boasting in talking so, if I did not believe a word of it."

"Then you do believe it?"

But Hugh was too much of a Scotchman to give a hasty opinion, or rather a direct answer—even when half-tipsy; especially when such was evidently desired. He only shook and nodded his head at the same moment.

"Do you really mean you would meet her if you could?"

"I do."

"Then, if all tales are true, you may, without much difficulty. For the coachman told me only to-day, that you may see her light in the window of that room almost any night, towards midnight. He told me, too (for I made quite a friend of him to-day, on purpose to hear his tales), that one of the maids, who left the other day, told the groom—and he told the coachman— that she had once heard talking; and, peeping through the key-hole of a door that led into that part of the old house, saw a figure, dressed exactly like the picture of Lady Euphrasia, wandering up and down, wringing her hands and beating her breast, as if she were in terrible trouble. She had a light in her hand which burned awfully blue, and her face was the face of a corpse, with pale-green spots."

"You think to frighten me, Funkelstein, and make me tremble at what I said a minute ago. Instead of repeating that. I say now: I will sleep in Lady Euphrasia's room this night, if you like."

"I lay you a hundred guineas you won't!" cried the Bohemian.

"Done!" said Hugh, offering him his hand. Funkelstein took it; and so the bet was committed to the decision of courage.

"Well, gentlemen," interposed Mr. Arnold at last, "you might have left a corner for me somewhere. Without my permission you will hardly settle your wager."

"I beg your pardon, Mr. Arnold," said Funkelstein. "We got rather excited over it, and forgot our manners. But I am quite willing to give it up, if Mr. Sutherland will."

"Not I," said Hugh;—"that is, of course, if Mr. Arnold has no objection."

"Of course not. My house, ghost and all, is at your service, gentlemen," responded Mr. Arnold, rising.

They went to the drawing-room. Mr. Arnold, strange to say, was in a good humour. He walked up to Mrs. Elton, and said:

"These wicked men have been betting, Mrs. Elton."

"I am surprised they should be so silly," said she, with a smile, taking it as a joke.

"What have they been betting about?" said Euphra, coming up to her uncle.

"Herr von Funkelstein has laid a hundred guineas that Mr. Sutherland will not sleep in Lady Euphrasia's room to-night."

Euphra turned pale.

"By sleep I suppose you mean spend the night?" said Hugh to Funkelstein. "I cannot be certain of sleeping, you know."

"Of course, I mean that," answered the other; and, turning to Euphrasia, continued:

"I must say I consider it rather courageous of him to dare the spectre as he does, for he cannot say he disbelieves in her. But come and sing me one of the old songs," he added, in an under tone.

Euphra allowed him to lead her to the piano; but instead of singing a song to him, she played some noisy music, through which he and she contrived to talk for some time, without being overheard; after which he left the room. Euphra then looked round to Hugh, and begged him with her eyes to come to her. He could not resist, burning with jealousy as he was.

"Are you sure you have nerve enough for this, Hugh?" she said, still playing.

"I have had nerve enough to sit still and look at you for the last half hour," answered Hugh, rudely.

She turned pale, and glanced up at him with a troubled look. Then, without responding to his answer, said:

"I daresay the count is not over-anxious to hold you to your bet."

"Pray intercede for me with the count, madam," answered Hugh, sarcastically. "He would not wish the young fool to be frightened, I daresay. But perhaps he wishes to have an interview with the ghost himself, and grudges me the privilege."

She turned deadly pale this time, and gave him one terrified glance, but made no other reply to his words. Still she played on.

"You will arm yourself?"

"Against a ghost? Yes, with a stout heart."

"But don't forget the secret door through which we came that night, Hugh. I distrust the count."

The last words were spoken in a whisper, emphasized into almost a hiss.

"Tell him I shall be armed. I tell you I shall meet him bare-handed. Betray me if you like."

Hugh had taken his revenge, and now came the reaction. He gazed at Euphra; but instead of the injured look, which was the best he could hope to see, an expression of "pity and ruth" grew slowly in her face, making it more lovely than ever in his eyes. At last she seemed on the point of bursting into tears; and, suddenly changing the music, she began playing a dead-march. She kept her eyes on the keys. Once more, only, she glanced round, to see whether Hugh was still by her side; and he saw that her face was pale as death, and wet with silent tears. He had never seen her weep before. He would have fallen at her feet, had he been alone with her. To hide his feelings, he left the room, and then the house.

He wandered into the Ghost's Walk; and, finding himself there, walked up and down in it. This was certainly throwing the lady a bold challenge, seeing he was going to spend the night in her room.

The excitement into which jealousy had thrown him, had been suddenly checked by the sight of Euphra's tears. The reaction, too, after his partial intoxication, had already begun to set in; to be accounted for partly by the fact that its source had been chiefly champagne, and partly by the other fact, that he had bound himself in honour, to dare a spectre in her own favourite haunt.

On the other hand, the sight of Euphra's emotion had given him a far better courage than jealousy or wine could afford. Yet, after ten minutes passed in the shadows of the Ghost's Walk, he would not have taken the bet at ten times its amount.

But to lose it now would have been a serious affair for him, the disgrace of failure unconsidered. If he could have lost a hundred guineas, it would have been comparatively a slight matter; but to lose a bet, and be utterly unable to pay it, would be disgraceful—no better than positive cheating. He had not thought of this at the time. Nor, even now, was it more than a passing thought; for he had not the smallest desire to recede. The ambition of proving his courage to Euphra, and, far more, the strength just afforded him by the sight of her tears, were quite sufficient to carry him on to the ordeal. Whether they would carry him through it with dignity, he did not ask himself.

And, after all, would the ghost appear? At the best, she might not come; at the very worst, she would be but a ghost; and he could say with Hamlet—

"for my soul, what can it do to that,

Being a thing as immortal as itself?"

But then, his jealousy having for the moment intermitted, Hugh was not able to say with Hamlet—

"I do not set my life at a pin's fee;"

and that had much to do with Hamlet's courage in the affair of the ghost.

He walked up and down the avenue, till, beginning to feel the night chilly, he began to feel the avenue eerie; for cold is very antagonistic to physical courage. But what refuge would he find in the ghost's room?

He returned to the drawing-room. Von Funkelstein and Euphra were there alone, but in no proximity. Mr. Arnold soon entered.

"Shall I have the bed prepared for you, Mr. Sutherland?" said Euphra.

"Which of your maids will you persuade to that office?" said Mr. Arnold, with a facetious expression.

"I must do it myself," answered Euphra, "if Mr. Sutherland persists."

Hugh saw, or thought he saw, the Bohemian dart an angry glance at Euphra, who shrank under it. But before he could speak, Mr. Arnold rejoined:

"You can make a bed, then? That is the housemaid's phrase, is it not?"

"I can do anything another can, uncle."

"Bravo! Can you see the ghost?"

"Yes," she answered, with a low lingering on the sibilant; looking round, at the same time, with an expression that implied a hope that Hugh had heard it; as indeed he had.

"What! Euphra too?" said Mr. Arnold, in a tone of gentle contempt.

"Do not disturb the ghost's bed for me," said Hugh. "It would be a pity to disarrange it, after it has lain so for an age. Besides, I need not rouse the wrath of the poor spectre more than can't be helped. If I must sleep in her room, I need not sleep in her bed. I will lie on the old couch. Herr von Funkelstein, what proof shall I give you?"

"Your word, Mr. Sutherland," replied Funkelstein, with a bow.

"Thank you. At what hour must I be there."

"Oh! I don't know. By eleven I should think. Oh! any time before midnight. That's the ghost's own, is it not? It is now—let me see—almost ten."

"Then I will go at once," said Hugh, thinking it better to meet the gradual approach of the phantom-hour in the room itself, than to walk there through the desolate house, and enter the room just as the fear would be gathering thickest within it. Besides, he was afraid that his courage might have broken down a little by that time, and that he would not be able to conceal entirely the anticipative dread, whose inroad he had reason to apprehend.

"I have one good cup of tea yet, Mr. Sutherland," said Euphra. "Will you not strengthen your nerves with that, before we lead you to the tomb?"

"Then she will go with me," thought Hugh. "I will, thank you, Miss Cameron."

He approached the table at which she stood pouring out the cup of tea. She said, low and hurriedly, without raising her head:

"Don't go, dear Hugh. You don't know what may happen."

"I will go, Euphra. Not even you shall prevent me."

"I will pay the wager for you—lend you the money."

"Euphra!"—The tone implied many things.

Mr. Arnold approached. Other conversation followed. As half-past ten chimed from the clock on the chimney-piece, Hugh rose to go.

"I will just get a book from my room," he said; "and then perhaps Herr von Funkelstein will be kind enough to see me make a beginning at least."

"Certainly I will. And I advise you to let the book be Edgar Poe's Tales."

"No. I shall need all the courage I have, I assure you. I shall find you here?"

"Yes."

Hugh went to his room, and washed his face and hands. Before doing so, he pulled off his finger a ring of considerable value, which had belonged to his father. As he was leaving the room to return to the company, he remembered that he had left the ring on the washhand-stand. He generally left it there at night; but now he bethought himself that, as he was not going to sleep in the room, it might be as well to place it in the escritoire. He opened the secret place, and laid the diamond beside his poems and the crystal ring belonging to Mr. Arnold. This done, he took up his book again, and, returning to the drawing-room, found the whole party prepared to accompany him. Mr. Arnold had the keys. Von Funkelstein and he went first, and Hugh followed with Euphra.

"We will not contribute to your discomfiture by locking the doors on the way, Mr. Sutherland," said Mr. Arnold.

"That is, you will not compel me to win the wager in spite of my fears," said Hugh.

"But you will let the ghost loose on the household," said the Bohemian, laughing.

"I will be responsible for that," replied Mr. Arnold.

Euphra dropped a little behind with Hugh.

"Remember the secret passage," said she. "You can get out when you will, whether they lock the door, or not. Don't carry it too far, Hugh."

"The ghost you mean, Euphra.—I don't think I shall," said Hugh, laughing. But as he laughed, an involuntary shudder passed through him.

"Have I stepped over my own grave?" thought he.

They reached the room, and entered. Hugh would have begged them to lock him in, had he not felt that his knowledge of the secret door, would, although he intended no use of it, render such a proposal dishonourable. They gave him the key of the door, to lock it on the inside, and bade him good night. They were just leaving him, when Hugh on whom a new light had broken at last, in the gradual restoration of his faculties, said to the Bohemian:

"One word with you, Herr von Funkelstein, if you please."

Funkelstein followed him into the room; when Hugh half-closing the door, said:

"I trust to your sympathy, as gentleman, not to misunderstand me. I wagered a hundred guineas with you in the heat of after-dinner talk. I am not at present worth a hundred shillings."

"Oh!" began Funkelstein, with a sneer, "if you wish to get off on that ground—"

"Herr von Funkelstein," interrupted Hugh, in a very decided tone, "I pointed to your sympathy as a gentleman, as the ground on which I had hoped to meet you now. If you have difficulty in finding that ground, another may be found to-morrow without much seeking."

Hugh paused for a moment after making this grand speech; but Funkelstein did not seem to understand him: he stood in a waiting attitude. Hugh therefore went on:

"Meantime, what I wanted to say is this:—I have just left a ring in my room, which, though in value considerably below the sum mentioned between us, may yet be a pledge of my good faith, in as far as it is of infinitely more value to me than can be reckoned in money. It was the property of one who by birth, and perhaps by social position as well, was Herr von Funkelstein's equal. The ring is a diamond, and belonged to my father."

Von Funkelstein merely replied:

"I beg your pardon, Mr. Sutherland, for misunderstanding you. The ring is quite an equivalent." And making him a respectful bow, he turned and left him.

CHAPTER XXIV
THE LADY EUPHRASIA

The black jades of swart night trot foggy rings 'Bout heaven's brow. 'Tis now stark dead night.

JOHN MARSTON.—Second Part of Antonio and Mellida.

As soon as Hugh was alone, his first action was to lock the door by which he had entered; his next to take the key from the lock, and put it in his pocket. He then looked if there were any other fastenings, and finding an old tarnished brass bolt as well, succeeded in making it do its duty for the first time that century, which required some persuasion, as may be supposed. He then turned towards the other door. As he crossed the room, he found four candles, a decanter of port, and some biscuits, on a table—placed there, no doubt, by the kind hands of Euphra. He vowed to himself that he would not touch the wine. "I have had enough of that for one night," said he. But he lighted the candles; and then saw that the couch was provided with plenty of wraps for the night. One of them—he recognised to his delight— was a Cameron tartan, often worn by Euphra. He buried his face in it for a moment, and drew from it fresh courage. He then went into the furthest recess, lifted the tapestry, and proceeded to fasten the concealed door. But, to his discomfiture, he could find no fastening upon it. "No doubt," thought he, "it does fasten, in some secret way or other." But he could discover none. There was no mark of bolt or socket to show whence one had been removed, nor sign of friction to indicate that the door had ever been made secure in such fashion. It closed with a spring.

"Then," said Hugh, apostrophising the door, "I must watch you."

As, however, it was not yet near the time when ghosts are to be expected, and as he felt very tired, he drank one glass of the wine, and throwing himself on the couch, drew Euphra's shawl over him, opened his book, and began to read. But the words soon vanished in a bewildering dance, and he slept.

He started awake in that agony of fear in which I suppose most people have awaked in the night, once or twice in their lives. He felt that he was not alone. But the feeling seemed, when he recalled it, to have been altogether different from that with which we recognise the presence of the most unwelcome bodily visitor. The whole of his nervous skeleton seemed to shudder and contract. Every sense was intensified to the acme of its acuteness; while the powers of volition were inoperative. He could not move a finger.

The moment in which he first saw the object I am about to describe, he could not recall. The impression made seemed to have been too strong for the object receiving it, destroying thus its own traces, as an overheated brand-iron would in dry timber. Or it may be that, after such a pre-sensation, the cause of it could not surprise him.

He saw, a few paces off, bending as if looking down upon him, a face which, if described as he described it, would be pronounced as far past the most liberal boundary-line of art, as itself had passed beyond that degree of change at which a human countenance is fit for the upper world no longer, and must be hidden away out of sight. The lips were dark, and drawn back from the closed teeth, which were white as those of a skull. There were spots—in fact, the face corresponded exactly to the description given by Funkelstein of the reported ghost of Lady Euphrasia. The dress was point for point correspondent to that in the picture. Had the portrait of Lady Euphrasia been hanging on the wall above, instead of the portrait of the unknown nun, Hugh would have thought, as far as dress was concerned, that it had come alive, and stepped from its frame—except for one thing: there was no ring on the thumb.

It was wonderful to himself afterwards, that he should have observed all these particulars; but the fact was, that they rather burnt themselves in upon his brain, than were taken notice of by him. They returned upon him afterwards by degrees, as one becomes sensible of the pain of a wound.

But there was one sign of life. Though the eyes were closed, tears flowed from them; and seemed to have worn channels for their constant flow down this face of death, which ought to have been lying still in the grave, returning to its dust, and was weeping above ground instead. The figure stood for a moment, as one who would gaze, could she but open her heavy, death-rusted eyelids. Then, as if in hopeless defeat, she turned away. And then, to crown the horror literally as well as figuratively, Hugh saw that her hair sparkled and gleamed goldenly, as the hair of a saint might, if the aureole were combed down into it. She moved towards the door with a fettered pace, such as one might attribute to the dead if they walked;— to the dead body, I say, not to the living ghost; to that which has lain in the prison-hold, till the joints are decayed with the grave-damps, and the muscles are stiff with more than deathly cold. She dragged one limb after the other slowly and, to appearance, painfully, as she moved towards the door which Hugh had locked.

When she had gone half-way to the door, Hugh, lying as he was on a couch, could see her feet, for her dress did not reach the ground. They were bare, as the feet of the dead ought to be, which are about to tread softly in the realm of Hades, But how stained and mouldy and iron-spotted, as if the rain had been soaking through the spongy coffin, did the dress show beside the pure whiteness of those exquisite feet! Not a sign of the tomb was upon them. Small, living, delicately formed, Hugh, could he have forgot the face they bore above, might have envied the floor which in their nakedness they seemed to caress, so lingeringly did they move from it in their noiseless progress.

She reached the door, put out her hand, and touched it. Hugh saw it open outwards and let her through. Nor did this strike him as in the smallest degree marvellous. It closed again behind her, noiseless as her footfalls.

The moment she vanished, the power of motion returned to him, and Hugh sprang to his feet. He leaped to the door. With trembling hand he inserted the key, and the lock creaked as he turned it.

In proof of his being in tolerable possession of his faculties at the moment, and that what he was relating to me actually occurred, he told me that he remembered at once that he had heard that peculiar creak, a few moments before Euphra and he discovered that they were left alone in this very chamber. He had never thought of it before.

Still the door would not open: it was bolted as well, and the bolt was very stiff to withdraw. But at length he succeeded.

When he reached the passage outside, he thought he saw the glimmer of a light, perhaps in the picture-gallery beyond. Towards this he groped his way.—He could never account for the fact, that he left the candles burning in the room behind him and went forward into the darkness, except by supposing that his wits had gone astray, in consequence of the shock the apparition had occasioned them.—When he reached the gallery, there was no light there; but somewhere in the distance he saw, or fancied, a faint shimmer.

The impulse to go towards it was too strong to be disputed with. He advanced with outstretched arms, groping. After a few steps, he had lost all idea of where he was, or how he ought to proceed in order to reach any known quarter. The light had vanished. He stood.—Was that a stealthy step he heard beside him in the dark? He had no time to speculate, for the next moment he fell senseless.

CHAPTER XXV
NEXT MORNING

Darkness is fled: look, infant morn hath drawn Bright silver curtains 'bout the couch of night; And now Aurora's horse trots azure rings, Breathing fair light about the firmament. Stand; what's that?

JOHN MARSTON.—Second Part of Antonio and Mellida.

When he came to himself, it was with a slow flowing of the tide of consciousness. His head ached. Had he fallen down stairs?—or had he struck his head against some projection, and so stunned himself? The last he remembered was—standing quite still in the dark, and hearing something. Had he been knocked down? He could not tell.—Where was he? Could the ghost have been all a dream? and this headache be nature's revenge upon last night's wine?—For he lay on the couch in the haunted chamber, and on his bosom lay the book over which he had dropped asleep.

Mingled with all this doubt, there was another. For he remembered that, when consciousness first returned, he felt as if he had seen Euphra's face bending down close over his.—Could it be possible? Had Euphra herself come to see how he had fared?—The room lay in the grey light of the dawn, but Euphra was nowhere visible. Could she have vanished ashamed through the secret door? Or had she been only a phantasy, a projection outwards of the form that dwelt in his brain; a phenomenon often occurring when the last of sleeping and the first of waking are indistinguishably blended in a vague consciousness?

But if it was so, then the ghost?—what of it? Had not his brain, by the events of the preceding evening, been similarly prepared with regard to it? Was it not more likely, after all, that she too was the offspring of his own imagination—the power that makes images—especially when considered, that she exactly corresponded to the description given by the Bohemian?— But had he not observed many points at which the Count had not even hinted?—Still, it was as natural to expect that an excited imagination should supply the details of a wholly imaginary spectacle, as that, given the idea of Euphra's presence, it should present the detail of her countenance; for the creation of that which is not, belongs as much to the realm of the imagination, as the reproduction of that which is.

It seemed very strange to Hugh himself, that he should be able thus to theorize, before even he had raised himself from the couch on which, perhaps, after all, he had lain without moving, throughout that terrible night, swarming with the horrors of the dead that would not sleep. But the long unconsciousness, in which he had himself visited the regions of death, seemed to have restored him, in spite of his aching head, to perfect mental equilibrium. Or, at least, his brain was quiet enough to let his mind work. Still, he felt very ghastly within. He raised himself on his elbow, and looked into the room. Everything was the same as it had been the night before, only with an altered aspect in the dawn-light. The dawn has a peculiar terror of its own, sometimes perhaps even more real in character, but very different from the terrors of the night and of candle-light. The room looked as if no ghost could have passed through its still old musty atmosphere, so perfectly reposeful did it appear; and yet it seemed as if some umbra, some temporary and now cast-off body of the ghost, must be lying or lingering somewhere about it. He rose, and peeped into the recess where the cabinet stood. Nothing was there but the well remembered carving and blackness. Having once yielded to the impulse, he could not keep from peering every moment, now into one, and now into another of the many hidden corners. The next suggesting itself for examination, was always one he could not see from where he stood:—after all, even in the daylight, there might be some dead thing there—who could tell? But he remained manfully at his post till the sun rose; till bell after bell rang from the turret; till, in short, Funkelstein came to fetch him.

"Good morning, Mr. Sutherland," said he. "How have you slept?"

"Like a—somnambulist," answered Hugh, choosing the word for its intensity. "I slept so sound that I woke quite early."

"I am glad to hear it. But it is nearly time for breakfast, for which ceremony I am myself hardly in trim yet."

So saying, Funkelstein turned, and walked away with some precipitation. What occasioned Hugh a little surprise; was, that he did not ask him one question more as to how he had passed the night. He had, of course, slept in the house, seeing he presented himself in deshabille.

Hugh hastened to his own room, where, under the anti-ghostial influences of the bath, he made up his mind not to say a word about the apparition to any one.

"Well, Mr. Sutherland, how have you spent the night?" said Mr. Arnold, greeting him.

"I slept with profound stupidity," answered Hugh; "a stupidity, in fact, quite worthy of the folly of the preceding wager."

This was true, as relating to the time during which he had slept, but was, of course, false in the impression it gave.

"Bravo!" exclaimed Mr. Arnold, with an unwonted impulsiveness. "The best mood, I consider, in which to meet such creations of other people's brains! And you positively passed a pleasant night in the awful chamber? That is something to tell Euphra. But she is not down yet. You have restored the character of my house, Mr. Sutherland; and next to his own character, a man ought to care for that of his house. I am greatly in your debt, sir."

At this moment, Euphra's maid brought the message, that her mistress was sorry she was unable to appear at breakfast.

Mrs. Elton took her place.

"The day is so warm and still, Mr. Arnold, that I think Lady Emily might have a drive to-day. Perhaps Miss Cameron may be able to join us by that time."

"I cannot think what is the matter with Euphra," said Mr. Arnold. "She never used to be affected in this way."

"Should you not seek some medical opinion?" said Mrs. Elton. "These constant headaches must indicate something wrong."

The constant headache had occurred just once before, since Mrs. Elton had formed one of the family. After a pause, Mr. Arnold reverted to the former subject.

"You are most welcome to the carriage, Mrs. Elton. I am sorry I cannot accompany you myself; but I must go to town to-day. You can take Mr. Sutherland with you, if you like. He will take care of you."

"I shall be most happy," said Hugh.

"So shall we all," responded Mrs. Elton kindly. "Thank you, Mr. Arnold; though I am sorry you can't go with us."

"What hour shall I order the carriage?"

"About one, I think. Will Herr von Funkelstein favour us with his company?"

"I am sorry," replied Funkelstein; "but I too must leave for London to-day. Shall I have the pleasure of accompanying you, Mr. Arnold?"

"With all my heart, if you can leave so early. I must go at once to catch the express train."

"I shall be ready in ten minutes."

"Very well."

"Pray, Mrs. Elton, make my adieus to Miss Cameron. I am concerned to hear of her indisposition."

"With pleasure. I am going to her now. Good-bye."

As soon as Mrs. Elton left the breakfast-room, Mr. Arnold rose, saying:

"I will walk round to the stable, and order the carriage myself. I shall then be able, through your means, Mr. Sutherland, to put a stop to these absurd rumours in person. Not that I mean to say anything direct, as if I placed any importance upon it; but, the coachman being an old servant, I shall be able through him, to send the report of your courage and its result, all over the house."

This was a very gracious explanation of his measures. As he concluded it, he left the room, without allowing time for a reply.

Hugh had not expected such an immediate consequence of his policy, and felt rather uncomfortable; but he soon consoled himself by thinking, "At least it will do no harm."

While Mr. Arnold was speaking, Funkelstein had been writing at a side-table. He now handed Hugh a cheque on a London banking-house for a hundred guineas. Hugh, in his innocence, could not help feeling ashamed of gaining such a sum by such means; for betting, like tobacco-smoking, needs a special training before it can be carried out quite comfortably, especially by the winner, if he be at all of a generous nature. But he felt that to show the least reluctance would place him at great disadvantage with a man of the world like the count. He therefore thanked him slightly, and thrust the cheque into his trowsers-pocket, as if a greater sum of money than he had ever handled before were nothing more for him to win, than the count would choose it to be considered for him to lose. He thought with himself: "Ah! well, I need not make use of it;" and repaired to the school-room.

Here he found Harry waiting for him, looking tolerably well, and tolerably happy. This was a great relief to Hugh, for he had not seen him at the breakfast-table—Harry having risen early and breakfasted before; and he had felt very uneasy lest the boy should have missed him in the night (for they were still bed-fellows), and should in consequence have had one of his dreadful attacks of fear.—It was evident that this had not taken place.

CHAPTER XXVI
AN ACCIDENT

There's a special providence in the fall of a sparrow
Hamlet.

When Mrs. Elton left the breakfast table, she went straight to Miss Cameron's room to inquire after her, expecting to find her maid with her. But when she knocked at the door, there was no reply.

She went therefore to her own room, and sent her maid to find Euphra's maid.

She came.

"Is your mistress going to get up to-day, Jane?" asked Mrs. Elton.

"I don't know, ma'am. She has not rung yet."

"Have you not been to see how she is?"

"No, ma'am."

"How was it you brought that message at breakfast, then?"

Jane looked confused, and did not reply.

"Jane!" said Mrs. Elton, in a tone of objurgation.

"Well, ma'am, she told me to say so," answered Jane.

"How did she tell you?"

Jane paused again.

"Through the door, ma'am," she answered at length; and then muttered, that they would make her tell lies by asking her questions she couldn't answer; and she wished she was out of the house, that she did.

Mrs. Elton heard this, and, of course, felt considerably puzzled.

"Will you go now, please, and inquire after your mistress, with my compliments?"

"I daren't, ma'am."

"Daren't! What do you mean?"

"Well, ma'am, there is something about my mistress—" Here she stopped abruptly; but as Mrs. Elton stood expectant, she tried to go on. All she could add, however, was—"No, ma'am; I daren't."

"But there is no harm in going to her room."

"Oh, no, ma'am. I go to her room, summer and winter, at seven o'clock every morning," answered Jane, apparently glad to be able to say something.

"Why won't you go now, then?"

"Why—why—because she told me—" Here the girl stammered and turned pale. At length she forced out the words—"She won't let me tell you why," and burst into tears.

"Won't let you tell me?" repeated Mrs. Elton, beginning to think the girl must be out of her mind. Jane looked hurriedly over her shoulder, as if she expected to see her mistress standing behind her, and then said, almost defiantly:

"No, she won't; and I can't."

With these words, she hurried out of the room, while Mrs. Elton turned with baffled bewilderment to seek counsel from the face of Margaret. As to what all this meant, I am in doubt. I have recorded it as Margaret told it to Hugh afterwards—because it seems to indicate something. It shows evidently enough, that if Euphra had more than a usual influence over servants in general, she had a great deal more over this maid in particular. Was this in virtue of a power similar to that of Count Halkar over herself? And was this, or something very different, or both combined, the art which he had accused her of first exercising upon him? Might the fact that her defeat had resulted in such absolute subjection, be connected with her possession of a power similar to his, which she had matched with his in vain? Of course I only suggest these questions. I cannot answer them.

At one o'clock, the carriage came round to the door; and Hugh, in the hope of seeing Euphra alone, was the first in the hall. Mrs. Elton and Lady Emily presently came, and proceeded to take their places, without seeming to expect Miss Cameron. Hugh helped them into the carriage; but, instead of getting in, lingered, hoping that Euphra was yet going to make her appearance.

"I fear Miss Cameron is unable to join us," said Mrs. Elton, divining his delay.

"Shall I run up-stairs, and knock at her door?" said Hugh.

"Do," said Mrs. Elton, who, after the unsatisfactory conversation she had held with her maid, had felt both uneasy and curious, all the morning.

Hugh bounded up-stairs; but, just as he was going to knock, the door opened, and Euphra, appeared.

"Dear Euphra! how ill you look!" exclaimed Hugh.

She was pale as death, and dark under the eyes; and had evidently been weeping.

"Hush! hush!" she answered. "Never mind. It is only a bad headache. Don't take any notice of it."

"The carriage is at the door. Will you not come with us?"

"With whom?"

"Lady Emily and Mrs. Elton."

"I am sick of them."

"I am going, Euphra."

"Stay with me."

"I must go. I promised to take care of them."

"Oh, nonsense! What should happen to them? Stay with me."

"No. I am very sorry. I wish I could."

"Then I must go with you, I suppose." Yet her tone expressed annoyance.

"Oh! thank you," cried Hugh in delight. "Make haste. I will run down, and tell them to wait."

He bounded away, and told the ladies that Euphra would join them in a few minutes.

But Euphra was cool enough to inflict on them quite twenty minutes of waiting; by which time she was able to behave with tolerable propriety. When she did appear at last, she was closely veiled, and stepped into the carriage without once showing her face. But she made a very pretty apology for the delay she had occasioned; which was certainly due, seeing it had been perfectly intentional. She made room for Hugh; he took his place beside her; and away they drove.

Euphra scarcely spoke; but begged indulgence, on the ground of her headache. Lady Emily enjoyed the drive very much, and said a great many pleasant little nothings.

"Would you like a glass of milk?" said Mrs. Elton to her, as they passed a farm-house on the estate.

"I should—very much," answered Lady Emily.

The carriage was stopped, and the servant sent to beg a glass of milk. Euphra, who, from riding backward with a headache, had been feeling very uncomfortable for some time, wished to get out while the carriage was waiting. Hugh jumped out, and assisted her. She walked a little way, leaning on his arm, up to the house, where she had a glass of water; after which she said she felt better, and returned with him to the carriage. In getting in again, either from the carelessness or the weakness occasioned by suffering, her foot slipped from the step, and she fell with a cry of alarm. Hugh caught her as she fell; and she would not have been much injured, had not the horses started and sprung forward at the moment, so that the hind wheel of the carriage passed over her ankle. Hugh, raising her in his arms, found she was insensible.

He laid her down upon the grass by the roadside. Water was procured, but she showed no sign of recovering.—What was to be done? Mrs. Elton thought she had better be carried to the farm-house. Hugh judged it better to take her home at once. To this, after a little argument, Mrs. Elton agreed.

They lifted her into the carriage, and made what arrangements they best could to allow her to recline. Blood was flowing from her foot; and it was so much swollen that it was impossible to guess at the amount of the injury. The foot was already twice the size of the other, in which Hugh for the first time recognised such a delicacy of form, as, to his fastidious eye and already ensnared heart, would have been perfectly enchanting, but for the agony he suffered from the injury to the other. Yet he could not help the thought crossing his mind, that her habit of never lifting her dress was a very strange one, and that it must have had something to do with the present accident. I cannot account for this habit, but on one of two suppositions; that of an affected delicacy, or that of the desire that the beauty of her feet should have its full power, from being rarely seen. But it was dreadful to think how far the effects of this accident might permanently injure the beauty of one of them.

Hugh would have walked home that she might have more room, but he knew he could be useful when they arrived. He seated himself so as to support the injured foot, and prevent, in some measure, the torturing effects of the motion of the carriage. When they had gone about half-way, she opened her eyes feebly, glanced at him, and closed them again with a moan of pain.

He carried her in his arms up to her own room, and laid her on a couch. She thanked him by a pitiful attempt at a smile. He mounted his horse, and galloped for a surgeon.

The injury was a serious one; but until the swelling could be a little reduced, it was impossible to tell how serious. The surgeon, however, feared that some of the bones of the ankle might be crushed. The ankle seemed to be dislocated, and the suffering was frightful. She endured it well, however—so far as absolute silence constitutes endurance.

Hugh's misery was extreme. The surgeon had required his assistance; but a suitable nurse soon arrived, and there was no pretext for his further presence in the sick chamber. He wandered about the grounds. Harry haunted his steps like a spaniel. The poor boy felt it much; and the suffering abstraction of Hugh sealed up his chief well of comfort. At length he went to Mrs. Elton, who did her best to console him.

By the surgeon's express orders, every one but the nurse was excluded from Euphra's room.

CHAPTER XXVII
MORE TROUBLES

Come on and do your best
To fright me with your sprites: you're powerful at it.
You smell this business with a sense as cold As is a dead man's nose.
A Winter's Tale.

When Mr. Arnold came home to dinner, and heard of the accident, his first feeling, as is the case with weak men, was one of mingled annoyance and anger. Hugh was the chief object of it; for had he not committed the ladies to his care? And the economy of his house being partially disarranged by it, had he not a good right to be angry? His second feeling was one of concern for his niece, which was greatly increased when he found that she was not in a state to see him. Still, nothing must interfere with the order of things; and when Hugh went into the drawing-room at the usual hour, he found Mr. Arnold standing there in tail coat and white neck-cloth, looking as if he had just arrived at a friend's house, to make one of a stupid party. And the party which sat down to dinner was certainly dreary enough, consisting only, besides the host himself, of Mrs. Elton, Hugh, and Harry. Lady Emily had had exertion enough for the day, and had besides shared in the shock of Euphra's misfortune.

Mr. Arnold was considerably out of humour, and ready to pounce upon any object of complaint. He would have attacked Hugh with a pompous speech on the subject of his carelessness, but he was rather afraid of his tutor now;—so certainly will the stronger get the upper hand in time. He did not even refer to the subject of the accident. Therefore, although it filled the minds of all at table, it was scarcely more than alluded to. But having nothing at hand to find fault with more suitable, he laid hold of the first wise remark volunteered by good Mrs. Elton; whereupon an amusing pas de deux immediately followed; for it could not be called a duel, inasmuch as each antagonist kept skipping harmlessly about the other, exploding theological crackers, firmly believed by the discharger to be no less than bomb-shells. At length Mrs. Elton withdrew.

"By the way, Mr. Sutherland," said Mr. Arnold, "have you succeeded in deciphering that curious inscription yet? I don't like the ring to remain long out of my own keeping. It is quite an heirloom, I assure you."

Hugh was forced to confess that he had never thought of it again.

"Shall I fetch it at once?" added he.

"Oh! no," replied Mr. Arnold. "I should really like to understand the inscription. To-morrow will do perfectly well."

They went to the drawing-room. Everything was wretched. However many ghosts might be in the house, it seemed to Hugh that there was no soul in it except in one room. The wind sighed fitfully, and the rain fell in slow, soundless showers. Mr. Arnold felt the vacant oppression as well as Hugh. Mrs Elton having gone to Lady Emily's room, he proposed back gammon; and on that surpassing game, the gentlemen expended the best part of two dreary hours. When Hugh reached his room he was too tired and spiritless for any intellectual effort; and, instead of trying to decipher the ring, went to bed, and slept as if there were never a ghost or a woman in the universe.

His first proceeding, after breakfast next day, was to get together his German books; and his next to take out the ring, which was to be subjected to their analytical influences. He went to his desk, and opened the secret place. There he stood fixed.—The ring was gone. His packet of papers was there, rather crumpled: the ring was nowhere. What had become of it? It was not long before a conclusion suggested itself. It flashed upon him all at once.

"The ghost has got it," he said, half aloud. "It is shining now on her dead finger. It was Lady Euphrasia. She was going for it then. It wasn't on her thumb when she went. She came back with it, shining through the dark—stepped over me, perhaps, as I lay on the floor in her way."

He shivered, like one in an ague-fit.

Again and again, with that frenzied, mechanical motion, which, like the eyes of a ghost, has "no speculation" in it, he searched the receptacle, although it freely confessed its emptiness to any asking eye. Then he stood gazing, and his heart seemed to stand still likewise.

But a new thought stung him, turning him almost sick with a sense of loss. Suddenly and frantically he dived his hand into the place yet again, useless as he knew the search to be. He took up his papers, and scattered them loose. It was all unavailing: his father's ring was gone as well.

He sank on a chair for a moment; but, instantly recovering, found himself, before he was quite aware of his own resolution, halfway down stairs, on his way to Mr. Arnold's room. It was empty. He rang for his servant. Mr. Arnold had gone away on horseback, and would not be home till dinner-time. Counsel from Mrs. Elton was hopeless. Help from Euphra he could not ask. He returned to his own room. There he found Harry waiting for him. His neglected pupil was now his only comforter. Such are the revenges of divine goodness.

"Harry!" he said, "I have been robbed."

"Robbed!" cried Harry, starting up. "Never mind, Mr. Sutherland; my papa's a justice of the peace. He'll catch the thief for you."

"But it's your papa's ring that they've stolen. He lent it to me, and what if he should not believe me?"

"Not believe you, Mr. Sutherland? But he must believe you. I will tell him all about it; and he knows I never told him a lie in my life."

"But you don't know anything about it, Harry."

"But you will tell me, won't you?"

Hugh could not help smiling with pleasure at the confidence his pupil placed in him. He had not much fear about being believed, but, at the best, it was an unpleasant occurrence.

The loss of his own ring not only added to his vexation, but to his perplexity as well. What could she want with his ring? Could she have carried with her such a passion for jewels, as to come from the grave to appropriate those of others as well as to reclaim her own? Was this her comfort in Hades, 'poor ghost'?

Would it be better to tell Mr. Arnold of the loss of both rings, or should he mention the crystal only? He came to the conclusion that it would only exasperate him the more, and perhaps turn suspicion upon himself, if he communicated the fact that he too was a loser, and to such an extent; for Hugh's ring was worth twenty of the other, and was certainly as sacred as Mr. Arnold's, if not so ancient. He would bear it in silence. If the one could not be found, there could certainly be no hope of the other.

Punctual as the clock, Mr. Arnold returned. It did not prejudice him in favour of the reporter of bad tidings, that he begged a word with him before dinner, when that was on the point of being served. It was, indeed, exceeding impolitic; but Hugh would have felt like an impostor, had he sat down to the table before making his confession.

"Mr. Arnold, I am sorry to say I have been robbed, and in your house, too."

"In my house? Of what, pray, Mr. Sutherland?"

Mr. Arnold had taken the information as some weak men take any kind of information referring to themselves or their belongings—namely, as an insult. He drew himself up, and lowered portentously.

"Of your ring, Mr. Arnold."

"Of—my—ring?"

And he looked at his ring-finger, as if he could not understand the import of Hugh's words.

"Of the ring you lent me to decipher," explained Hugh.

"Do you suppose I do not understand you, Mr. Sutherland? A ring which has been in the family for two hundred years at least! Robbed of it? In my house? You must have been disgracefully careless, Mr. Sutherland. You have lost it."

"Mr. Arnold," said Hugh, with dignity, "I am above using such a subterfuge, even if it were not certain to throw suspicion where it was undeserved."

Mr. Arnold was a gentleman, as far as his self-importance allowed. He did not apologize for what he had said, but he changed his manner at once.

"I am quite bewildered, Mr. Sutherland. It is a very annoying piece of news—for many reasons."

"I can show you where I laid it—in the safest corner in my room, I assure you."

"Of course, of course. It is enough you say so. We must not keep the dinner waiting now. But after dinner I shall have all the servants up, and investigate the matter thoroughly."

"So," thought Hugh with himself, "some one will be made a felon of, because the cursed dead go stalking about this infernal house at midnight, gathering their own old baubles. No, that will not do. I must at least tell Mr. Arnold what I know of the doings of the night."

So Mr. Arnold must still wait for his dinner; or rather, which was really of more consequence in the eyes of Mr. Arnold, the dinner must be kept waiting for him. For order and custom were two of Mr. Arnold's divinities; and the economy of his whole nature was apt to be disturbed by any interruption of their laws, such as the postponement of dinner for ten minutes. He was walking towards the door, and turned with some additional annoyance when Hugh addressed him again:

"One moment, Mr. Arnold, if you please."

Mr. Arnold merely turned and waited.

"I fear I shall in some degree forfeit your good opinion by what I am about to say, but I must run the risk."

Mr. Arnold still waited.

"There is more about the disappearance of the ring than I can understand."

"Or I either, Mr. Sutherland."

"But I must tell you what happened to myself, the night that I kept watch in Lady Euphrasia's room."

"You said you slept soundly."

"So I did, part of the time."

"Then you kept back part of the truth?"

"I did."

"Was that worthy of you?"

"I thought it best: I doubted myself."

"What has caused you to change your mind now?"

"This event about the ring."

"What has that to do with it? How do you even know that it was taken on that night?"

"I do not know; for till this morning I had not opened the place where it lay: I only suspect."

"I am a magistrate, Mr. Sutherland: I would rather not be prejudiced by suspicions."

"The person to whom my suspicions refer, is beyond your jurisdiction, Mr. Arnold."

"I do not understand you."

"I will explain myself."

Hugh gave Mr. Arnold a hurried yet circumstantial sketch of the apparition he believed he had seen.

"What am I to judge from all this?" asked he, coldly, almost contemptuously.

"I have told you the facts; of course I must leave the conclusions to yourself, Mr. Arnold; but I confess, for my part, that any disbelief I had in apparitions is almost entirely removed since—"

"Since you dreamed you saw one?"

"Since the disappearance of the ring," said Hugh.

"Bah!" exclaimed Mr. Arnold, with indignation. "Can a ghost fetch and carry like a spaniel? Mr. Sutherland, I am ashamed to have such a reasoner for tutor to my son. Come to dinner, and do not let me hear another word of this folly. I beg you will not mention it to any one."

"I have been silent hitherto, Mr. Arnold; but circumstances, such as the commitment of any one on the charge of stealing the ring, might compel me to mention the matter. It would be for the jury to determine whether it was relevant or not."

It was evident that Mr. Arnold was more annoyed at the imputation against the nocturnal habits of his house, than at the loss of the ring, or even its possible theft by one of his servants. He looked at Hugh for a moment as if he would break into a furious rage; then his look gradually changed into one of suspicion, and, turning without another word, he led the way to the dining-room, followed by Hugh. To have a ghost held in his face in this fashion, one bred in his own house, too, when he had positively declared his absolute contempt for every legend of the sort, was more than man could bear. He sat down to dinner in gloomy silence, breaking it only as often as he was compelled to do the duties of a host, which he performed with a greater loftiness of ceremony than usual.

There was no summoning of the servants after dinner, however. Hugh's warning had been effectual. Nor was the subject once more alluded to in Hugh's hearing. No doubt Mr. Arnold felt that something ought to be done; but I presume he could never make up his mind what that something ought to be. Whether any reasons for not prosecuting the inquiry had occurred to him upon further reflection, I am unable to tell. One thing is certain; that from this time he ceased to behave to Hugh with that growing cordiality which he had shown him for weeks past. It was no great loss to Hugh; but he felt it; and all the more, because he could not help associating it with that look of suspicion, the remains of which were still discernible on Mr. Arnold's face. Although he could not determine the exact direction of Mr. Arnold's suspicions, he felt that they bore upon something associated with the crystal ring, and the story of the phantom lady. Consequently, there was little more of comfort for him at Arnstead.

Mr. Arnold, however, did not reveal his change of feeling so much by neglect as by ceremony, which, sooner than anything else, builds a wall of separation between those who meet every day. For the oftener they meet, the thicker and the faster are the bricks and mortar of cold politeness, evidently avoided insults, and subjected manifestations of dislike, laid together.

CHAPTER XXVIII
A BIRD'S-EYE VIEW

O, cocks are crowing a merry midnight,
I wot the wild-fowls are boding day;
Give me my faith and troth again,
And let me fare me on my way.

Sae painfully she clam the wa',
She clam the wa' up after him;
Hosen nor shoon upon her feet,
She hadna time to put them on.

Scotch Ballad.—Clerk Saunders.

Dreary days passed. The reports of Euphra were as favourable as the nature of the injury had left room to expect. Still they were but reports: Hugh could not see her, and the days passed drearily. He heard that the swelling was reduced, and that the ankle was found not to be dislocated, but that the bones were considerably injured, and that the final effect upon the use of the parts was doubtful. The pretty foot lay aching in Hugh's heart. When Harry went to bed, he used to walk out and loiter about the grounds, full of anxious fears and no less anxious hopes. If the night was at all obscure, he would pass, as often as he dared, under Euphra's window; for all he could have of her now was a few rays from the same light that lighted her chamber. Then he would steal away down the main avenue, and thence watch the same light, whose beams, in that strange play which the intellect will keep up in spite of—yet in association with—the heart, made a photo-materialist of him. For he would now no longer believe in the pulsations of an ethereal medium; but—that the very material rays which enlightened Euphra's face, whether she waked or slept, stole and filtered through the blind and the gathered shadows, and entered in bodily essence into the mysterious convolutions of his brain, where his soul and heart sought and found them.

When a week had passed, she was so far recovered as to be able to see Mr. Arnold; from whom Hugh heard, in a somewhat reproachful tone, that she was but the wreck of her former self. It was all that Hugh could do to restrain the natural outbreak of his feelings. A fortnight passed, and she saw Mrs. Elton and Lady Emily for a few moments. They would have left before, but had yielded to Mr. Arnold's entreaty, and were staying till Euphra should be at least able to be carried from her room.

One day, when the visitors were out with Mr. Arnold, Jane brought a message to Hugh, requesting him to walk into Miss Cameron's room, for she wanted to see him. Hugh felt his heart flutter as if doubting whether to stop at once, or to dash through its confining bars. He rose and followed the maid. He stood over Euphra pale and speechless. She lay before him wasted and wan; her eyes twice their former size, but with half their former light; her fingers long and transparent; and her voice low and feeble. She had just raised herself with difficulty to a sitting posture, and the effort had left her more weary.

"Hugh!" she said, kindly.

"Dear Euphra!" he answered, kissing the little hand he held in his.

She looked at him for a little while, and the tears rose in her eyes.

"Hugh, I am a cripple for life."

"God forbid, Euphra!" was all he could reply.

She shook her head mournfully. Then a strange, wild look came in her eyes, and grew till it seemed from them to overflow and cover her whole face with a troubled expression, which increased to a look of dull agony.

"What is the matter, dear Euphra?" said Hugh, in alarm. "Is your foot very painful?"

She made no answer. She was looking fixedly at his hand.

"Shall I call Jane?"

She shook her head.

"Can I do nothing for you?"

"No," she answered, almost angrily.

"Shall I go, Euphra?"

"Yes—yes. Go."

He left the room instantly. But a sharp though stifled cry of despair drew him back at a bound. Euphra had fainted.

He rang the bell for Jane; and lingered till he saw signs of returning consciousness.

What could this mean? He was more perplexed with her than ever he had been. Cunning love, however, soon found a way of explaining it—A way?—Twenty ways—not one of them the way.

Next day, Lady Emily brought him a message from Euphra—not to distress himself about her; it was not his fault.

This message the bearer of it understood to refer to the original accident, as the sender of it intended she should: the receiver interpreted it of the occurrence of the day before, as the sender likewise intended. It comforted him.

It had become almost a habit with Hugh, to ascend the oak tree in the evening, and sit alone, sometimes for hours, in the nest he had built for Harry. One time he took a book with him; another he went without; and now and then Harry accompanied him. But I have already said, that often after tea, when the house became oppressive to him from the longing to see Euphra, he would wander out alone; when, even in the shadows of the coming night, he would sometimes climb the nest, and there sit, hearing all that the leaves whispered about the sleeping birds, without listening to a word of it, or trying to interpret it by the kindred sounds of his own inner world, and the tree-talk that went on there in secret. For the divinity of that inner world had abandoned it for the present, in pursuit of an earthly maiden. So its birds were silent, and its trees trembled not.

An aging moon was feeling her path somewhere through the heavens; but a thin veil of cloud was spread like a tent under the hyaline dome where she walked; so that, instead of a white moon, there was a great white cloud to enlighten the earth,—a cloud soaked full of her pale rays. Hugh sat in the oak-nest. He knew not how long he had been there. Light after light was extinguished in the house, and still he sat there brooding, dreaming, in that state of mind in which to the good, good things come of themselves, and to the evil, evil things. The nearness of the Ghost's Walk did not trouble him, for he was too much concerned about Euphra to fear ghost or demon. His mind heeded them not, and so was beyond their influence.

But while he sat, he became aware of human voices. He looked out from his leafy screen, and saw once more, at the end of the Ghost's Walk, a form clothed in white. But there were voices of two. He sent his soul into his ears to listen. A horrible, incredible, impossible idea forced itself upon him—that the tones were those of Euphra and Funkelstein. The one voice was weak and complaining; the other firm and strong.

"It must be some horrible ghost that imitates her," he said to himself; for he was nearly crazy at the very suggestion.

He would see nearer, if only to get rid of that frightful insinuation of the tempter. He descended the tree noiselessly. He lost sight of the figure as he did so. He drew near the place where he had seen it. But there was no sound of voices now to guide him. As he came within sight of the spot, he saw the white figure in the arms of another, a man. Her head was lying on his shoulder. A moment after, she was lifted in those arms and borne towards the house, —down the Ghost's Avenue.

A burning agony to be satisfied of his doubts seized on Hugh. He fled like a deer to the house by another path; tried, in his suspicion, the library window; found it open, and was at Euphra's door in a moment. Here he hesitated. She must be inside. How dare he knock or enter?

If she was there, she would be asleep. He would not wake her. There was no time to lose. He would risk anything, to be rid of this horrible doubt.

He gently opened the door. The night-light was burning. He thought, at first, that Euphra was in the bed. He felt like a thief, but he stole nearer. She was not there. She was not on the couch. She was not in the room. Jane was fast asleep in the dressing-room. It was enough.

He withdrew. He would watch at his door to see her return, for she must pass his door to reach her own. He waited a time that seemed hours. At length—horrible, far more horrible to him than the vision of the ghost— Euphra crept past him, appearing in the darkness to crawl along the wall against which she supported herself, and scarcely suppressing her groans of pain. She reached her own room, and entering, closed the door.

Hugh was nearly mad. He rushed down the stair to the library, and out into the wood. Why or whither he knew not.

Suddenly he received a blow on the head. It did not stun him, but he staggered under it. Had he run against a tree? No. There was the dim bulk of a man disappearing through the boles. He darted after him. The man heard his footsteps, stopped, and waited in silence. As Hugh came up to him, he made a thrust at him with some weapon. He missed his aim. The weapon passed through his coat and under his arm. The next moment, Hugh had wrenched the sword-stick from him, thrown it away, and grappled with— Funkelstein. But strong as Hugh was, the Bohemian was as strong, and the contest was doubtful. Strange as it may seem—in the midst of it, while each held the other unable to move, the conviction flashed upon Hugh's mind, that, whoever might have taken Lady Euphrasia's ring, he was grappling with the thief of his father's.

"Give me my ring," gasped he.

An imprecation of a sufficiently emphatic character was the only reply. The Bohemian got one hand loose, and Hugh heard a sound like the breaking of glass. Before he could gain any advantage—for his antagonist seemed for the moment to have concentrated all his force in the other hand—a wet handkerchief was held firmly to his face. His fierceness died away; he was lapt in the vapour of dreams; and his senses departed.

CHAPTER XXIX
HUGH'S AWAKING

But ah! believe me, there is more than so, That works such wonders in the minds of men; I, that have often proved, too well it know; And whoso list the like assays to ken, Shall find by trial, and confess it then, That beauty is not, as fond men misdeem, An outward show of things that only seem!

But ye, fair dames, the world's dear ornaments, And lively images of heaven's light, Let not your beams with such disparagements Be dimmed, and your bright glory darkened quite; But, mindful still of your first country's sight, Do still preserve your first informed grace, Whose shadow yet shines in your beauteous face.

SPENSER.—Hymn in Honour of Beauty.

When Hugh came to himself, he was lying, in the first grey of the dawn, amidst the dews and vapours of the morning woods. He rose and looked around him. The Ghost's Walk lay in long silence before him. Here and there a little bird moved and peeped. The glory of a new day was climbing up the eastern coast of heaven. It would be a day of late summer, crowned with flame, and throbbing with ripening life. But for him the spirit was gone out of the world, and it was nought but a mass of blind, heartless forces.

Possibly, had he overheard the conversation, the motions only of which he had overseen the preceding night, he would, although equally perplexed, have thought more gently of Euphra; but, in the mood into which even then he must have been thrown, his deeper feelings towards her could hardly have been different from what they were now. Although he had often felt that Euphra was not very good, not a suspicion had crossed his mind as to what he would have called the purity of her nature. Like many youths, even of character inferior to his own, he had the loftiest notions of feminine grace, and unspottedness in thought and feeling, not to say action and aim. Now he found that he had loved a woman who would creep from her chamber, at the cost of great suffering, and almost at the risk of her life, to meet, in the night and the woods, a man no better than an assassin—probably a thief. Had he been more versed in the ways of women, or in the probabilities of things, he would have judged that the very extravagance of the action demanded a deeper explanation than what seemed to lie on the surface.

Yet, although he judged Euphra very hardly upon those grounds, would he have judged her differently had he actually known all? About this I am left to conjecture alone.

But the effect on Hugh was different from what the ordinary reader of human nature might anticipate. Instead of being torn in pieces by storms of jealousy, all the summer growths of his love were chilled by an absolute frost of death. A kind of annihilation sank upon the image of Euphra. There had been no such Euphra. She had been but a creation of his own brain. It was not so much that he ceased to love, as that the being beloved—not died, but—ceased to exist. There were moments in which he seemed to love her still with a wild outcry of passion; but the frenzy soon vanished in the selfish feeling of his own loss. His love was not a high one—not such as thine, my Falconer. Thine was love indeed; though its tale is too good to tell, simply because it is too good to be believed; and we do men a wrong sometimes when we tell them more than they can receive.

Thought, Speculation, Suggestion, crowded upon each other, till at length his mind sank passive, and served only as the lists in which the antagonist thoughts fought a confused battle without herald or umpire.

But it is amazing to think how soon he began to look back upon his former fascination with a kind of wondering unbelief. This bespoke the strength of Hugh's ideal sense, as well as the weakness of his actual love. He could hardly even recall the feelings with which, on some well-remembered occasion, he had regarded her, and which then it had seemed impossible he should ever forget. Had he discovered the cloven foot of a demon under those trailing garments—he could hardly have ceased to love her more suddenly or entirely. But there is an aching that is worse to bear than pain.

I trust my reader will not judge very hardly of Hugh, because of the change which had thus suddenly passed upon his feelings. He felt now just as he had felt on waking in the morning and finding that he had been in love with a dream-lady all the night: it had been very delightful, and it was sad that it was all gone, and could come back no more. But the wonder to me is, not that some loves will not stand the test of absence, but that, their nature being what it is, they should outlast one week of familiar intercourse.

He mourned bitterly over the loss of those feelings, for they had been precious to him. But could he help it? Indeed he could not; for his love had been fascination; and the fascination having ceased, the love was gone.

I believe some of my readers will not need this apology for Hugh; but will rather admire the facility with which he rose above a misplaced passion, and dismissed its object. So do not I. It came of his having never loved. Had he really loved Euphra, herself, her own self, the living woman who looked at him out of those eyes, out of that face, such pity would have blended with the love as would have made it greater, and permitted no indignation to overwhelm it. As it was, he was utterly passive and helpless in the matter. The fault lay in the original weakness that submitted to be so fascinated; that gave in to it, notwithstanding the vague expostulations of his better nature, and the consciousness that he was neglecting his duty to Harry, in order to please Euphra and enjoy her society. Had he persisted in doing his duty, it would at least have kept his mind more healthy, lessened the absorption of his passion, and given him opportunities of reflection, and moments of true perception as to what he was about. But now the spell was broken at once, and the poor girl had lost a worshipper. The golden image with the feet of clay might arise in a prophet's dream, but it could never abide in such a lover's. Her glance was powerless now. Alas, for the withering of such a dream! Perhaps she deserved nothing else; but our deserts, when we get them, are sad enough sometimes.

All that day he walked as in a dream of loss. As for the person whom he had used to call Euphra, she was removed to a vast distance from him. An absolutely impassable gulf lay between them.

She sent for him. He went to her filled with a sense of insensibility. She was much worse, and suffering great pain. Hugh saw at once that she knew that all was over between them, and that he had seen her pass his door, or had been in her room, for he had left her door a little open, and she had left it shut. One pathetic, most pitiful glance of deprecating entreaty she fixed upon him, as after a few moments of speechless waiting, he turned to leave the room—which would have remained deathless in his heart, but that he interpreted it to mean: "Don't tell;" so he got rid of it at once by the grant of its supposed request. She made no effort to detain him. She turned her face away, and, hard-hearted, he heard her sob, not as if her heart would break— that is little—but like an immortal woman in immortal agony, and he did not turn to comfort her. Perhaps it was better—how could he comfort her? Some kinds of comfort—the only kinds which poor mortals sometimes have to give—are like the food on which the patient and the disease live together; and some griefs are soonest got rid of by letting them burn out. All the fire-engines in creation can only prolong the time, and increase the sense of burning. There is but one cure: the fellow-feeling of the human God, which converts the agony itself into the creative fire of a higher life.

As for Von Funkelstein, Hugh comforted himself with the conviction that they were destined to meet again.

The day went on, as days will go, unstayed, unhastened by the human souls, through which they glide silent and awful. After such lessons as he was able to get through with Harry,—who, feeling that his tutor did not want him, left the room as soon as they were over—he threw himself on the couch, and tried to think. But think he could not. Thoughts passed through him, but he did not think them. He was powerless in regard to them. They came and went of their own will: he could neither say come nor go. Tired at length of the couch, he got up and paced about the room for hours. When he came to himself a little, he found that the sun was nearly setting. Through the top of a beech-tree taller than the rest, it sent a golden light, full of the floating shadows of leaves and branches, upon the wall of his room. But there was no beauty for him in the going down of the sun; no glory in the golden light; no message from dream-land in the flitting and blending and parting, the constantly dissolving yet ever remaining play of the lovely and wonderful shadow-leaves. The sun sank below the beech-top, and was hidden behind a cloud of green leaves, thick as the wood was deep. A grey light instead of a golden filled the room. The change had no interest for him. The pain of a lost passion tormented him—the aching that came of the falling together of the ethereal walls of his soul, about the space where there had been and where there was no longer a world.

A young bird flew against the window, and fluttered its wings two or three times, vainly seeking to overcome the unseen obstacle which the glass presented to its flight. Hugh started and shuddered. Then first he knew, in the influence of the signs of the approaching darkness, how much his nerves had suffered from the change that had passed. He took refuge with Harry. His pupil was now to be his consoler; who in his turn would fare henceforth the better, for the decay of Hugh's pleasures. The poor boy was filled with delight at having his big brother all to himself again; and worked harder than ever to make the best of his privileges. For Hugh, it was wonderful how soon his peace of mind began to return after he gave himself to his duty, and how soon the clouds of disappointment descended below the far horizon, leaving the air clear above and around. Painful thoughts about Euphra would still present themselves; but instead of becoming more gentle and sorrowful as the days went on, they grew more and more severe and unjust and angry. He even entertained doubts whether she did not know all about the theft of both rings, for to her only had he discovered the secret place in the old desk. If she was capable of what he believed, why should she not be capable of anything else? It seemed to him most simple and credible. An impure woman might just as well be a thief too.—I am only describing Hugh's feelings.

But along with these feelings and thoughts, of mingled good and bad, came one feeling which he needed more than any—repentance. Seated alone upon a fallen tree one day, the face of poor Harry came back to him, as he saw it first, poring over Polexander in the library; and, full of the joy of life himself, notwithstanding his past troubles, strong as a sunrise, and hopeful as a Prometheus, the quivering perplexity of that sickly little face smote him with a pang. "What might I not have done for the boy! He, too, was in the hands of the enchantress, and, instead of freeing him, I became her slave to enchain him further." Yet, even in this, he did Euphra injustice; for he had come to the conclusion that she had laid her plans with the intention of keeping the boy a dwarf, by giving him only food for babes, and not good food either, withholding from him every stimulus to mental digestion and consequent hunger; and that she had objects of her own in doing so—one perhaps, to keep herself necessary to the boy as she was to the father, and so secure the future. But poor Euphra's own nature and true education had been sadly neglected. A fine knowledge of music and Italian, and the development of a sensuous sympathy with nature, could hardly be called education. It was not certainly such a development of her own nature as would enable her to sympathise with the necessities of a boy's nature. Perhaps the worst that could justly be said of her behaviour to Harry was, that, with a strong inclination to despotism, and some feeling of loneliness, she had exercised the one upon him in order to alleviate the other in herself. Upon him, therefore, she expended a certain, or rather an uncertain kind of affection, which, if it might have been more fittingly spent upon a lapdog, and was worth but little, might yet have become worth everything, had she been moderately good.

Hugh did not see Euphra again for more than a fortnight.

CHAPTER XXX
CHANGES

Hey, and the rue grows bonny wi' thyme! And the thyme it is withered, and rue is in prime.

Refrain of an old Scotch song, altered by BURNS.

He hath wronged me; indeed he hath; —at a word, he hath; —
believe me; Robert Shallow, Esquire, saith he is wronged.

Merry Wives of Windsor.

At length, one evening, entering the drawing-room before dinner, Hugh found Euphra there alone. He bowed with embarrassment, and uttered some commonplace congratulation on her recovery. She answered him gently and coldly. Her whole air and appearance were signs of acute suffering. She did not make the slightest approach to their former familiarity, but she spoke without any embarrassment, like one who had given herself up, and was, therefore, indifferent. Hugh could not help feeling as if she knew every thought that was passing in his mind, and, having withdrawn herself from him, was watching him with a cold, ghostly interest. She took his arm to go into the dining-room, and actually leaned upon it, as, indeed, she was compelled to do. Her uncle was delighted to see her once more. Mrs. Elton addressed her with kindness, and Lady Emily with sweet cordiality. She herself seemed to care for nobody and nothing. As soon as dinner was over, she sent for her maid, and withdrew to her own room. It was a great relief to Hugh to feel that he was no longer in danger of encountering her eyes.

Gradually she recovered strength, though it was again some days before she appeared at the dinner-table. The distance between Hugh and her seemed to increase instead of diminish, till at length he scarcely dared to offer her the smallest civility, lest she should despise him as a hypocrite. The further she removed herself from him, the more he felt inclined to respect her. By common consent they avoided, as much as before, any behaviour that might attract attention; though the effort was of a very different nature now. It was wretched enough, no doubt, for both of them.

The time drew near for Lady Emily's departure.

"What are your plans for the winter, Mrs. Elton?" said Mr. Arnold, one day.

"I intend spending the winter in London," she answered.

"Then you are not going with Lady Emily to Madeira?"

"No. Her father and one of her sisters are going with her."

"I have a great mind to spend the winter abroad myself; but the difficulty is what to do with Harry."

"Could you not leave him with Mr. Sutherland?"

"No. I do not choose to do that."

"Then let him come to me. I shall have all my little establishment up, and there will be plenty of room for Harry."

"A very kind offer. I may possibly avail myself of it."

"I fear we could hardly accommodate his tutor, though. But that will be very easily arranged. He could sleep out of the house, could he not?"

"Give yourself no trouble about that. I wish Harry to have masters for the various branches he will study. It will teach him more of men and the world generally, and prevent his being too much influenced by one style of thinking."

"But Mr. Sutherland is a very good tutor."

"Yes. Very."

To this there could be no reply but a question; and Mr. Arnold's manner not inviting one, the conversation was dropped.

Euphra gradually resumed her duties in the house, as far as great lameness would permit. She continued to show a quiet and dignified reserve towards Hugh. She made no attempts to fascinate him, and never avoided his look when it chanced to meet hers. But although there was no reproach any more than fascination in her eyes, Hugh's always fell before hers. She walked softly like Ahab, as if, now that Hugh knew, she, too, was ever conscious.

Her behaviour to Mrs. Elton and Lady Emily was likewise improved, but apparently only from an increase of indifference. When the time came, and they departed, she did not even appear to be much relieved.

Once she asked Hugh to help her with a passage of Dante, but betrayed no memory of the past. His pleased haste to assist her, showed that he at least, if fancy-free, was not memory-clear. She thanked him very gently and truly, took up her book like a school-girl, and limped away. Hugh was smitten to the heart. "If I could but do something for her!" thought he; but there was nothing to be done. Although she had deserved it, somehow her behaviour made him feel as if he had wronged her in ceasing to love her.

One day, in the end of September, Mr. Arnold and Hugh were alone after breakfast. Mr. Arnold spoke:

"Mr. Sutherland, I have altered my plans with regard to Harry. I wish him to spend the winter in London."

Hugh listened and waited. Mr. Arnold went on, after a slight pause:

"There I wish him to reap such advantages as are to be gained in the metropolis. He has improved wonderfully under your instruction; and is now, I think, to be benefited principally by a variety of teachers. I therefore intend that he shall have masters for the different branches which it is desirable he should study. Consequently I shall be compelled to deny him your services, valuable as they have hitherto been."

"Very well, Mr. Arnold," said Mr. Sutherland, with the indifference of one who feels himself ill-used. "When shall I take my leave of him?"

"Not before the middle of the next month, at the earliest. But I will write you a cheque for your salary at once."

So saying, Mr. Arnold left the room for a moment, and returning, handed Hugh a cheque for a year's salary. Hugh glanced at it, and offering it again to Mr. Arnold, said:

"No, Mr. Arnold; I can claim scarcely more than half a year's salary."

"Mr. Sutherland, your engagement was at so much a year; and if I prevent you from fulfilling your part of it, I am bound to fulfil mine. Indeed, you might claim further provision."

"You are very kind, Mr. Arnold."

"Only just," rejoined Mr. Arnold, with conscious dignity. "I am under great obligation to you for the way in which you have devoted yourself to Harry."

Hugh's conscience gave him a pang. Is anything more painful than undeserved praise?

"I have hardly done my duty by him," said he.

"I can only say that the boy is wonderfully altered for the better, and I thank you. I am obliged to you: oblige me by putting the cheque in your pocket."

Hugh persisted no longer in his refusal; and indeed it had been far more a feeling of pride than of justice that made him decline accepting it at first. Nor was there any generosity in Mr. Arnold's cheque; for Hugh, as he admitted, might have claimed board and lodging as well. But Mr. Arnold was one of the ordinarily honourable, who, with perfect characters for uprightness, always contrive to err on the safe side of the purse, and the doubtful side of a severely interpreted obligation. Such people, in so doing, not unfrequently secure for themselves, at the same time, the reputation of generosity.

Hugh could not doubt that his dismissal was somehow or other connected with the loss of the ring; but he would not stoop to inquire into the matter. He hoped that time would set all right; and, in fact, felt considerable indifference to the opinion of Mr. Arnold, or of any one in the house, except Harry.

The boy burst into tears when informed of his father's decision with regard to his winter studies, and could only be consoled by the hope which Hugh held out to him—certainly upon a very slight foundation—that they might meet sometimes in London. For the little time that remained, Hugh devoted himself unceasingly to his pupil; not merely studying with him, but walking, riding, reading stories, and going through all sorts of exercises for the strengthening of his person and constitution. The best results followed both for Harry and his tutor.

CHAPTER XXXI
EXPLANATIONS

I have done nothing good to win belief, My life hath been so faithless; all the creatures Made for heaven's honours, have their ends, and good ones; All but... false women... When they die, like tales Ill-told, and unbelieved, they pass away.

I will redeem one minute of my age, Or, like another Niobe, I'll weep Till I am water.

BEAUMONT AND FLETCHER.—The Maid's Tragedy.

The days passed quickly by; and the last evening that Hugh was to spend at Arnstead arrived. He wandered out alone. He had been with Harry all day, and now he wished for a few moments of solitude. It was a lovely autumn evening. He went into the woods behind the house. The leaves were still thick upon the trees, but most of them had changed to gold, and brown, and red; and the sweet faint odours of those that had fallen, and lay thick underfoot, ascended like a voice from the grave, saying: "Here dwelleth some sadness, but no despair." As he strolled about among them, the whole history of his past life arose before him. This often happens before any change in our history, and is surest to take place at the approach of the greatest change of all, when we are about to pass into the unknown, whence we came.

In this mood, it was natural that his sins should rise before him. They came as the shadows of his best pleasures. For now, in looking back, he could fix on no period of his history, around which the aureole, which glorifies the sacred things of the past, had gathered in so golden a hue, as around the memory of the holy cottage, the temple in which abode David, and Janet, and Margaret. All the story glided past, as the necromantic Will called up the sleeping dead in the mausoleum of the brain. And that solemn, kingly, gracious old man, who had been to him a father, he had forgotten; the homely tenderness which, from fear of its own force, concealed itself behind a humorous roughness of manner, he had—no, not despised—but forgotten, too; and if the dim pearly loveliness of the trustful, grateful maiden had not been quite forgotten, yet she too had been neglected, had died, as it were, and been buried in the churchyard of the past, where the grass grows long over the graves, and the moss soon begins to fill up the chiselled records. He was ungrateful. He dared not allow to himself that he was unloving; but he must confess himself ungrateful.

Musing sorrowfully and self-reproachfully, he came to the Ghost's Avenue. Up and down its aisle he walked, a fit place for remembering the past, and the sins of the present. Yielding himself to what thoughts might arise, the strange sight he had seen here on that moonlit night, of two silent wandering figures—or could it be that they were one and the same, suddenly changed in hue?—returned upon him. This vision had been so speedily followed by the second and more alarming apparition of Lady Euphrasia, that he had hardly had time to speculate on what the former could have been. He was meditating upon all these strange events, and remarking to himself that, since his midnight encounter with Lady Euphrasia, the house had been as quiet as a church-yard at noon, when all suddenly, he saw before him, at some little distance, a dark figure approaching him. His heart seemed to bound into his throat and choke him, as he said to himself: "It is the nun again!" But the next moment he saw that it was Euphra. I do not know which he would have preferred not meeting alone, and in the deepening twilight: Euphra, too, had become like a ghost to him. His first impulse was to turn aside into the wood, but she had seen him, and was evidently going to address him. He therefore advanced to meet her. She spoke first, approaching him with painful steps.

"I have been looking for you, Mr. Sutherland. I wanted very much to have a little conversation with you before you go. Will you allow me?"

Hugh felt like a culprit directly. Euphra's manner was quite collected and kind; yet through it all a consciousness showed itself, that the relation which had once existed between them had passed away for ever. In her voice there was something like the tone of wind blowing through a ruin.

"I shall be most happy," said he.

She smiled sadly. A great change had passed upon her.

"I am going to be quite open with you," she said. "I am perfectly aware, as well as you are, that the boyish fancy you had for me is gone. Do not be offended. You are manly enough, but your love for me was boyish. Most first loves are childish, quite irrespective of age. I do not blame you in the least."

This seemed to Hugh rather a strange style to assume, if all was true that his own eyes had reported. She went on:

"Nor must you think it has cost me much to lose it."

Hugh felt hurt, at which no one who understands will be surprised.

"But I cannot afford to lose you, the only friend I have," she added.

Hugh turned towards her with a face full of manhood and truth.

"You shall not lose me, Euphra, if you will be honest to yourself and to me."

"Thank you. I can trust you. I will be honest."

At that moment, without the revival of a trace of his former feelings, Hugh felt nearer to her than he had ever felt before. Now there seemed to be truth between them, the only medium through which beings can unite.

"I fear I have wronged you much," she went on. "I do not mean some time ago." Here she hesitated.—"I fear I am the cause of your leaving Arnstead."

"You, Euphra? No. You must be mistaken."

"I think not. But I am compelled to make an unwilling disclosure of a secret—a sad secret about myself. Do not hate me quite—I am a somnambulist."

She hid her face in her hands, as if the night which had now closed around them did not hide her enough. Hugh did not reply. Absorbed in the interest which both herself and her confession aroused in him, he could only listen eagerly. She went on, after a moment's pause:

"I did not think at first that I had taken the ring. I thought another had. But last night, and not till then, I discovered that I was the culprit."

"How?"

"That requires explanation. I have no recollection of the events of the previous night when I have been walking in my sleep. Indeed, the utter absence of a sense of dreaming always makes me suspect that I have been wandering. But sometimes I have a vivid dream, which I know, though I can give no proof of it, to be a reproduction of some previous somnambulic experience. Do not ask me to recall the horrors I dreamed last night. I am sure I took the ring."

"Then you dreamed what you did with it?"

"Yes, I gave it to—"

Here her voice sank and ceased. Hugh would not urge her.

"Have you mentioned this to Mr. Arnold?"

"No. I do not think it would do any good. But I will, if you wish it," she added submissively.

"Not at all. Just as you think best."

"I could not tell him everything. I cannot tell you everything. If I did, Mr. Arnold would turn me out of the house. I am a very unhappy girl, Mr. Sutherland."

From the tone of these words, Hugh could not for a moment suppose that Euphra had any remaining design of fascination in them.

"Perhaps he might want to keep you, if I told him all; but I do not think, after the way he has behaved to you, that you could stay with him, for he would never apologize. It is very selfish of me; but indeed I have not the courage to confess to him."

"I assure you nothing could make me remain now. But what can I do for you?"

"Only let me depend upon you, in case I should need your help; or—"

Here Euphra stopped suddenly, and caught hold of Hugh's left hand, which he had lifted to brush an insect from his face.

"Where is your ring?" she said, in a tone of suppressed anxiety.

"Gone, Euphra. My father's ring! It was lying beside Lady Euphrasia's."

Euphra's face was again hidden in her hands. She sobbed and moaned like one in despair. When she grew a little calmer, she said:

"I am sure I did not take your ring, dear Hugh—I am not a thief. I had a kind of right to the other, and he said it ought to have been his, for his real name was Count von Halkar—the same name as Lady Euphrasia's before she was married. He took it, I am sure."

"It was he that knocked me down in the dark that night then, Euphra."

"Did he? Oh! I shall have to tell you all.—That wretch has a terrible power over me. I loved him once. But I refused to take the ring from your desk, because I knew it would get you into trouble. He threw me into a somnambulic sleep, and sent me for the ring. But I should have remembered if I had taken yours. Even in my sleep, I don't think he could have made me do that. You may know I speak the truth, when I am telling my own disgrace. He promised to set me free if I would get the ring; but he has not done it; and he will not."

Sobs again interrupted her.

"I was afraid your ring was gone. I don't know why I thought so, except that you hadn't it on, when you came to see me. Or perhaps it was because I am sometimes forced to think what that wretch is thinking. He made me go to him that night you saw me, Hugh. But I was so ill, I don't think I should have been able, but that I could not rest till I had asked him about your ring. He said he knew nothing about it."

"I am sure He has it," said Hugh. And he related to Euphra the struggle he had had with Funkelstein and its result. She shuddered.

"I have been a devil to you, Hugh; I have betrayed you to him. You will never see your ring again. Here, take mine. It is not so good as yours, but for the sake of the old way you thought of me, take it."

"No, no, Euphra; Mr. Arnold would miss it. Besides, you know it would not be my father's ring, and it was not for the value of the diamond I cared most about it. And I am not sure that I shall not find it again. I am going up to London, where I shall fall in with him, I hope."

"But do take care of yourself. He has no conscience. God knows, I have had little, but he has none."

"I know he has none; but a conscience is not a bad auxiliary, and there I shall have some advantage of him. But what could he want that ring of Lady Euphrasia's for?"

"I don't know. He never told me."

"It was not worth much."

"Next to nothing."

"I shall be surer to find that than my own. And I will find it, if I can, that Mr. Arnold may believe I was not to blame."

"Do. But be careful."

"Don't fear. I will be careful."

She held out her hand, as if to take leave of him, but withdrew it again with the sudden cry:

"What shall I do? I thought he had left me to myself, till that night in the library."

She held down her head in silence. Then she said, slowly, in a tone of agony:

"I am a slave, body and soul.—Hugh!" she added, passionately, and looking up in his face, "do you think there is a God?"

Her eyes glimmered with the faint reflex from gathered tears, that silently overflowed.

And now Hugh's own poverty struck him with grief and humiliation. Here was a soul seeking God, and he had no right to say that there was a

God, for he knew nothing about him. He had been told so; but what could that far-off witness do for the need of a desolate heart? She had been told so a million of times. He could not say that he knew it. That was what she wanted and needed.

He was honest, and so replied:

"I do not know. I hope so."

He felt that she was already beyond him; for she had begun to cry into the vague, seemingly heartless void, and say:

"Is there a God somewhere to hear me when I cry?"

And with all the teaching he had had, he had no word of comfort to give. Yes, he had: he had known David Elginbrod.

Before he had shaped his thought, she said:

"I think, if there were a God, he would help me; for I am nothing but a poor slave now. I have hardly a will of my own."

The sigh she heaved told of a hopeless oppression.

"The best man, and the wisest, and the noblest I ever knew," said Hugh, "believed in God with his whole heart and soul and strength and mind. In fact, he cared for nothing but God; or rather, he cared for everything because it belonged to God. He was never afraid of anything, never vexed at anything, never troubled about anything. He was a good man."

Hugh was surprised at the light which broke upon the character of David, as he held it before his mind's eye, in order to describe it to Euphra. He seemed never to have understood him before.

"Ah! I wish I knew him. I would go to that man, and ask him to save me. Where does he live?"

"Alas! I do not know whether he is alive or dead—the more to my shame. But he lives, if he lives, far away in the north of Scotland."

She paused.

"No. I could not go there. I will write to him."

Hugh could not discourage her, though he doubted whether a real communication could be established between them.

"I will write down his address for you, when I go in," said he. "But what can he save you from?"

"From no God," she answered, solemnly. "If there is no God, then I am sure that there is a devil, and that he has got me in his power."

Hugh felt her shudder, for she was leaning on his arm, she was still so lame. She continued:

"Oh! if I had a God, he would right me, I know."

Hugh could not reply. A pause followed.

"Good-bye. I feel pretty sure we shall meet again. My presentiments are generally true," said Euphra, at length.

Hugh kissed her hand with far more real devotion than he had ever kissed it with before.

She left him, and hastened to the house 'with feeble speed.' He was sorry she was gone. He walked up and down for some time, meditating on the strange girl and her strange words; till, hearing the dinner bell, he too must hasten in to dress.

Euphra met him at the dinner-table without any change of her late manner. Mr. Arnold wished him good night more kindly than usual. When he went up to his room, he found that Harry had already cried himself to sleep.

CHAPTER XXXII
DEPARTURE

I fancy deemed fit guide to lead my way,
And as I deemed I did pursue her track;
Wit lost his aim, and will was fancy's prey;
The rebel won, the ruler went to wrack.
But now sith fancy did with folly end,
Wit, bought with loss—will, taught by wit, will mend.
SOUTHWELL.—David's Peccavi.

After dinner, Hugh wandered over the well-known places, to bid them good-bye. Then he went up to his room, and, with the vanity of a young author, took his poems out of the fatal old desk; wrote: "Take them, please, such as they are. Let me be your friend;" inclosed them with the writing, and addressed them to Euphra. By the time he saw them again, they were so much waste paper in his eyes.

But what were his plans for the future?

First of all, he would go to London. There he would do many things. He would try to find Funkelstein. He would write. He would make acquaintance with London life; for had he not plenty of money in his pocket? And who could live more thriftily than he?—During his last session at Aberdeen, he had given some private lessons, and so contrived to eke out his small means. These were wretchedly paid for, namely, not quite at the rate of sevenpence-halfpenny a lesson! but still that was something, where more could not be had.—Now he would try to do the same in London, where he would be much better paid. Or perhaps he might get a situation in a school for a short time, if he were driven to ultimate necessity. At all events, he would see London, and look about him for a little while, before he settled to anything definite.

With this hopeful prospect before him, he next morning bade adieu to Arnstead. I will not describe the parting with poor Harry. The boy seemed ready to break his heart, and Hugh himself had enough to do to refrain from tears. One of the grooms drove him to the railway in the dog-cart. As they came near the station, Hugh gave him half-a-crown. Enlivened by the gift, the man began to talk.

"He's a rum customer, that ere gemman with the foring name. The colour of his puss I couldn't swear to now. Never saw sixpence o' his'n. My opinion is, master had better look arter his spoons. And for missus—well, it's a pity! He's a rum un, as I say, anyhow."

The man here nodded several times, half compassionately, half importantly.

Hugh did not choose to inquire what he meant. They reached the station, and in a few minutes he was shooting along towards London, that social vortex, which draws everything towards its central tumult.

But there is a central repose beyond the motions of the world; and through the turmoil of London, Hugh was journeying towards that wide stillness—that silence of the soul, which is not desolate, but rich with unutterable harmonies.